Pearl Bound

Natalie G. Bergman

Copyright

Author Website: **www.nataliebergman.com**

FIRST EDITION

ISBNs
Paperback (Amazon KDP): 979-8-9996271-1-7
eBook (Amazon Kindle): 979-8-9996271-0-0
Paperback (Draft2Digital): 979-8-9996271-2-4
eBook (Draft2Digital): 979-8-9996271-3-1
Audiobook (Lantern Media): 979-8-9996271-4-8

Library of Congress Control Number: 2025922880 (print)

CONTENT WARNING
This work contains mature themes and depictions of violence and trauma that may be distressing to some readers.

Dedication

* * *

TO KIM, MY PARTNER IN ALL THINGS

Contents

Part One

Chapter 1

A Spark In The Snow

Upstate New York - Winter 1883 - Moira

Hunger twisted my stomach, sharp and unrelenting—a cruel reminder that promises don't fill bellies. The wood smoke stung my eyes, and an icy wind whistled through the cracks in our cabin's walls, as if to jeer at us. Sean had promised me that life in America would be better than our cramped Dublin tenement. If only...

Back home, peat fires had warmed both body and soul. Neighbors had packed together like herring, their songs and stories slipping through walls thin as paper. Here, we faced the wilderness, hunger, bitter cold, all alone.

I turned to the hearth where our little lass sat and played with a scrappy tabby. Eve, just three, giggled as she tormented the poor beastie with her sticky fingers. I hate cats. During the summer, I had tossed it out of the cabin more times than I could count. But when the snow arrived, I relented. He kept the rodents at bay and our child entertained.

Eve had Sean's mischievous green eyes and his red hair. Meanwhile, I'd spotted more than a few white strands in my own reflection lately. Sean's mother would've said white hairs came from guarding

3

secrets. Lately, though, it felt like the secrets were guarding me—watching, waiting, whispering when no one else could hear. My own mother had said such whispers ran in our blood, though the gift had skipped me like a stone across water.

With temperatures below freezing, Eve and I had spent the day cloistered inside. Sean had left at dawn to hunt, but now the sun bled out behind the mountains, painting the sky in bruised shades of purple and gray. I peered through the frost-rimed window, willing a shadow to emerge from the snow-covered woods. The acid tang of fear burned upward from my gut to my throat.

Where was Sean...?

He should've been back hours ago. A cold sweat prickled at the back of my neck, and my hands trembled as I gripped the edge of the window frame.

I forced myself to turn away and keep busy, pulling out the last of the day's soda bread, a nub of butter, and my final jar of huckleberry preserves. The knife trembled in my hand as I sliced the bread, the silence pressing so heavy I could hear the crackle of wood burning, and the faint scratch of something—mice, perhaps?—beneath the floorboards.

I exhaled sharply, the sound too loud in the suffocating quiet and glanced over at Eve. She'd gotten up and stood now beneath the mantel. Her sparkling green eyes were fixed on the ceramic bird perched above—a fragile, glistening thing that seemed to shiver in the firelight. It was the last gift from Sean's mother before we left Ireland, a relic of a home that now felt as distant as the stars.

"I want," she whispered, her voice unnervingly low, almost hollow. A chill snaked down my spine, the same sensation that haunted my dreams. Dreams where shadows murmured secrets in voices I didn't recognize, always just before I woke gasping in the dark.

The room shifted, almost imperceptibly, as though the air itself was holding its breath.

Eve's gaze never left the bird as she whispered again, her voice colder now, sharper. "Jump."

The tabby moved as if summoned, its muscles twitching beneath its fur like a puppet pulled by invisible strings. My breath caught in my throat as I watched its eyes glaze over with an unnatural sheen. Its sinewy body coiled, then sprang upward with impossible precision. One swipe of a paw, and the fragile bird tumbled, its gleaming surface catching the firelight like a falling star.

The hair on the back of my neck stood on end. I'd seen Eve do strange things before—toys moving just out of reach, flames dancing in unusual patterns—but this was different. This was control, pure and deliberate. The thought sent ice through my veins.

The bird's neck snapped against the floorboards, its delicate head rolling into the shadows. The sound hung in the air, sharp and final, like the toll of a distant church bell.

"Off with you!" I snapped at the cat. He bolted. His yellow eyes glinting like tiny flames as he vanished into the dim corners of the cabin.

Eve shoved the broken pieces under the rug with frantic determination. Another time, I would have smiled at her effort to cover her mischief, but not tonight, with my nerves frayed and my stomach a hollow ache. I needed to tell Sean about what I'd seen—the cat acting as if bewitched. Would he dismiss it as fancy, as he had when I'd mentioned the shadows that seemed to follow our child? Or would he believe me?

As I approached Eve, my shadow arched long and dark over her. "Hand it over," I said, sharper than I intended, thanks to the unrelenting tension in my chest.

Eve's lip quivered as she reached beneath the rug and offered up the head and body of the little bird. Her small hands trembled and her emerald green eyes, (so like Sean's), filled with tears that seemed to cut straight through me, though I couldn't tell if it was guilt or grief that twisted the knife.

I opened my mouth to scold her, the words poised on the tip of my tongue when...

Crack! A rifle shot split the frozen air. The sound ricocheted through my chest like a bullet. For one terrible moment, my heart forgot how to beat.

I rushed to the window. The frost nipped at my fingertips, as I pressed them to the glass. Relief surged through me—there he was, Sean, rifle in one hand and a brace of rabbits in the other, trudging through the drifts. Tonight, at least, we would eat.

But then black as the deepest shadows, a raven swooped toward Sean with an unholy grace, its eyes gleaming with cruel intent. I'd seen it before, circling the cabin like an omen. We weren't the only ones starving this winter.

Talons slashed through the air. Sean's yelp of pain sliced through the air, chilling my blood. It dove again, relentless, claws reaching for the rabbits · but Sean lifted his rifle and it roared. Once last screech, and the foul creature vanished into the darkening sky.

I flung the door open, a gust of frigid air rushing in with Sean. He stood there, blood streaking his cheek and frost clinging to his whiskers, but his tired smile broke through it all. While Eve squealed and danced around his legs, I helped him with his coat, leaning close under the pretense of examining the scratches on his face.

"Something's happened with the child," I whispered, my lips barely moving. "The cat—it wasn't natural, Sean. She made it—"

"Hush now," he murmured, squeezing my hand. "You've been alone too long with your thoughts." But beneath his dismissive words, I caught the flicker of worry in his eyes, the way his gaze lingered on Eve a heartbeat too long. He'd seen things too, I knew, though he'd never admit it. The weight of unspoken fears hung between us like frost in the air.

He held up the rabbits triumphantly. "Who's hungry?" he asked, his warm voice melting away my fear.

"Dada!" Eve tugged on her father's hand. Sean knelt to meet the child's eager embrace. "Look what I've got for you," he said, producing a small wooden toy from his pocket. Its surface was rough, but the shape was unmistakable—a horse.

"Ooh!" Eve exclaimed, pressing a sticky kiss to Sean's cheek. "It's Buttercup!" she declared, cradling the toy as though it were alive. My mind flickered to the real Buttercup, huddled in the barn. I prayed the cold hadn't taken her.

"Aye, lass, just like her," Sean replied.

Eve took the toy back to the warm hearth.

"Ach, Sean, you'll be spoiling her," I said, though the corner of my mouth betrayed a faint smile.

"Sure, tis a father's duty," he replied with an easy shrug. Sean came over and wrapped his arms around me, his embrace a steadying comfort. I let myself lean into him, drawing warmth and reassurance from his familiar scent of spice and tobacco. For a moment, it eased my fears, softening the edges of my worry. But then I stepped back, reaching for a clean cloth to gently dab away the blood and dirt from the cuts on his cheek.

"Well, how is it?" Sean asked.

"Not too bad," I said. "You'll live."

"Thanks be," he said, as he sat on his favorite chair and tugged off his ice-crusted boots. Eve sat cross-legged before the hearth, her new toy clutched tightly in her hands, the flickering firelight casting strange, shifting patterns over her face.

I was in the middle of skinning the rabbits, when I paused to glance at my little family. Sean was whittling a new piece of wood, but Eve began to wave her tiny hands, the motion strange and deliberate, like a conductor commanding an orchestra.

My breath caught as I watched her command the flames with an unearthly precision. It sent shivers down my spine.

The flames in the hearth flared higher, licking greedily at the mantel.

"Sean!" I cried, the knife slipping from my hand.

Sean looked up to see the wood catch on fire with a sudden

7

crackle, embers spitting into the air. "Holy Mother of God!" Sean's voice cracked like a whip.

"Get the bairn!" I cried, running for the water pail. I brought the full bucket and began to fling handfuls of water at the growing flames, the fire hissing and snapping as it clung stubbornly to the wood. Heat prickled at my cheeks, smoke stung my eyes, but I couldn't stop—not when this cabin was all that kept us from freezing to death.

Sean lunged toward Eve, his arms outstretched to pull her away from the flames. But as he touched her, a searing burst of light erupted from her small frame—a crackling surge that filled the room with a blinding brightness.

The force slammed into Sean, hurling him backward until his head struck the wall. The sound that followed wasn't just a crack—it was the sound of our world splitting apart, echoing through the cabin like the toll of a death knell. The flames in the hearth surged and twisted, casting writhing shadows that seemed to reach for us with hungry fingers.

I stumbled to Sean's side, my legs moving as though weighed down with chains. "Sean!" The word tore from my throat, but it sounded distant, as though the space between us had stretched into an endless chasm. His head lolled at an unnatural angle, and when my trembling hands found the back of his skull, they came away coated in his life's blood. The crimson seemed to pulse in the firelight, each drop holding a reflection of the flames.

A sound erupted from deep within me—not quite a scream, but something older, something primal. It rattled the windows and made the flames dance and dip, as if even they recoiled from my grief.

Eve's face contorted, her features twisting into something I barely recognized. The power that had flowed through her seemed to turn inward, and she doubled over, retching onto the rough-hewn floorboards. Then she collapsed, her small frame folding in on itself like a flower touched by frost. The wooden horse slipped from her limp fingers, its fall marking the seconds between before and after.

I knelt beside Sean's body, my bloodied hands trembling in my lap like wounded birds. The hearth's dying embers cast an orange glow across the scene, and sorrow settled over me like a burial shroud. Through a teary haze I watched dark stains spread across the floor-boards, seeping into the wood's hungry grain. Would these boards forever remember this night, I wondered, holding the memory of our tragedy in their rings and knots?

When Eve stirred, she moved with an otherworldly grace, and a cold shiver climbed my bones like an old warning come awake. Her eyelids fluttered like moth wings seeking flame, and for a heartbeat, everything stood still. Then her gaze found mine. Those eyes—Sean's eyes—were impossibly wide, holding something ancient and terrible in their depths. Her body began to shake, as though the very air around her had turned to needles. Her mouth opened in a rictus of pain —

Then the screaming began. Not the wails of a child, but some-thing that spoke of deeper horrors—each cry carrying echoes of ancient powers awakening. The sound pierced me like winter wind through threadbare cloth, each shriek a reminder of what had been unleashed.

"Eve," I whispered, my voice a fragile thing against the storm of her cries. "Eve, darling, it's..." But comfort died on my tongue, bitter as winter berries. Nothing about this was right, or natural, or bearable.

The firelight painted devils' shadows on her tear-streaked face, her green eyes wild as summer storms. Her tiny fists opened and closed like flower buds in a time-turned nightmare, her body trem-bling as though it housed something vast and terrible trying to break free. I remained frozen in place, instinct warning that any movement might shatter whatever tenuous bounds still held that power in check.

Time stretched like molasses in winter, her cries rising and falling like a tide of sorrow that threatened to drown us both. The hours bled together until finally, mercifully, exhaustion claimed her. Her small body went limp as a rag doll, the terrible power seemingly spent. With shaking hands, I wrapped her in the blanket Sean's mother had knitted—another relic of a life that now felt centuries distant. I held her close as dawn's gray fingers crept through the cabin windows, painting everything in the color of ash.

Somehow in the early morning, I found the strength to stand, to walk. Every step away from Sean's body felt like a betrayal, but I couldn't look back. His blood had frozen in the weave of my dress, crackling with each movement like the crust of ice over deep water. The cold bit through to my bones as I stumbled through snowdrifts that seemed to reach for us with frozen fingers.

The path to the Andersen's cabin stretched before me like a ribbon of torment. Ivar and Hedda were our nearest neighbors, though we'd kept our distance save for the occasional sharing of winter stores. The thought of explaining what had happened—what Eve had done—made bile rise in my throat. But our cabin had become a tomb, haunted by more than just death. Every shadow held memories, every creak of the boards whispered accusations.

When Hedda opened her door, the lamplight spilled across her face, painting her shock in shades of amber. I must have looked like something risen from a grave—clothes stiff with frozen blood, eyes hollow as winter caves, body trembling on the knife's edge of collapse. Eve stirred in my arms, whimpering like a wounded thing, and reality crashed back over me in a wave.

"Sean..." The name caught in my throat like a shard of ice. "There was..." But how could I speak of what I'd witnessed? What words could possibly contain the horror of watching my child's power tear our world apart?

Hedda asked no questions. One look at my face told her enough —or perhaps not nearly so. She drew us inside, her gentle touch almost unbearable in its kindness. As I crossed her threshold, the last thread of strength holding me together unraveled. The world tilted, darkened, and mercifully disappeared.

I surfaced from unconsciousness hours later, every muscle crying out with cold and loss. Eve was curled against me like a comma, her face finally peaceful in sleep. The familiar scent of pipe smoke drew my gaze to Ivar, who watched us from his chair with eyes dark as well water. Hedda sat by the hearth, her usually busy hands still in her lap, her needlepoint forgotten. Concern and wariness flashed across her features in equal measure.

"You've been through a hard trial, ja," she murmured, her accent thick with sympathy. "Rest now, Moira. The details, they can wait."

But even as her gentle words washed over me, I felt the truth writhing in my chest like a living thing. Rest was a luxury forever lost to me now. Whatever ancient power had claimed Sean's life, whatever force flowed through my child's veins, it wasn't finished with us.

Chapter 2

The Binding

Moira

The morning after the funeral mocked me with clear skies—a brightness I couldn't bear. My hands trembled over each item I packed: his coat, still holding his special scent of spice and tobacco; the pinewood cutting board he'd made for me. Every object was a shard of memory, cutting deep.

I found myself clenching Sean's whittling knife, the handle worn smooth by his hands. My thumb traced the small notch near the handle where he'd carved our wedding date. He'd always loved working with wood — a tangible thing he could shape with his own two hands. "Old magic's naught but fairy stories," he'd say whenever my mother spoke of our bloodline's power, of the ancient forces that ran through our veins like river water through mountain stone. Even when strange things happened around Eve, he'd turn away, jaw set with a stubborn determination I'd once found so endearing. Just days ago he'd wielded the knife to shape dreams from wood for our little girl. Now, I pressed it to my chest as if I could somehow keep a piece of him close to my heart. Tears welled as I slipped it into my pocket. The weight of it against my hip was a constant reminder that he was gone—truly gone—though my mind still couldn't grasp how the world could keep turning without him in it.

Hedda had come back with me, helping gather what little we could carry. What wouldn't fit in the wagon, I offered to her. In exchange, she hugged me tightly and pressed a small leather coin pouch into my hands before taking her leave.

Exhausted but determined, I lifted Eve—bundled in Sean's old wool coat—onto the wagon's front bench. Buttercup pawed the ground, steam rising from her nostrils like ghostly sighs. Eve sniffled, rocking back and forth, caught in her own private storm.

The memory surged unbidden: the searing flash, Sean's body crumpling, my hands slick with his blood. My chest constricted, but I forced the thoughts away. I had to keep moving.

"Da..." Eve whimpered. The sound cut through me like a blade, as her tears brimmed before spilling over.

I tossed the last bag onto the wagon floor with a loud thunk, then clambered up beside her. Her crying grated against my frayed nerves, relentless and unbearable. Before I could stop myself, I snapped. "For the last time, Da's gone!"

The words tore from my throat, sharp and jagged. The moment they left my lips, guilt bit deep. How could I blame her for clinging to him, when I was doing the same with every breath?

Since that terrible night, even the smallest movement of Eve's hands made my heart stutter. The memory of her conductor's gesture before the flames erupted haunted me. I couldn't stop seeing it—the way she'd commanded the fire like it was her plaything, just as she'd done with that poor cat. How many signs had I ignored? How many times had I dismissed Sean's mother's warnings as mere superstition?

My hand jerked up instinctively, half-born of frustration, half from fear — fear of my own child. The air around her shimmered faintly, and I froze, the memory of Sean's final moments flashing through my mind.

Eve cried silently now, her small shoulders shaking as we passed the church. Sean's body lay inside, waiting for spring's thaw to be buried. I'd dismissed his mother's cryptic warnings as superstition, but now they rang like a death knell in my ears. If only we'd listened. If only we'd stayed in Ireland, where my family could've helped me bear this burden.

The horse's hooves crunched through the snow as we made our way deeper into the woods. A familiar caw echoed through the trees —the same haunting sound that had preceded Sean's death. I clucked at the horse to pick up her pace and clutched the reins tighter, remembering how that dark messenger had swooped down at him with evil purpose. Icicles hung from the branches, glinting like frozen daggers, and shadows seemed to follow our progress with hungry interest.

Finally, we arrived at a ramshackle cottage, its windows obscured by layers of grime and cobwebs. Eve had fallen asleep, her small body slumped against me. Sliding from the bench, I cradled her as I approached the door. Before I could knock, it swung open, revealing an old woman with a halo of silver curls. Her sharp eyes, bright with recognition, bore into me.

"Moira Kelly!" Fiona said in a deep Irish brogue. "What drives you to my door in dead o' winter? And where's that handsome fella o' yours?"

"Sean...." My throat tightened as tears welled. I swallowed hard. How could I explain? How could I tell her that my own family's bloodline had shown itself in our daughter—with devastating consequences?

Fiona's expression softened as she read my face. She knew my mother's people, knew the whispers that ran through our blood even if they'd passed me by. Without a word, she stepped aside and gestured for us to enter.

Inside, the cottage was dimly lit, but unlike the familiar warm glow of our hearth, these flames cast strange shadows that seemed to dance with intent. The air was thick with the mingling scents of dried herbs and woodsmoke. Every surface held some token of the old ways—the ways Sean and I had turned our backs on, seeking a new

14

life in a new world. Now that choice had come full circle, leaving me to gather up the scattered pieces of our shattered dreams.

Bundles of flowers and feathers hung from the rafters alongside animal bones and tattered skins. The space felt alive, charged with an energy that prickled my skin. Fiona waved us towards a seat at her worn table.

I sat in silence across from Fiona, Eve still curled in my lap. The old woman reached into a cloth bag, pulling out a handful of runes, crystals, and knuckle bones. They clattered across the tabletop as she cast them, her gaze narrowing as she studied their placement. After a long pause, she sighed.

"It's not the wee one's fault," Fiona said, her tone laced with sorrow that made my stomach churn.

"I bloody know, all right?! Will you help us or no?" The words came out sharper than I had meant them to, my grief and fear spilling over. "His mother..." I stopped, remembering her icy cold hands gripping mine before we left. And her eyes—so like Sean's, so like Eve's.

Eve's eyes fluttered open and fixed on one of the hanging bundles of herbs, and for a moment, I saw that same terrible focus I'd witnessed with the ceramic bird. My hands trembled as I watched the bundle sway, though no breeze stirred the air. But Fiona's presence seemed to settle something in Eve—whether it was the old woman's power or simply her calm acceptance, I couldn't tell. I felt the child relax against my chest.

Fiona's gaze didn't waver. "The old powers choose their vessels, and we've nought to say about it." She rose and pulled a mound of straw into the center of the floor. "Bring the bairn here," she said. "It's in the blood—strong and wild."

I hesitated, memories of that night flickering through my mind like dark moths. Though I held Eve daily out of necessity, these moments—when the old magic stirred so close to the surface—made my heart flutter like a trapped bird. Some deep maternal instinct still drew me to cradle her, even as another part of me whispered of the devastation her power could unleash. Sean would never have hesitated this way; he'd remained fearless with her until the very end, reaching for her with a father's pure love even as the magic blazed forth to consume him. Drawing in a steadying breath, I carried Eve to the straw and gently laid her down. My arms felt achingly empty as I stepped back, that endless dance between love and fear leaving me dizzy.

Eve's bright green eyes scanned the room, lingering on the bundles of herbs and bones overhead.

Fiona knelt beside her, brushing a comforting hand over her hair. "Don't be afraid, little one," she murmured. "Stay still now, and hush."

Eve nodded, her pale face calm despite everything.

Fiona reached for a piece of chalk and began drawing a pentacle around the child with swift, deliberate movements.

"Candles, if you please," Fiona said without looking up.

I fetched the tapers, placing one at each point of the pentacle. Fiona lit a bundle of dried herbs from the flames, the pungent smoke curling upward as she began to chant. Her voice rose and fell, weaving an ancient melody that vibrated in my very bones.

Fiona paused in her chanting, head tilting as if listening to voices I couldn't hear. Then she moved to the windows with purposeful steps, her weathered hands reaching for the latches. "They must be welcomed properly," she murmured, "the ones who watch at the threshold between worlds." The windows creaked open, letting in a rush of winter air that made the candle flames dance and weave. The smoke from the herbs seemed to twist into shapes—wings and claws and hungry, reaching things.

CAW! CAW! CAW!

Three ravens swept through the open window, their black wings slicing the air like knives. Their unblinking stares settled on Eve—not me—as if something inside her had summoned them. My breath caught, dredging up the memory of the raven that had circled our cabin before attacking Sean.

But Eve's face lit with a strange delight, her green eyes tracking

16

the birds' movements as if reading words written in their flight. She lifted one small hand toward them, fingers splaying like the feathers of a wing. The ravens drew closer, their obsidian eyes reflecting the candlelight, and my heart lurched—but there was no malice in their approach, no echo of that terrible day. They circled her like a living crown, their wings stirring the herb-sweet air, and my daughter smiled as if greeting old friends.

Fiona froze. "The Morrigan," she whispered. Her sharp eyes met mine, heavy with meaning, then bowed her head.

"The Morrigan...?" I echoed, uncertain.

"She's no mere goddess, Moira, " Fiona replied, her eyes sharp as winter stars. "The Morrigan is the Phantom Queen—a weaver of fates, a guardian of bloodlines older than the stones of Ireland. Those flames that took Sean weren't just fire, child. They were the raw power of the old world, untamed and hungry. The same force that drove ravens to guard our ancestors now flows through your daughter's veins. The Celtic magic in Eve is linked to the Morrigan herself —a power as untamed as the old lands."

The candles flickered, then snuffed out entirely. In the sudden gloom, a soft white light began to glow from Eve's chest. It pulsed faintly, the energy within her shifting and coalescing.

My throat tightened as I watched Fiona's gnarled hands gather the light, compressing it until it hardened into a small, luminous pearl. She held it up, her expression unreadable, then turned to me.

"This," she said, "is her power, her inheritance. You'll need to teach her, Moira. About the power that runs through your bloodline. If you don't..." She trailed off, the unspoken warning clear.

Fiona pressed the pearl into a bronze Celtic cross, then tied it to a leather cord. My hands trembled as she placed it in my palm. It was warm, almost alive, and unbearably heavy for its size. I slipped it over my neck. The pearl gleamed faintly against my skin, its weight both physical and intangible.

"When the time comes, crush it," Fiona said.

"Understood," I replied, though nothing felt clear. I was alone now, burdened with a legacy I barely grasped and a daughter I was too afraid to hold.

The ravens watched in silence before rising as one, their wings stirring the air as they disappeared into the gray sky. I stared after them, a hollow ache settling in my chest.

Sean's mother had tried to warn us. But it had been Sean's choice to turn his back on my family's strange inheritance, and I, a fool in love, had followed.

Now he was gone, and I was here—widowed and alone with our child, left to bear the consequences. As the candlelight caught Eve's sleeping face, I realized my greatest fear wasn't just what Eve could do, but what she might become.

Part Two

Chapter 3

An Injured Sparrow

Tarrytown, New York - Spring 1899 - Eve

The sparrow's heart fluttered against my dry, chapped palms like a trapped secret. I'd found the fallen hatchling in the vegetable garden of the Tarrytown Inn, where Ma and I had been stuck these past months, toiling for low pay and little thanks.

My hands were a mess from the scouring I'd done the previous night, nails ragged from my dreadful habit of biting them to the quick. Mostly, I didn't realize I was doing it; but even when I did, I couldn't stop myself. I found it strangely soothing. Ma found it appalling – but that was a small potato on the list of things that Moira Kelly didn't fancy about her daughter. I sighed.

I'd been fetching wood for the kitchen's stove and fireplace, when I spotted the garden tabby, ready to pounce. "Shoo!" I called out, my voice shaky even to my own ears. The cat fixed me with those knowing golden eyes before dashing off, as if to say I had no business giving orders to anyone.

The tiny bird lay there on the soggy soil, one leg bent peculiar. Poor thing was too frightened to peep. I couldn't leave it there to die, though Ma would surely scold me for bringing in another stray. I tucked the injured bird in my apron pocket and hurried back to the dark kitchen, my arms full of wood.

A large cast-iron pot was suspended above the fireplace.. The fireplace sputtered weakly as I added logs, though it did little to warm the dreary space. A proper healer's surgery would smell of carbolic acid and clean linen, not old cabbage and yesterday's fish.

Ma always said I spent too much time dreaming of better things instead of accepting what we had. But how could I not dream when the kitchen walls pressed in so close, years of grease and smoke making the air feel thick and stale?

I kept a small brown leather bag hidden on a tucked-away shelf - my secret medicine kit that I'd pieced together from what I could afford from my wages. Ma would call it more foolishness, but I couldn't help wanting to learn healing.

I laid out witch hazel and cotton strips, my rough hands feeling clumsy with such delicate work. Sometimes when I tended hurt creatures, a peculiar warmth spread through my fingers. Today as I tended the bird, an odd tingling crept into my fingertips. For a moment I thought I saw silver light glowing from my hands, but I blinked hard. Just tricks from the fire, surely.

The tiny bird cheeped and shivered, tickling my rough palms with her soft down. "Shhh... you'll be alright," I cooed. The bird wasn't convinced. Neither was I, to be honest.

Outside, wagons clattered past on muddy Orchard Street, where most of Tarrytown's businesses sat in their neat brick rows. Candy-striped awnings flapped above shop windows displaying silks and fancy goods I could never afford. The Claremont Hotel across the way boasted gas lights, while we made do with oil lamps. They wouldn't hire Irish folks like us - we weren't good enough for their fine establishment. Instead, we got their overflow of hoity-toity folks who had nowhere else to stay. Tarrytown bustled with travelers stopping by on their way up to posh Poughkeepsie (where the fanciest of country estates were located) or down to New York City. But Ma and

I were nowhere posh, just another grimy inn in another dull river town.

The ostentatious Music Hall stood proud nearby, built by some chocolate magnate with more money than sense. Now the Rockefellers and Vanderbilts were building gaudy mansions uphill in their new "Millionaire's Colony." And here we were, scraping by below. I'd spent my last penny on medical supplies while their ladies wore silk gloves that cost more than my monthly wage.

Well, Ma might be okay with being a drudge for the rest of her life, but not me. I sat there, holding that little bird, thinking about how Ma was forty-eight years and still cleaning folks' dirty linen. I shivered, and the bird peeped in response.

I glanced up at the kitchen clock. A few precious moments before the morning rush. I pulled out a dogeared book – Florence Hartley's "Ladies' Book of Etiquette and Manual of Politeness." Several affluent young guests had been reading it lately, and one had left it behind. It wasn't the most thrilling read, but books were far too dear for me to be particular.

I missed New York City. Even the Bowery, rough and crowded as it was, had an excitement to it, and I wasn't so lonesome. In New York I had friends who were close to my age. Plus, there were the most incredible libraries. I'd spent many a Sunday afternoon curled up with a good book. But it was not to be for us Kelly women. After leaving a disastrous job in Hell's Kitchen, we had bounced around from one small town to another as servant work became available, so I didn't have much of a chance to really befriend anyone. Next week would be exactly one year working at this Inn, and I was hoping Ma would allow me to go out on my own on my day off, now that I'd turned eighteen.

While the kettle heated up, I figured I'd bone up on how to "behave like a lady." I did try to sometimes practice those skills by chatting with the female visitors, but they seldom stayed very long. "Besides," Ma had often berated me, "The fancy folk don't want to chat with the help. Keep your head down, your hands busy, and stay out of their way."

I had just found the spot I'd left off from, "Many believe that politeness is but a mask worn in the world to conceal bad passions and impulses" – when a nasty prickle crawled up my spine. The air seemed to thicken, like just before a storm.

I looked up to find Owen Turner strutting in. My stomach turned at the sight of him - a tall, pimply beanpole, who stroked that wisp of a mustache like it was a prize stallion. Though he was only twenty-two, he acted like his years made him wise as Solomon. He loved boasting about being great-nephew to Andrew Carnavoy, though everyone knew the Turners weren't in that league. He'd been at the Inn three endless days, negotiating lumber contracts for his uncle.

"Whatcha readin'?" He reeked of stale tobacco and that awful cologne he doused himself in. Before I could answer, he snatched my book away. The bird in its box gave an alarmed peep, and something inside me shifted—like a door creaking open to a dark room.

"Owen!" I squeaked, hating how small my voice sounded.

"Well now, Eve, that's 'Master Owen' to you..." He loomed closer, and the kitchen seemed to darken, though the morning sun still streamed through the window.

I swallowed hard. "Master Owen, please give back my book." The politeness felt like ashes in my mouth.

He smirked at the title. "Ah, excellent... Allow me to teach you how to be a good and pleasing lady and wife." Then he leaned down, lips puckered, smelling of chew and meanness.

Owen slid the sparrow box to one side of the table and grabbed a chair. The little bird peeped in alarm. Before I could move, he grabbed my chin, forcing me to look into eyes dead as stones. His tongue pushed past my teeth, until I choked and gagged.

I felt frozen solid – couldn't have moved to save my life – when suddenly a strange vibration filled my mind along with a bright light. The air crackled with something that felt ancient and familiar, though I couldn't say why. Silver energy rippled between us, and Owen reeled back, blood spurting from his nose onto his silk vest.

"What in blazes?!" His voice mixed fear and rage, as he yanked out his handkerchief.

The door burst open as Ma marched in, arms full of dirty linens. Her eyes found mine first, then the blood, then the strange shimmer still hanging in the air - though maybe I only imagined that last part. Her hand flew to her pendant, face draining of color before she masked it with a servile smile.

Quick as a blink, Moira turned to give Owen her best smile. "Mornin'. Oh, Mr. Turner, are you okay?" Ma's voice was smooth as butter, though I saw how her knuckles whitened around the linens she held.

"Yes, yes—just a little nosebleed. I'm fine." He dabbed at his face with the silk handkerchief he'd pulled from his breast pocket, but his eyes held a murderous gleam.

"So glad to hear it. I believe your uncle has been looking for you. Upstairs, in the smoking lounge," Ma said.

My face burned watching Ma bow and scrape to someone who'd just... but that was Ma's way. Always practical, always surviving.

My thumbnail found its way to my mouth as Owen brushed past, whispering, "I'm not done with you." I shuddered.

As soon as he was gone, Ma's eyes sparked fire. "Eve—how many times have I warned you about being alone with young men?" Her voice trembled, whether from anger or fear, I couldn't tell.

"Honestly, Ma! I wasn't seeking his attention. I was hiding behind my book here in the kitchen. If I could have put up a 'do not disturb' sign, I would have."

Ma dumped the laundry in the barrel, her movements sharp. "Did you hit him?"

"Of course not! I didn't touch him... wish I could say the same about him. Bastard stuck his disgusting tongue down my throat. I gagged, then there was a flash of light. All of a sudden his nose spurted blood."

Something crossed Ma's face then – something I couldn't quite read before it vanished.

"Good mornin', ladies." Dina bustled in from the garden, baskets overflowing with vegetables and eggs. She was my only friend here - originally from Jamaica with her lovely island lilt and bright don't-miss-a-thing eyes. I saw Ma notice how my face lit up at Dina's arrival. Ma sighed and turned away to get the tea trays ready.

"I just saw Master Turner—his nose sprung a leak?" Dina chuckled, twisting off carrot tops and dunking the veggies in water.

"The shite tried to force me to kiss him. Again..."

"Language!" Ma snapped. I ignored her.

Dina clicked her tongue. "The young master is trouble. And his uncle has money, which means he can be a nasty kind of trouble, indeed."

"I try to avoid him..." My voice sounded small.

"Won't help. Men like that, once they start, they don't like to be stopped," Dina said, scrubbing vegetables.

My heart sank as I helped Ma with tea trays, trying to ignore her frowns. She'd been angry at the whole world, especially me, since Da died when I was just a bairn.

"Ma, I'm worried Dina's right. Master Turner's a regular. We need to leave," I whispered. It wasn't the first time I'd tried to convince her. Each time, Ma found some reason to stay put.

"You really ought to consider getting the chores done, instead of sticking your nose in a book," Ma snipped through clenched teeth. "Let me remind you, missy, that we are at this bloody inn because you begged to come and work here..."

"I thought it would be a good opportunity to rub shoulders with higher-class customers," I countered. "You agreed with me at the time. How was I to know there'd be so many piggish men traveling through here?"

"You'll come to learn, dear daughter, that there are dreadful men to be encountered everywhere," Ma replied, her voice heavy with things unsaid. She began arranging teacups with sharp, precise movements - the way she always did when she was trying to avoid conversation.

I'd seen it before - that look she got whenever change loomed. Like a hunted animal, frozen between the safety of its den and the promise of open fields. Sometimes I wondered if it had something to do with Da's death, though she never spoke of it. Whatever the reason, Ma preferred the devil she knew to the one she didn't.

"What about the Rennards at Greythorne? Ma, you know Dina's brother works for them?" I pressed on, though I knew it was dangerous to push her too hard. Last time I'd suggested leaving, she'd barely spoken to me for days, her hand constantly worrying that pendant of hers.

"Yes, Mr. Rennard is richer than god himself," Dina said.

"Could you ask about work there? As soon as possible?" My voice trembled with a hope I'd learned to guard. The bird in its box stirred, as if sensing my desperation. "They have a proper nurse on staff, Ma. Think of what I could learn—"

"Always dreaming above your station," Ma muttered, but her tone lacked its usual bite. Her fingers found her pendant again, twisting it the way she did when she was torn about something. We'd been having this same argument since I was fifteen - me always pushing for something better, her always pulling us back to what was safe. Or what she thought was safe.

Dina paused, watching Ma carefully. She'd seen this dance between us before - my pushing, Ma retreating. The kitchen grew quiet save for the crackle of the fire - which seemed to rise slightly higher as we waited for Ma's answer.

"The Rennards are good people," Dina offered softly. "They take care of their own."

Ma's hand tightened around her pendant, and I saw that familiar fear flash across her face - the one that appeared whenever there was talk of change. But this time, something was different. Maybe it was Owen's attack, or maybe she'd finally grown tired of watching me chase a future we could never reach here.

Ma set down her tray and gave Dina a long look. "Cook, give the Rennards a call if you'd be so kind. If they have an opportunity for us, we will hear it at least."

I flung my arms around Ma, feeling her familiar stiffness before she reluctantly returned my embrace. Such a rare victory!

"Will do, Mrs. Kelly. Maybe the timing will be better," Dina smiled, though something in her eyes suggested she knew more than she let on. She'd been the one to comfort me after every failed attempt to convince Ma to leave, the one who understood my dreams of something more.

"Eve," Ma shrugged me off. "Add the cream and sugar, then take the tea tray to table four."

"Yes, of course, Ma."

My spirits soared thinking of working for the Rennards. With their great wealth, surely they must be people of the highest quality - not like Owen Turner at all. Perhaps this time would be different. Perhaps this time Ma would finally let us reach for something better.

Chapter 4

A Warning

Eve

I woke early, thanks to my churning stomach. The new tailor-made outfit I'd spent the last of my pay on at Mrs. Kenny's hung ready. She was considered the best seamstress in Tarry-town, and had convinced me to purchase a crisp white shirtwaist with a charcoal gray worsted wool skirt and matching jacket – the latest fashion for a young working woman, and the first new outfit I'd bought in ages. Once on, it did boost my confidence a bit. Most of my clothes were second-hand out of necessity, though Ma was adept at turning tatters into passable garments—another skill I'd neither inherited nor desired to master.

With the last of my toiletries packed away, I stepped out onto the Inn's front porch, my grip white-knuckled on my suitcase. I gazed down bustling Orchard Street, the unknown future stretching before me like a vast, uncharted wilderness.

Smack! Ma slammed her suitcase down next to me, making her mood quite clear.

"Bloody hell!" I yelped.

Ma's eyes flashed. "Watch yourself!"

I bit my lip, tasting blood. "Sorry, Ma."

Ma's gaze raked over my new outfit, her lips thinning to a white line. "Must have cost a pretty penny."

I smoothed my skirt, fighting the urge to fidget under her scrutiny. "I just thought—"

"Did you now?" she cut me off.

I stopped myself from snapping back, seeing how nervous she was, too. Ma had a tell—whenever she was anxious, her fingers would fiddle with that old Celtic shield pendant she kept around her neck. Today, she was rubbing the little pearl inside as if it were a genie in a lantern.

"I'm still not sure this is the right thing to do, lass." Ma's tough exterior dropped for a moment as she sighed. "Leaving the Inn so fast. Going to who-knows-where, to do who-knows-what."

"Well yes, but you must agree—we deserve better pay, better treatment," I said.

Ma's eyes flashed. "Deserve?! The world doesn't care what we deserve, girl. It's safer to know our place and stay in it."

I bristled. How could we move forward if Ma was always looking back? No wonder I'm afraid, I thought. I come by it honestly.

Dina emerged from the garden, a wicker basket brimming with fresh escarole, carrots and ramps balanced on her hip. Her eyes darted between Ma and me, reading the tension in our stances.

"Mornin'," she said, her usual cheerful lilt strained. She set the basket down and enveloped me in a tight hug, whispering, "You take care now, you hear?"

I nodded against her shoulder, inhaling her comforting scent of spices and baking bread. "I'll miss you," I murmured, my voice catching.

"Now, now. None of that," Dina said. "You'll be too busy in that grand house to think of us common folk."

I opened my mouth to protest, but Dina cut me off with a wink. "My sister says they have a big library filled with all sorts of books. Maybe you can sneak one here and there without them folks noticing, hey?" Dina said.

My eyes lit up at the thought of an entire private library at my fingertips. Who was I kidding though... It wasn't like they were going to let the help touch their expensive treasures.

Ma cleared her throat, her foot tapping an impatient rhythm on the wooden porch.

Dina's smile faltered for a moment as she turned to Ma. "Mrs. Kelly, I'm sure you'll keep our girl grounded up there with all them fancy folk."

Moira's lips thinned. "Aye, that I will."

A heavy silence fell, broken by the front door opening behind us. Out slithered the reptilian Owen Turner, pipe in hand. "Cook, there you are!" he hollered. "I'll take one of those omelets you made me yesterday. You know what, better make it two: I'm famished."

Dina shared an eye roll with me. "Happy to, Master Turner." Dina gave a quick sigh, then "Best of luck to you both. Give my love to Bette and Isaiah, won't you?"

I nodded, words failing me as she hurried inside.

Owen took his sweet time standing on the porch way too close to us. He fiddled with re-lighting his pipe, only to puff a thick cloud of pungent tobacco smoke into the air.

The man's disgusting smoke and even more vile personality made me feel queasy. I tried to distract myself by looking down the road.

Suddenly, Ma jabbed me in the side with her elbow. I hadn't even realized I'd been biting my nails again. Damn! A little blood appeared at the corner of my right thumb's cuticle. Ashamed, I tucked my rough hands behind my back.

"Ah, that'll be the Rennard carriage," Owen mused as an elegant horse-drawn carriage turned onto Orchard Street and headed towards the Inn. Owen sucked on his pipe, watching it approach through the hazy air. "Loads of money and yet, no taste."

I clenched my jaw to stop myself from making a savage retort. I could feel my body almost vibrate with anger towards him.

Across from the Inn, a raven landed on a shop awning and

croaked loudly. A second raven, then a third, descended side by side. Were they staring at us? My skin prickled.

Ma's hand flew to her pendant, her whispered words barely audible: 'The Morrigan.'

A chill ran down my spine at the unfamiliar name. I looked at Ma with curiosity. It wasn't like her to reference old Irish myths and stories – she mostly refused to discuss the past at all. I mused for a moment – I had heard that name before. But where?

Owen finished his tobacco, tapped out his pipe, leaned in, and whispered in my ear. "A parting gift." He pressed a small box into my hands, his smirk setting my teeth on edge.

Owen headed down the front steps, clearly intending to welcome the Rennards.

"What is it?" Ma asked in a whisper.

My fingers trembled as I opened the little box. A tiny broken body lay inside. The fledgling's neck bent at an impossible angle. My vision blurred and a strangled gasp escaped me as I snapped the box shut. What kind of a monster...?

Ma looked at Owen, who stood several yards away from us, her voice quivering with quiet rage. "Bollocks! I suppose it's a good thing we're getting away."

I sniffed away my tears and nodded. Ma kindly took the box with the dead bird from me and walked it around the back of the inn. Och, ye rotten little man! May the devil take you! I prayed to whoever was listening that I'd never see his face again.

Ma returned to the porch, just as an opulent carriage of the finest mahogany and lustrous leathers came to a stop. Pulled by four large gray bays (each animal must have been over sixteen hands high) the carriage's side was emblazoned by a large crest – silver on a background of deep burgundy with a fierce little fox posed in the center of the shield. Even the wheel spokes gleamed.

Owen went to the window of the carriage and began to chat with whomever was inside.

Moira and I straightened up, and it was then that I became aware of the birds. Where there had been just three ravens, one by one, more now materialized. They settled silently on nearby rooftops, shop awnings, and tree branches. Their collective gaze felt heavy, expectant - as if they were harbingers of some impending doom. Some croaked and ruffled their feathers, while others shuffled back and forth along their perches, beady eyes fixed below.

If Ma noticed, she was doing her damndest to keep a straight face. I followed her lead.

The coachman was a large-framed fellow with impressive whiskers and eyes like raisins in a plum-pudding face. He hopped down and motioned for Owen to step aside as he set a wooden step on top of the mud. The carriage door opened with a flourish. He offered an arm, and an older woman clambered out, dressed in slightly dated, but clearly expensive attire. Her sharp blue eyes pierced me with disdain.

Oh well, I sighed. That old biddy's going to be a tough nut to crack.

On the woman's head was one of those ridiculous chapeaus with a stuffed bird poised in flight. I felt a pang of sorrow for the poor little fledgling Owen had killed.

"Ah Mrs. Price, how was your voyage home from Europe?" Owen asked.

"Long and uncomfortable," she complained, then softened. "And how is your dear Uncle Andrew?"

I looked downward to signal respect as the two chatted away. With my eyes cast down, I caught the emergence of a shapely leg and ankle graced with an elegant navy leather shoe. Out of the carriage stepped a strikingly beautiful young woman, holding a floral silk parasol with a cherry wood handle. She carefully avoided the larger puddles of mud, holding her skirts up higher than she would probably have liked. Finally, she looked up and cast a warm smile towards us. I bit my tongue to stop from making a sound.

She was the epitome of the Gibson Girl – perfection personified. I'd seen women like her in magazines, but never in person.

I became acutely aware of my callused hands, chewed fingernails, and old clunky work shoes. Despite polishing them last night, the scuffs and scrapes were too deep to conceal. The young woman's smile was warm, but I couldn't shake the feeling that I was a bug under glass, being examined and found wanting.

"Saskia, my dear," Owen purred, "you look lovelier than ever."

Oh! Magazine Girl must be Miss Saskia Rennard!

I watched as Owen grasped the young woman's hand and brought her knuckles to his lips for a kiss. I shuddered in silence but was amused to observe a moment of distaste flash across Miss Rennard's face.

"Hello, Owen," she replied, politely. "What a lovely surprise to see you here...We're only stopping for a moment, so we will need to postpone catching up to a future date," she said with a honey smooth voice. "My best to your cousin, Gloria!"

Annoyed by the dismissal, he snapped, "In that case, I shall bid you my adieus." He pivoted and headed up the stairs to gobble up his breakfast before irritating all manner of people.

Miss Rennard approached us. "Mrs. Kelly? Miss Kelly, I presume?" she enquired. Gorgeous blonde tresses of hair piled in generous waves atop a perfectly symmetrical face, with clear grey eyes, high cheekbones, and a peaches and cream complexion.

"Aye," Moira said, and curtsied. I stood there, mouth agape, until Ma elbowed me, and I matched the gesture. My cheeks reddened.

"A pleasure to meet you both," said Miss Rennard. "My name is Saskia Rennard, and this is my Aunt, Mrs. Winifred Price. And, our hounds' master and drover, Mr. Maxwell."

The walrus-looking man sneered in greeting at the mention of his name. He tipped his cap, but his eyes crawled first over me, then over Ma. I suppressed a shudder.

"A pleasure," said Ma. "Many thanks for passage to your family estate. We are honored by the opportunity."

"It wasn't my choice," Mrs. Price snapped.

Ma's lips pressed tight in a flat line. Her eyes sparked before she lowered them.

Miss Rennard ignored her Aunt. "It's no trouble. Father asked us to stop. We've only just returned from a year-long sojourn in Europe," Miss Rennard explained, waving her parasol in the air.

As if triggered by the innocuous gesture, the sky exploded into a maelstrom of black feathers and sharp beaks.

Screams pierced the air as the ravens dive-bombed our group. Ma grabbed me and pulled me violently to her breast. Poor Mrs. Price screamed in abject horror one of the birds screeched in her ears as it tore at her hat. Was the hat the provocation? I wondered.

Miss Rennard used her parasol as a weapon. She swung it towards one of the ravens and managed to bat at it, but that seemed to just agitate it. It clawed at the shoulder of her dress before flapping off. More ravens hopped off a nearby branch and swooped down.

Without a thought, I pulled away from my mother, ran down the steps, and planted myself solidly in front of Miss Rennard and her Aunt. My voice ripped from my throat in a primal scream: 'STOP!'

To my amazement - and horror - the birds froze mid-attack, their eyes locked on me. The sudden silence was deafening. An energy coursed through my body, making my fingertips tingle. What have I done?

My skin crawled as dozens of beady little eyes stared at me from every direction. Odd prickles tingled in the tips of my fingers and toes – I shook my hands to get rid of the strange sensation.

Just then, Maxwell drew a pistol from his belt and fired into the air with an explosive clap! The birds erupted again into chaos, taking flight at the sound of the gunshot. "Black-feathered bastards!" Maxwell shouted after the fleeing birds.

Passersby had paused to watch the chaos – in turns stunned and bemused by the birds' behavior. I ignored the busybodies, and turned to check on Miss Rennard. "Are you hurt, Miss?"

"One of those hell birds clawed me," Miss Rennard responded. She pointed to her shoulder, where the silk had been torn.

"May I take a look?" I asked.

"Certainly." Miss Rennard was a little surprised by my request.

I moved the fabric aside and could see a deep scratch with beads of blood, glistening red.

"We will need to clean this before we go," I said with as much authority as I could muster. I retrieved my bag and pulled out my trusty medical kit.

"You're a veritable Florence Nightingale," Miss Rennard smiled, as I poured a bit of witch hazel onto a clean cloth and dabbed at her clawed skin.

Meanwhile, Mrs. Price sat on the steps, hat and hair askew. "Well, I am not alright. That was madness!" Ma tut-tutted to reassure her, but Mrs. Price was not having it. She waved Ma away.

"Maxwell! Help me off these steps! I don't want to stay another moment in this horrid town."

"Yes, Ma'am." He hurried over and took her by the arm. She climbed back into the carriage far faster than she'd seemed capable.

As I finished cleaning the wound, Miss Rennard put her hand on top of mine. "Thank you, Miss Kelly, that feels a lot better."

I could feel my cheeks heat. I hadn't realized I was holding my breath until I replied, "My pleasure." Not wanting to appear forward, I quickly turned and put my things back in my bag.

When I glanced up, I felt Ma staring at me with her familiar displeased look. *What now*, I wondered. I just shrugged and carried on.

Miss Rennard leaned inside the carriage and talked quietly to her Aunt, while Ma and I brought our bags to the carriage to help Maxwell load them. Aunt Winifred had no concern about the hired help hearing her.

"...don't know what Theodore is thinking, bringing in more of... their kind," the older woman hissed.

"Now, Aunt Winifred, you know Father has his reasons," Miss Rennard replied, her voice low but firm.

"Reasons! Ha! Mark my words, girl. No good will come of this.

These... people... they bring nothing but trouble. As for now, they can sit next to Maxwell on the riding board!" Mrs. Price howled.

Miss Rennard, apologetic, turned to us. "Mrs. Kelly, Miss Kelly, please join Maxwell up above." She waved her hand to encourage us.

"Of course, Miss Rennard," Ma replied, before I could respond. After the carriage door was closed, though, Ma turned and shot me a look that told me exactly how she felt about our new employers. Ma's pessimism made my stomach flip-flop. Determined not to be negative, I shook off her attitude and focused on being excited to start this new chapter of our lives.

Maxwell gave us each a hand up onto the riding board, although I did not appreciate it when his clammy grip on my hand lingered, and his eyes gravitated towards my chest. Ma didn't notice, as she was busy getting herself sorted. I did my best to divert my attention.

Finally, Maxwell took the reins, and with a low whistle the horses began to pull the carriage. They set off up Orchard Street on their way north toward Poughkeepsie. Block by block, house by house, Tarrytown faded away behind us, A great sense of relief bubbled up within me. *It's really happening.*

As the carriage rolled northward, the gentle sway of the journey lulled me into a reverie, my mind painting pictures of the grand house awaiting us. I imagined myself in a world of polished silver and crisp linens, far removed from the grime and drudgery of the Inn. Still, as the miles passed, a faint unease crept in. Mrs. Price's disdainful glare and Maxwell's lingering clammy touch sent a shiver down my spine. Might they be tiny warnings of what lay ahead?

As Poughkeepsie drew nearer, I steeled myself. Whatever Greythorne held - opportunity or obstacle - I was determined to face it head-on, my mother's warnings echoing in the back of my mind.

Chapter 5

A Curious Thing

Saskia

I gazed outside as we rolled out of Poughkeepsie, watching the sky grow darker with each passing mile. The vibrant bustle of the town faded behind us, replaced by an eerie quiet, only broken by the rhythmic clop of hooves and the creak of the carriage wheels. My attention drifted to the exquisite gold Lalique bracelet I had acquired from my Parisian admirer, the Marquis d'Limousin. Each link, adorned with alternating diamonds and amethysts, shimmered in the dappled light streaming through the window, casting fragments of white and aquamarine across the carriage's walls and ceiling. It was a true art nouveau masterpiece, and I cherished it deeply.

"Saskia," Aunt Winnie glanced up from a letter she had just finished reading, her eyes scrutinizing me. "It seems your Papa has a surprise in store for you once we arrive at Greythorne." My aunt relished in the thrill of secrets, be they trivial or significant.

"Is it the Hanoverian stallion I wrote to him about?" I eagerly asked, my heart racing. The singular prospect I truly longed for was the chance to ride and compete in local equestrian events in Dutchess County. I had honed my riding skills in Paris, and with the assistance of a local trainer, I had gained newfound confidence in jumping and dressage. I couldn't wait for my father and Teddy to take me hunting again; I was itching to surprise them with how much I had improved.

Her eyes crinkled with amusement. "I shan't tell you—it would ruin the surprise." I tried my best to coax the information from her, but she artfully changed the subject. "Now that we are back," Aunt Winnie continued, "perhaps this year your father will be persuaded to host a summer ball and invite the most eligible bachelors from the finest families."

I scowled, and my unenthusiastic reaction didn't go unnoticed by my perceptive aunt. "Seriously, dear, you need to change your attitude about settling down. Your Father is counting on you to do your bit."

Not wishing to ignite an argument, I resorted to flattery. "Well, Aunt Winnie, it's hardly my fault that I have such an independent, strong-willed role model to admire, to say nothing of your *joie de vivre*. You answer to no one. You travel as you wish and speak your mind freely," I said, my words ringing with truth. "A husband would only serve to limit those freedoms."

"Now, Saskia, I'm just making a silk purse out of a sow's ear. I was already married and overseeing the estate with my dear Walter, may he rest in peace, at your age. I promise you, your life won't end once you are married..."

Sighing, I recognized I needed a break from Aunt Winifred's relentless probing. I feigned a yawn and settled into a corner of the carriage, feeling glum about my enforced return. Yet, a small, serendipitous bright spot lay in the young woman seated just feet above me. She felt worlds apart from my refined circle, yet there was an allure, a mystery that both intrigued and unsettled me. Although she lacked the poise and polish of ma cherie Isabel, her openness was enchanting. Her eagerness to care for others, demonstrated by her little kit of salves and balms, captured my admiration. And...she had somehow commanded those ravens. A shiver traveled down my spine as I recalled the uncanny stillness that had enveloped the birds at her command. What other secrets might this intriguing girl be hiding?

Aunt Winifred began to snore loudly, her head lolling against the cabin's headrest. Poor thing had experienced quite the shock that morning and, unlike me, had little tolerance for wildlife. With great annoyance, she had removed her precious bird hat upon settling inside the carriage. One of the ravens had clawed at it, and the dead bird clinging to the chapeau barely held on. While I felt a twinge of sympathy for my Aunt, I couldn't help but think the raven had done her a fashion favor.

In stark contrast to Aunt Winifred, who found all rural pastimes most unpleasant, I had spent countless hours outdoors with my father and brother. We cherished our time riding, hunting, and fishing. The estate my father had purchased was grand by Northeast standards, replete with forests, a creek, and an expansive pond. Teddy and I had explored and hunted these grounds to our hearts' content during our youth. Frankly, I would choose tracking game over the tedious feminine pursuits of embroidery and practicing the pianoforte any day.

Suddenly, a wad of tobacco splattered against the carriage window. *Ugh.* I struck the handle of my parasol against the roof of the carriage. From above, Maxwell called down, "Sorry, ma'am." The noise jolted my aunt from her slumber. "What's going on?" she mumbled.

"Nothing to worry about. Maxwell spat out some chew. *C'est une mauvaise habitude.* Why men indulge in such distastefulness..."

"Aah, Saskia. Men must have their little pleasures." Aunt Winifred's voice drifted as she closed her eyes again.

I had worked diligently on my French during my time in Paris. Initially, the Parisians had snubbed me for my atrocious accent, but I was determined not to become fodder for their amusement. Now, as I returned to New York, I decided that incorporating French phrases into my everyday speech would help solidify my grasp on the language. And honestly, everything just seemed to sound better in French, *n'est-ce pas?*

The coach jerked to an abrupt stop. "We can't possibly have arrived yet?" Aunt Winifred asked, her eyes open but still sleepy.

I shook my head in response. Maxwell leapt down and approached the carriage window, carrying a bundle of rags. "Sorry, ladies, I just need to make a quick stop." He trundled off into the bushes, seeking a semblance of privacy.

Oh Lord, I thought to myself.

"Ugh! The man is so uncouth!" Aunt Winifred wrinkled her nose in disapproval. Despite our differences, it seemed we could both agree on our assessment of Maxwell. My father seemed to like him well enough, having worked at Greythorne for as long as I could remember. In contrast, Aunt Winifred longed for Theodore to hire what she deemed a "better class" of servant—those she believed were more trustworthy and genteel. Of course, it wasn't her money that was at stake, leaving her with no real say in the matter.

Regardless, I relished a break from my grumpy aunt. I swung open the carriage door, feeling the sun break through the clouds and brighten my spirits. "Auntie, I'll just stretch my legs."

"Stay close!" she commanded.

As I stepped out, Miss Kelly's voice rang from above. "May I join you?"

"Of course," I replied, delight sweeping through me. I closed the carriage door and reassured my aunt I would return shortly. She leaned back, her eyes drifting shut before I finished speaking.

Miss Kelly climbed down, and we began to stroll along a charming, tree-lined country lane. Lush grasses flourished against the backdrop of rolling green hills, not a carriage in sight. Taking a deep breath, I relished the invigorating scent of fresh air. "I hear your home is beautiful," she remarked as we skirted a mud puddle.

"Indeed. *C'est magnifique.*" I noticed the puzzled look she shot my way. Perhaps she hadn't learned any French.

"How long were you in France?" she queried.

"My Aunt and I spent much of the past year in Paris," I shared.

Eve's eyes lit with excitement. "Sounds wonderful."

I nodded, the memories flooding back. "It truly is. The *crème de la crème* gather there. The music, the salons, the museums, the restaurants, the fashion—it's all distinctly magical. You must visit someday."

She shrugged. "Perhaps."

Realizing my prattling about Paris might seem a touch pretentious, I added, "At any rate, I'd still be there if Father hadn't called me home."

"And what of the lady of the house?" she ventured delicately.

I chuckled, appreciating the formality in her tone. "That's me. My mother died delivering my little brother. I scarcely remember her."

"I'm so sorry... I don't remember my Da well either... He passed away when I was very young," Eve murmured, a hint of sorrow shading her voice.

I shrugged, accepting this as part of life. "My father is my rock," I stated firmly. "A more honorable and generous man does not exist. You're going to love working at Greythorne. When my father takes a shine to someone, he truly does all he can to assist them."

Eve nodded, but then her attention shifted as something in the field ahead caught her eye. She pivoted with glee. "Do you mind if we head that way? Towards those blooms?"

Curiosity drove me to follow her toward a patch of golden flowers. "What are they?" I inquired.

"Chamomile. Excellent for tea and all sorts of remedies." She knelt to pick the delicate yellow blooms.

At that moment, I felt a pressing urge to relieve myself. Glancing around, I noticed we were quite alone—Maxwell, Aunt Winifred, and Mrs. Kelly nowhere in sight. "Might as well seek my own relief," I thought. Spotting a secluded spot, I walked over and began to hike up my skirts.

Miss Kelly turned away to give me some privacy, but I noticed the nape of her neck flush a deep crimson. I studied her back for a moment, intrigued by her glossy copper curls. Then, suddenly, the air

42

grew thick with an oppressive stillness. A chill coursed down my spine, and the hairs on my neck stood alert. It seemed the peaceful field held its breath, aware of an impending danger.

CH-CH-CH-CH-CH...

The unmistakable sound of a rattlesnake pierced the air. I froze mid-action. Snakes abounded in the countryside, but the rattler's warning indicated I had strayed too close. I couldn't see where it was, and that realization sent a jolt of panic through me. Ever so cautiously, I reached down with one arm while remaining as still as possible.

"Miss Rennard! Snake!"

I turned my head slowly, and caught a glimpse of the dull chevroned pattern of browns and grays as the snake coiled like living rope. A pair of coal-black eyes fixed on me, its pink forked tongue flicking in and out a mere four feet away. The rattler's tail shook ominously, and my heart pounded in my chest, each second stretching into eternity as I faced the deadly creature.

Miss Kelly's eyes dilated, and she suddenly spoke the word "No!" in a voice deeper than usual. An energy rippled through the air, making my skin prickle. For an instant, I could have sworn I saw an otherworldly flash in her eyes. The air crackled, and I felt a fleeting sensation of power emanating from her.

The snake paused, its arrow-shaped head craning toward me, flicking its tongue in anticipation. It was all the time I needed. I deftly reached beneath my skirts to my garter, pulling out my silver derringer in one fluid motion. The pearl-inlaid handle fit comfortably in my grip, reassuring and steady. I pivoted, raised the pistol, and sighted along the short barrel. If I missed, there was no doubt the rattler would lunge and strike.

I drew in a deep breath, held steady, and aimed carefully. With a slow squeeze of the trigger, just as my father had taught me, I fired.

BLAM!

The derringer kicked back, smoke wafting, the report echoing in my ears. The snake's head exploded into a fine, red mist. The air filled with the acrid scent of gunpowder mixed with the metallic tang of blood.

The headless snake thrashed wildly, its blood spraying across the nearby flowers and grasses. I stood up, dropping my skirts as I hurriedly examined my dress for any stains. Thankfully, I found none—a relief, as my French attire was nearly irreplaceable back in New York.

Miss Kelly's eyes rolled back, and she collapsed into a thick patch of grass. I rushed over, anxiety surging within me. "Miss Kelly, are you alright?" I asked, fear pulsating in my chest as I waited for a response. My heart raced as she lay there, unresponsive. After a tense moment, her eyes fluttered open, and she sat up quickly, catching her breath. "Yes, yes, thank you. The gunshot took me by surprise."

"Of course. I apologize for startling you with my pistol," I said, offering her my hand. She accepted it, and I noticed her rough palms and strong grip. With a heave, Eve stood and brushed herself off. There was something wondrous yet peculiar about this young woman —the birds, the snake... I couldn't resist asking, "Is snake charming another of your skills?"

"No, Miss, I wish..." She smiled shyly at me. "But may I ask, why do you keep a pistol?"

"Ah, well, it was a gift from my father on my eighteenth birthday," I replied. Then, with playful cheek, added, "And I keep it tucked away here—" I lifted my skirts to show the leather garter and holster strapped to my right thigh.

Eve blushed crimson, quickly bending down to retrieve the bundles of flowers she had collected before the disturbance. The snake's thrashing began to subside, blood pooling around its lifeless form.

At that point, Mrs. Kelly and Maxwell came rushing up across the field. "Eve! Miss Rennard! What happened?" Mrs. Kelly cried in alarm.

"It's alright, Ma," Eve responded. "Miss Rennard shot a snake, but neither of us are hurt."

I lifted the dead snake for them to see, its length impressive and girth substantial. Mrs. Kelly's eyes widened in disbelief, and I suspected she might faint at the sight.

"Good shot, Miss!" Maxwell beamed. "That'll make a fine belt."

"Here, why don't you take it?" I said, feeling a swell of pride as I handed him the snake.

Mrs. Kelly turned to me, worry etched across her face. "Your Aunt is worried sick. Come, Miss Rennard. Let us get you back to the carriage."

"Oh goodness, yes, let's hurry before her imagination runs wild." I winked at Miss Kelly, who beamed back at me with a radiant smile.

As we made our way back across the field, careful to keep watch for any more snakes basking in the sun, I couldn't help but notice Mrs. Kelly fidgeting nervously with a pearl pendant necklace resting on her ample bosom. She glanced up, noticing my eyes on her, and quickly tucked it away. I thought it rather silly; I had no interest in trifling pieces of cheap jewelry.

We reached the lane and quickly turned back toward the carriage. As we walked, I took surreptitious glances at Miss Kelly. What a fascinating creature she was... seemingly fearless, even without a pistol in hand. I looked forward to getting to know her better, even as a nagging voice in the back of my mind whispered that there was something deeper within her, hints of secrets that might draw me into perilous waters.

As we neared the carriage, an undeniable sense that our lives would become inexorably intertwined settled upon me, for better or for worse.

Chapter 6

The Road To Greythorne

Eve

For the remainder of the carriage ride, my mind was focused on the remarkable Miss Rennard. She was unlike anyone I'd ever met. A young woman with a pistol! Kept underneath her fancy silk dress! In a scarlet garter! And an amazing shot! She was a revelation.

I'd certainly had to take care of the occasional well-heeled young woman. On the whole, beneath the money, their lives and their minds were quite shallow and dull. For all their access to books and learning, their opportunities to travel, and most importantly of all, (at least to me), to actually accomplish something meaningful, they seemed mostly to stay put (alternating between their winter and summer places, with the occasional foray to a different big city for shopping or socializing). Their conversations swirled around a litany of who's-who, and chasing after the latest dazzling trend that they intended to adopt. Of course, special attention was paid to potential suitors, young and not-so-young, whom they evaluated much as I might study an apple before opting to buy it.

One such insipid lady was Miss Earlmore of the Newport Earl-mores. I cringed at the mere thought of her. She had passed through the Tarrytown Inn not a fortnight earlier, and much to her chagrin, her maid had up and quit on her just upon arrival. So I had the unexpected task of attending to the lady during her stay.

Within a few moments of being in her presence, I completely understood why the help had fled. The woman was the most indolent creature I had ever met. Miss Earlmore was so used to servants responding to her every bid and call, that I was surprised when she lifted her own teacup. In the course of a single day she went through three or four clothing changes, as she visited and called upon the Vanderbilts and other denizens of Millionaire's Row.

For each clothing change, I needed to drop what I was doing and rush to prepare her dresses and coats, which invariably involved unpacking and repacking her trunks in search of the particular outfit she sought for each visit. And then into the night she would go, arriving back at the Inn well past my usual bedtime, so that I had to await her return and force myself to stay awake. For all of this effort I was repaid in insults and criticism, accused of laziness and slowness, and disdained by her in front of her rotund and bewhiskered father, George Earlmore, as though I were too doltish to understand or be offended.

The Earlmores scowled and looked down their noses upon folks such as myself and Ma, calling us hardworking Irish immigrants "lazy, stupid, thieving bridgets." I'd seen the grotesque caricatures of servants such as ourselves in popular publications, including Puck. We were drawn with the faces of apes and said to possess only the dimmest wit. I found their notion of us as lazy to be ridiculous, considering that we were up before dawn and worked til nightfall without stop. Meanwhile, these young women spent much of their time sleeping in, being waited on, eating, gossiping, embroidering and generally lying about like plump, over-fussed Persian cats. They mostly functioned as family ornaments for proof of wealth, good breeding and marriage opportunities.

On the other hand, even from the short time since we had met this morning, it was obvious Miss Rennard was not at all like those spoiled girls. Though quite full of herself and annoyingly proud of her frenchiness (*Is that a word?*), she seemed to have a different level of energy and self-reliance. And, unlike her curmudgeon of an aunt, she did not seem like a bigot. Really, she was quite friendly and open. And if that hadn't been enough to win me over, when she pulled the little pistol from her garter, and obliterated that snake's head... Well, that's a moment I wouldn't soon forget.

I'd never known a woman to handle guns and pistols. My mother was deathly afraid of all such devices, and I suppose I'd learned that sort of fear from her. But now thinking on it, why shouldn't a woman be able to protect herself in such dire circumstances?

At any rate, my musings rambled on as did the carriage, until we came upon the most magnificent and ornate wrought-iron gates, painted in gold, embedded in a high stone wall. On the gates was the same boldly colored Rennard Family Crest as on the carriage.

"Faith and begorrah!" Ma exclaimed. She was as flabbergasted as I by the sight.

Maxwell chuckled and said "You haven't seen anything, yet." He hopped down off the riding board with a massive set of keys and approached the giant gates. He selected a huge bronze one. The gates must have been well engineered, because when he unlocked them, they swung open in perfect balance.

"What did I tell you, Ma?! We've landed in a pot of jam," I whispered.

"Well, they certainly spent a pretty penny on this wall," she replied. Always skeptical, she added, "Let's see if the insides match up with the out."

Maxwell grabbed the closer horse's bridle and walked the carriage through, then went to lock the gate behind us. The grounds were immaculate. We could see a crew of gardeners out trimming some of the shrubs. Off to our left sat a large glass greenhouse, filled with brightly-hued roses, lilacs, lilies and more, grown no doubt to decorate the various rooms of the manse. Past a small hillock, I saw just the hint of a --

CLANG! The gates struck hard and rang like an ominous bell. Put my hair on end. Maxwell clambered back up and guided the horses up the main entry concourse.

oh-Oh, oh-Oh! To our right, one of several pairs of magnificent white and black swans trumpeted, as they sailed atop the mirror surface of a delightful pond. A creek ran through to the pond, with stacked stone to create a pretty waterfall effect on one end. Both Ma and I were slack jawed.

Maxwell glanced at our reaction and laughed. "Told you!"

After the pond, we approached the main property: Greythorne Mansion. Colossal, stately walls of expertly-hewn grey stonework launched themselves from the verdant gardens up toward the sky. A crown of narrow gothic turrets, - an ostentatiousness I'd thought reserved for the likes of Manhattan's St. Patrick's Cathedral - aimed at the heavens with what looked like spearpoints of black slate. We had attended services there at the New York City Cathedral, Ma and I, only a few times and all before we had left Manhattan for good. But while St. Patrick's spires sought to channel the divine, Greythorne's appeared to me its inverse: dark, dominant, and disdainful all at once. The building loomed, a grand edifice devoted to the power of money.

"Just a moment please, ladies," said Maxwell as he hopped down. He grabbed the little wooden stool kept tucked away, and placed it with a flourish in front of the carriage door. Out stepped Miss Rennard.

Saskia's aunt clambered out of the carriage, with a grumble and even less grace. She stood beside the carriage, watching with her hawk-like eyes, as the luggage was unloaded.

Then it was our turn. Maxwell had unpleasantly sweaty hands, so I did my best to avoid any hand holding with the man. I scrambled down on my own. Ma followed with some assistance.

"*Bienvenue á* Greythorne," Miss Rennard announced to us with a swish of her arm.

"Thank you, Miss," Ma responded.

"I think you'll find that it's definitely a step up from the Tarry-town Inn," she said slyly.

I laughed. "We're happy to be here."

The butler, a gray-haired African American man, dressed in navy and gold-trimmed livery, came running down the steps to greet us. His handsome face and smile were heartwarming. This must be Dina's brother-in-law. I sensed a lot of wisdom from behind his lined face.

"Welcome home Mrs. Price, Miss Rennard," he had a pleasing baritone voice.

Miss Rennard gave him a warm smile. "So good to see you Isaiah. It's been too long."

Behind Isaiah followed a couple of young valets who hastily began to help Maxwell unload the carriage. One was a skinny ginger lad, the other a portly blond; perhaps they were just eighteen or so. Looked like they had been hired from a nearby village. They whisked the bags and trunks up the stairs and into the house.

The sound of rapid hoofbeats clattered through the afternoon air. A magnificent ebony Arabian horse cantered towards us. The rider was a handsome enough young man with similar coloring and features to Miss Rennard. He dismounted with ease, and approached with a large gregarious smile. His clothes were soiled with mud and blood. Strapped onto the stallion was a freshly killed deer, leaking its life out onto the horse's haunch. The buck had had its neck slashed twice, in a peculiar criss-cross pattern. I shuddered and looked away from the poor beast.

"Hallo, dear sister! Auntie!" The rider waved and hollered.

"Ah, Teddy...still playing in the muck?" Mrs. Price inquired.

I stifled a giggle.

"Nice to see you, too, Aunty," he responded.

Teddy pivoted to give his sister a hug, but Miss Rennard looked at his dirty clothes and put her hand up to stop him.

"*Arrêt*, Teddy! It's silk."

Teddy glanced down at his outfit as if noticing the filth for the first time. "Oh, sorry, of course. I'm just so glad to have you back. It's been such a *bore* being stuck here alone with Father. I've had to endure countless days listening to him drone on and on about business. All while you've been gallivanting around Europe...Even the riding and the hunting have been dull of late." He had the petulant manner of someone spoiled and entitled since birth.

Miss Rennard responded with mild irritation. "I wouldn't describe it as gallivanting..." She redirected her brother's attention towards us. "Teddy, meet the new help; Mrs. Moira Kelly and Miss Eve Kelly, recently of Tarrytown. Father had us pick them up."

"Delighted. Welcome to our cozy abode," he added.

Ma and I did a quick curtsey. As I looked up, I noticed his eyes evaluate me. He began to stare at my chest in a most discomforting way.

Ma pursed her lips into a thin white line of annoyance. If he weren't our employer, she would have given him an earful for looking at me so brazenly.

And then, to my surprise, Miss Rennard shook her head subtly but firmly towards her brother and he snapped out of it.

Was she trying to protect me? Again, I wondered, how unique and unpredictable she was.

Isaiah came over and offered to help carry our bags.

Typical of Ma, she waved him off. "Not necessary, we can manage our own things," she stated crisply.

Isaiah responded with a polite, "As you wish," and winked at me.

"Your sister-in-law, Dina, asked me to send you her regards," I said.

Isaiah flashed a warm smile towards me. "Much appreciated, Miss Kelly."

"Very well, please follow along," Miss Saskia encouraged us to head up the stairs.

"Maxwell, make sure the staff take care of this deer," Teddy commanded.

"Yessir." Maxwell waved over one of the stable hands, who jogged over and led the horse away.

We all followed in Miss Rennard's wake, up the stairs and into the gaping maw of Greythorne.

Stepping out of the bright afternoon sun, we found ourselves in a cool, palatial foyer of marble floors, stone columns and banks of windows. Animal heads of all sorts bedecked the walls amidst enormous oil portraits of various--ancestors, perhaps? Instead of the ornate Turkish or Persian rugs I had been expecting, several large pelts had been lain across the floor. Countless lifeless black marble eyes gazed up at me, as if to beseech me for some kind of aid that would never be rendered. It was clear we had entered a huntsman's abode.

Mrs. Price's face wrinkled in distaste as she looked around the space. "Good Lord, your brother has gone overboard with the taxidermy, Saskia. The place looks like a ghastly zoo. Your mother must be turning over in her grave!"

As she spoke, a dark, wood-paneled door swung open and out strode a tall, regal man, dressed in a well-tailored suit, with a neatly trimmed silvering beard. Mr. Theodore Rennard, presumably.

"No such thing, dear sister! Each one of these trophies was hard earned. Besides it brings your nephew great joy to preserve each one," Mr. Rennard radiated genuine warmth and charisma. I could see where Saskia had inherited her magnetism.

"Father!" Miss Rennard flounced over to Mr. Rennard. Her father picked her up as though she were still a child, swung her round in the air, skirts billowing, and gave her a big kiss on the cheek, before putting her back down. Both smiled from ear to ear after the greeting.

"I do believe you've grown a bit," said Mr. Rennard.

"I doubt it, Father. Not sure that that's likely."

Mr. Rennard sighed. "It's hard for me to accept that you are now twenty-one, dear; In my mind, I still picture you as that mischievous nine-year-old sneaking her mother's gowns from the attic."

"Hello, Theodore!" Aunt Winifred chimed in.

Mr. Rennard gave his sister a warm peck on her cheek.

"Winnie, so good to have your civilizing influence back at Greythorne. I trust it was no struggle to mind Saskia for so long? Did you finally make it to the Louvre as I had hoped?" Despite their age, a flash of sibling rivalry sparked across their faces. But before Winifred could respond, Mr. Rennard swiveled and faced my mother and I. "Oh, and this must be the new help?"

"Yes Papa. Mrs. Moira Kelly and Miss Eve Kelly, this is my father, Theodore Rennard, Senior."

We both did our best curtseys.

Teddy entered then, his boots smearing muck across the floors.

"Teddy! You're tracking mud," Miss Rennard chided.

Mr. Rennard interrupted, "Saskia, leave your brother alone. How was the morning hunt, son?"

"Bagged a large buck," answered Teddy. "Eight points, father. Excellent, given the time of year. The mounted head should make a superb addition to the collection..."

"Ah yes," Mr. Rennard paused. "Son, your - workshop, has become a bit of an abattoir of late. Perhaps you could clear out some of the less well-preserved specimens? Cook has complained of the smell, too."

"Of course, Father," said Teddy, looking rather crestfallen.

Mr. Rennard pivoted back to beam at us. "Welcome ladies. I'm so glad you are here. I hope that you will find Greythorne a pleasant place to work. Some of our employees, Isaiah and Bette for example, have been here for more than two decades. We do have high standards to maintain."

"Not to worry, sir. My daughter and I are more than capable," Ma was never one to cower before authority.

"Well, your timing is very helpful. Our head housekeeper, Mrs. Doyle, had just been asking for more help. I hold an annual private gathering here at Greythorne known as the Ambrose Hunt. We host industry titans. They're due to arrive in a few weeks for a weekend of fine food and to hunt in our little corner of Dutchess County."

"That sounds exciting, Sir." I replied. "We'll do our best to get up to steam quickly."

"Wonderful!" Mr. Rennard rubbed his hands together. "Mrs. Doyle keeps us running like a Swiss clock.

As if on cue, a tall narrow featured woman emerged at a brisk clip from a hallway. Likely in her late forties, the woman wore the typical severe black dress of a housekeeper, with a large collection of keys dangling from her waist. Her grey-speckled brown hair was pinned up high, and her dress and black leather shoes were immaculate.

"Indeed, sir," Mrs. Doyle offered her employer a brief smile. "Ladies, please follow me as I show you to the servants' quarters and get you settled."

"Nice to meet you, Mr. Rennard," I offered as Mrs. Doyle guided us out. "We're grateful for the chance to work here, sir." Ma pinched my elbow to get me to shut up. She hated if I spoke out of turn to our employers, when she dared not.

"And you, my dear," he replied.

We followed Mrs. Doyle through the mansion to the servants's wing. On our way, we glimpsed sitting rooms, a formal dining room, and a ball room - all were stunning. But the room that really wowed me was the library. Floor to ceiling wood paneled shelving, with hundreds of beautiful leather-bound books. Maybe there'd be a chance for me to spend a little time in there.

We arrived at a separate wing of the mansion, where the staff were housed. We had left the section lined with immense paintings and tapestries, and headed down a modest hallway. On our right, we passed the servants' kitchen and dining room - spotlessly clean and large enough to accommodate a large number of folks. In the kitchen a pair of scullery maids were busy setting out foodstuffs, presumably for the afternoon meal.

A young woman about my age came rushing towards us with cleaning and dusting tools in her hands. Her curvy form filled out the maid's uniform in a most flattering way.

Mrs. Doyle glanced at her pocket watch with a frown.

"Oy, Mrs. Doyle, who've you got here?" she asked with a strong Irish brogue.

"Miss Fitzgerald, you're late again," Mrs. Doyle sniped.

"Don't I know it! Already got an earful from Isaiah. Ah you must be the new help! Welcome! I'm Peggy," Peggy said.

"Nice to meet you," I replied. "I'm Eve Kelly and this is my ma, Moira."

Ma scowled at Peggy - already deducting points I could tell.

Peggy promptly ignored Ma and turned to me. "Miss Kelly, after you're settled in, I'll introduce you to me sister..."

"Please call me Eve! I look forward to it," I responded. I grew more excited by the moment for this new position. A new friend or two would be wonderful. It had been ages since I'd been at an Inn where anyone in service was my age.

"Miss Fitzgerald!" Mrs. Doyle was fast losing patience. "This is not afternoon tea at the Savoy. Please get to your chores."

Peggy nodded and rushed off.

Mrs. Doyle sighed, then guided us down the hall. She opened the door to a clean and tidy room with two neatly made beds, a chest of drawers, wash basin and a small closet. We even had a small window out onto the grounds. I looked outside at the flowering trees, lush green lawn and topiaries. Not far off, to my left, stood a large, freshly painted red barn.

"We added a bed, thinking that you may wish to room together, at least in the beginning," Mrs. Doyle said.

"Very thoughtful, thank you. It will do nicely," Ma said.

"I've called a meeting in the servants' hall at a quarter past - so you have ten minutes." Mrs. Doyle opened a wardrobe where a selection of women's uniforms stood at the ready.

"We'll be right there," Ma replied.

And, with that, the housekeeper took her leave.

As I stood at the window, Maxwell emerged from the barn, holding the leads on a highly energetic mix of coonhounds, pointers and foxhounds. The number and quality of the beasts was intimidating. I'd hate to be a fox or a rabbit on the run from that lot. At first, it seemed like the hounds were controlling the man, rather than the other way around. But then Maxwell gave a signal of some sort (inaudible through the glass), and darn if those hounds didn't immediately drop onto their haunches and focus on him intently.

A young boy servant ran ahead of Maxwell, carrying what looked like decoy ducks. He stood about a hundred yards away from the hounds.

Maxwell signaled to the boy, who blew a duck whistle and tossed the decoys high into the air. The hounds' massive heads followed the rise and fall of the ducks without moving a muscle.

Then Maxwell waved his hand and gave some sort of command, and the dogs tore across the green to get the decoy. The hounds' complete obedience, coupled with their speed and aggression, sent a shiver down my spine. As they approached the decoys, their jaws snapped and they barked and bugled.

The dogs came rushing up to the boy servant, teeth gnashing, eyes swirling. My heart pounded as I watch the young fellow tremble.

Then Maxwell blew a whistle, and the dogs stopped in their tracks, just inches from the young fellow. Maxwell waved, and the young servant relaxed and ambled back towards him.

"Eve! For heaven's sake!" Ma interrupted my reverie.

"Sorry, Ma." I turned around and came away from the window.

"No time for daydreaming, lass! Hurry up and get dressed, then come meet me in the servant's kitchen."

In contrast to me, Ma was fully dressed, and ready to go.

"Yes, will do."

Ma exited, giving me one parting frown. This part of my life was clearly going to be the same regardless where we were...I sighed as I began to change into the new uniform.

Chapter 7

Strange And Stranger

Eve

A silver blade flashed through the musty air and buried itself in the flesh with a meaty thwack! *Bloody hell!* I jumped out my skin at the sound. Ma grimaced.

The cleaver severed the leg from a pig's carcass. Bits of blood and gristle sprayed upward. Greythorne's Cook, Bette Franklin (Isaiah's wife) wielded the blade with precision and power. A broad, strong woman in her fifties, she had the same lovely island lilt as her sister, Dina, and seemed quite regal. Clearly the kitchen was her domain.

We were assembled in the kitchen to be instructed by the highly impressive and somewhat intimidating Mrs. Doyle.

"Mrs. Franklin, would you be so good as to pause the butchering for just a moment?" Mrs. Doyle smiled warmly at the cook: a gesture that was not returned.

Bette side-eyed Mrs. Doyle, but lowered the cleaver. I smiled at Bette's feistiness.

I had rushed to the kitchen, after doing the fastest uniform change ever. While Mrs. Doyle spoke, I covertly looked down to make sure all my buttons were done correctly, and my shoes buckled. Thankfully, everything was in order, and even better, this uniform was of far higher quality than the ones we had left behind in Tarrytown. I took a deep breath to stop focusing on myself. I looked up and studied the room.

There were a dozen all told, all dressed in matching uniforms, who stood by as Mrs. Doyle finished her instructions. "I look forward to us working together and doing our best, as Greythorne entertains such important guests."

Next to Peggy must be her sister, Nan. Similar in appearance yes, but her sister seemed quite dour. She had a turned down mouth and mournful eyes. Seemed like a little black rain cloud might be hovering over her head.

The room was bright, large and functional, with multiple heavy metal doored ovens, marble-carved sinks, oak cupboards, islands, and shelves. All were stocked with enormous copper and steel pots and pans, an impressive assortment of knives, whisks, ladles, and floral patterned serving platters and more. Lots of freshly picked carrots, radishes, tomatoes and onions were stacked up in crates along the far wall of the room.

Peggy raised her hand.

Mrs. Doyle nodded. "Go ahead."

"Mrs. Doyle, if you think it would be helpful, our younger sister, Frances, is available to serve starting next week."

"How old is she?"

Nan chimed in. "She's about to turn 18 -"

Peggy elbowed and interrupted her sister, "And very responsible. She's been helping the Binghams at their Hyde Park home, but they're going back to the city."

Mrs. Doyle considered, as she glanced around the mountain of supplies piled high in the kitchen. "Very well. It wouldn't hurt to have an extra pair of hands." With that the housekeeper clapped her hands twice, and the staff sharpened up. "Let's all head back to work."

The servants responded in unison, "Yes, ma'am."

"Mrs. Kelly, Miss Kelly, please stay behind for a moment," Mrs. Doyle directed.

"Yes, ma'am," we responded.

As people were heading out, Peggy and Nan came up behind me. I overheard Peggy scold her sister - "Next time, just let me do the talking!"

"Okay, okay!" Nan responded.

I smiled and turned around. Peggy pulled me over. "Nan, meet Eve Kelly."

"Hi Nan," I said cheerfully. "Nice to meet you."

"Nice to meet you." Nan responded as though she were attending a funeral.

Peggy elbowed her sister again, and Nan eked out a crooked smile.

Peg and Nan hurried off, while Mrs. Doyle approached Bette.

"Mrs. Franklin, please keep me abreast of any items that you are running low on. We must put forth our best of the best. Mr. Rennard's hunting guests arrive in ten days."

"I believe I have everything under control," Bette replied. "I already have Mr. Danforth scheduled to deliver oysters before the guests arrive, and his freshest catch of the day. Mr. Norbury has promised flour, sugar, salt and some fancy French cheeses. And the fellow who handles the ice is scheduled for later this afternoon and a refill next week as well. I told him we will need an extra large order."

"Very well," Mrs. Doyle sniffed her approval, then beckoned us over.

"Mrs. Kelly, I understand you were the head housekeeper at Tarrytown Inn?"

"Yes, ma'am," Ma replied.

"Excellent. I'm glad to have someone with experience on whom I can rely. I would like you to manage our meal services. This would include maintaining inventory of all the dishes, linens, silverware and ensuring everything is kept up to our rigorous standards. I will show you where everything is stored." Mrs. Doyle reached over to a cubby in the kitchen shelving where logbooks rested. She selected a navy leather-bound one and handed it to my mother. "Here is the logbook that I use to track all of the various crockery, crystal, *et cetera* that we need on hand. You are literate, yes?"

"Of course, Mrs. Doyle," Ma responded crisply.

"Very good, Mrs. Kelly. I look forward to working with you."

I was happy for my mother. Mrs. Doyle was giving Ma a modicum of responsibility and some independence. Hopefully this good fortune would trickle down to me in the form of a more cheery mother, which would make my life a little easier.

"And Miss Kelly?" She looked me up and down with a critical eye.

"Yes, Mrs. Doyle," I replied.

"Have you helped with service in a dining room setting?"

I nodded my head.

"Very well. I would like you to start as one of the house maids. You will assist with maintaining the spaces, setting tables for the various meal times, and clearing and cleaning after meals. From there, we shall see how you do with service in a formal setting. I believe you've already made the acquaintance of Miss Peggy Fitzgerald?"

"Yes, Mrs. Doyle," I said.

"You will join her and her sister Nan in that area of responsibility. Do not hesitate to come to me if you see anything at all that requires attention, repair or replacement. Understood?"

"Yes, Mrs. Doyle," I hated being repetitive, but I sensed that was all Mrs. Doyle wanted to hear.

"And now that Miss Rennard is home, she will also be asking for assistance with her personal necessaries....she has informed me that she does not need a full-time maid, but may ask for assistance from you or the other house maids at various points during the day."

I brightened at the thought, "Yes, ma'am."

Mrs. Doyle noted my reaction and shook her head. "Don't be too excited, it will mean that you will be at her beck and call - being a lady's maid is a lot of work and can be at all hours of the day or night."

"I understand, ma'am."

"Very well. You should find the Fitzgerald sisters in the foyer, arranging the freshly cut flowers brought in from the greenhouse," Mrs. Doyle said. With that, she turned and waved for my Ma to follow her to start the inventory process.

As I walked past Bette, the Cook called me over with a sharp tone of voice.

"Before you run off to play with flowers, I need you to go downstairs for me."

"Yes, of course, Bette," I replied.

Bette picked up the cleaver and flipped the pig's carcass around with a great heave. Her strength was truly impressive to me. "That's 'Mrs. Franklin' to you, fresh one!"

"Of course, Mrs. Franklin..."

"Bring up a small sack of flour and one of salt. It's through that door across from me. There are crates and everything should be labeled."

I nodded.

"You'll need that oil lamp - the basement has no light."

"Thanks," I mumbled. As I headed to the cellar door, I passed a sour-faced scullery maid, named Edna, who was busy kneading dough. "First day here, and already you're Miss Saskia's pet," she sneered.

What on earth?! "No idea what you're talking about," I snapped as I passed her to grab the oil lamp and head down the cellar steps.

I started down a flight of old stone stairs into a nearly pitch black space. The silence and chilly air felt quite sinister. I held the lantern up and walked cautiously down the steps into the cellar. The air grew bitingly cold with each subsequent step. *Perfect place for keeping meats fresh*; the gamey smells of curing venison and lamb filled my nostrils. I could hear a quiet *drip, drip, drip* sound.

I reached the bottom of the steps and raised the lamp, peering into the inky black space. A pair of wet black eyes glimmered back at me through the darkness. I shuddered.

As I raised the oil lamp, out of the shadows emerged the dim outline of a deer suspended from a hook in the ceiling. It was likely the buck that Teddy Jr had brought in earlier. I stepped closer. The buck had eight points on its antlers, and an unusually jagged criss-cross slit across its throat still streamed blood. From my medical books, I could tell it was venous rather than arterial - it was a slower flow. If it had been arterial, the poor thing would have already bled out. A long ragged cut along the belly to remove the stomach and bowels had flayed the skin back, exposing red muscle and sinew. Blood was starting to dry along the wound's edges.

Before I could stop myself, I reached out and touched the deer. Pinpricks ran up my hands and arms to the elbow, as if I had plunged my arm into stinging nettle. The deer BLINKED.

I GASPED. The colors before my eyes faded to shades of blue and grey.

I saw myself standing -like I was inside the deer's mind looking at me. Unbearable pain radiated from my chest to my crotch...

I let go as if I had touched a scalding fire, dropped onto my knees and tried to erase what I had just seen and felt.

Plip, plip, plip...

The deer's blood dripped onto the stone floor, joining a dark puddle that drained between the basement cobbles and into the sandy sub-floor.

I looked up at the meat hooks dangling from the ceiling. A wild boar carcass hung from one hook - but there was something odd about it. I stood up and raised the lantern...*Gah!*

The beast's face was entirely stripped of its skin. The Boar's red muscles, cloudy eyeballs and toothy grimace glinted at me. *Bloody hell!*

Animal skins were stretched out to dry on the walls. All around me, glinting metal hooks held guinea fowl, legs of ham, ducks, and sides of beef, hanging just inches from the gray hewn stone of the mansion's walls. I shivered and made sure not to brush up against any of them.

I took a few deep breaths to center myself, then walked around the space. Clearly labeled crates of wine, sacks of grain, jars of preserves and boxes of root vegetables lined several shelves around the room's perimeter. I perused each one, until I found the flour and salt. I carefully took out a cotton bag filled with flour and a similar one for the salt.

Along one wall gleamed three large steel-riveted steam boilers. They all had round semi-doors that one could open or close, with openings below to feed fuel. One was operational, with coal piles and cords of wood stacked neatly near it. The other two stood silent and cold.

I heard soft whispers, and clutched my head, panic rising within my chest. *What is happening to me?*

"Miss Kelly?!"

It was Bette, calling me from upstairs. I'd never been so happy to hear my name.

"Coming." I ran up the stairs only to collide into someone.

"Watch out!"

It was Teddy Jr.

He raised a fleshing knife up close to my face. He seemed to relish my frightened reaction as I almost leapt back a step.

"You don't want to accidentally end up on the pointy end of this blade."

"No sir, thank you sir," I said quickly as I rushed past him and emerged, squinting in the bright daylight of the kitchen. I put the lantern back on the hook.

"What took you so long?" Bette asked. She studied me with her head cocked to one side.

"First time down there - I was a bit lost. At any rate, here you go." I placed the bags next to Bette on a sideboard. "Your sister was a very good friend to me, at Tarrytown Inn," I shared.

Bette sniffed and replied coolly, "She's too much of a softie. Always kind to the strays."

Ouch!

Edna snickered as Bette turned away, and resumed her carving and butchering. I got the message and left to search out Peggy Fitzgerald.

After I exited the kitchen, I found Ma examining the contents of a hall linen closet. Still reeling with emotion from the cellar, I ran up and gave her a quick hug, which surprised us both. She was strong and broad shouldered and proud, and hugging her always felt more like a duty than a comfort. Still, I occasionally persevered in the vain hope that she might, one day, hug me back.

"Ma," I whispered. "The strangest thing. Down in the cellar, I touched a deer that was hanging on a hook to bleed out, and it was like I could see and feel its thoughts."

Instead of a modicum of reassurance, Ma reacted with anger. She pushed me off.

"For heaven's sake, lass! No more nonsense. And hush up, afore someone hears you spouting gibberish! Keep your head down, and your hands busy. Mrs. Doyle asked you to help with the bunches of fresh cut flowers ready for placing in vases around the foyer and main lower level rooms. Go and get started."

Feeling resentful and deflated, I responded with a flat "Yes, Ma."

A short time later, I was placing the flowers on various side tables in the foyer. A grand space of travertine marble columns and floors, yet sorely in need of more feminine touches. The dark old family portraits seemed to stare down at us with sinister expressions, and the dead animal pelts and taxidermy contributed a rather stern and grim effect.

Mrs. Price and Mr. Rennard Sr. were sitting in a drawing room. The door was open and Mrs. Price and I briefly made eye contact as I crossed the foyer. The sounds of their conversation came to me.

"And another thing, Theodore," Mrs. Price was saying, as she raised her voice. "I recommend you keep a close eye on those newly hired women. Can't trust those Irish. I'm certain that horrid O'Shaughnessy woman stole my favorite pearl earrings. Taking advantage of an old widow," Mrs. Price snapped. "The nerve!"

It seemed she deliberately wanted to make sure I overheard. I bristled at her comments, but clenched my jaw to stop a retort. I took a few deep breaths to calm myself, then carried on as though I'd heard nothing.

"Dear Sister," Mr. Rennard purred. "I do appreciate your concern. You always have the best interests of the Rennard family at heart. I simply cannot thank you enough for looking after Saskia in Europe."

"Your daughter is full of *joie de vivre,* as she would say. But she is a handful, Theo," Mrs. Price announced. "It's good that you summoned us back when you did. Scandal is easy to be found in Paris, and your daughter seemed to have a knack for courting it."

I found myself eavesdropping, while lightly adjusting the floral arrangement.

"Anything...compromising, I should know about?" Mr. Rennard's question had a steely edge.

The moment stretched as Mrs. Price considered her response. The grandfather clock nearby *ticked* and *tocked* loudly. I idly picked and fluffed at the baby's breath and daffodils in the vase, unable to stop myself from listening.

"No," said the widow, first with hesitation, then again with more sincerity. "No, nothing you need worry about. Teenage fun and a taste of freedom run amok."

"Runs in the family," Mr. Rennard teased. "I remember you well at that age."

"Ha!" Mrs. Price chortled. "Although I don't really understand why she needed to be away for an entire year. Rather indulgent. At her age, I was already -"

"Yes, yes Winnie, I know. You were already married to your dear Walter, may he rest in peace." He sighed, then continued, "The truth is, I wanted to give her a year of freedom, so she cannot complain later that she has never been free."

"Even with that, I am not sure that Saskia is ready to settle down. I worry that Paris has only whetted her appetite for novelty," Mrs. Price replied.

"She's like her Mother. Full of spirit, but secretly waiting to be tamed," Mr. Rennard said. "She just needs the right suitor to appear, and she will see her whole life coalesce in front of her. The way it was for you and Walter. How it went with me and Helen."

"For all of our sakes, I hope so." The chair creaked as Mrs. Price rose to exit the room.

While I still held a second bundle of flowers, I had inched past an empty vase and near the doorway leading into the study. I tried to avoid Mrs. Price as she exited but miscalculated. We bumped into one another.

"Watch where you're going, girl!" she snapped at me.

"Yes, Ma'am," I replied, lowering my head. "I'm sorry, Ma'am."

Above me, I heard my name called, "Miss Kelly." I looked up and saw Miss Rennard standing on the second floor leaning over the balustrade.

"Yes, Miss." I looked up, relieved.

"Would you come up and assist me in unpacking my trunks?" She tilted her head a little to the side as she asked. Her wavy hair glinted in the golden late afternoon light which streamed through the skylights.

"Of course, Miss. Be right there."

Thank goodness! What a blessing Miss Rennard was, coming to my rescue before I found some new way to run afoul of Mrs. Price. I muttered another apology to the matron, tossed the flowers into an empty vase, and scuttled across the foyer to the mahogany staircase.

I hurried upstairs and Miss Rennard led me to her grand suite. Oh my! It was really and truly grand. Elegant floral wallpaper on the walls, rich floor rugs, paintings on the walls - that were refreshingly not of either ancestors or prey, but instead of magnificent horses running across enchanting landscapes, and some still life of fruit or flowers or both. Her mahogany four-poster bed sported luxurious bed linens. She had an enormous closet filled with all sorts of dresses and folderol, but what caught my eye was her vast collection of riding attire: jodhpurs, riding jackets, gloves and more. It was clear she loved to ride.

She walked across the room and unlocked several large trunks, adorned with pasted travel labels for Paris, Rome and Istanbul. From the first of these she produced several of the finest dresses I had ever beheld. "These should be folded and brought to Deirdre in the washing. No one else, just Deirdre. She will know how to clean these *vetements.*"

"Of course," I responded. I began to lift out the lavish Parisian dresses in shimmery satin, rich velvet and handwoven lace, while Miss Rennard sat at her makeup table. She undid her hair pins, and long tresses fell about her shoulders as she brushed out her hair.

I mustn't stare, I scolded myself, but I was captivated by her glamour. Her grace and elegance seemed effortless. She inhaled radiance and exhaled beauty.

All of the sudden, I realized that Miss Rennard was studying me through the mirror's reflection. She seemed mildly amused.

I was mortified. I knew I had gone red as a beet, the flush running up my neck and back.

"T-Thank you for hiring us," I managed to stammer. Eyes cast downward, I went back to unpacking and untangling the various dresses, petticoats, and slips Saskia had piled upon the bed. "There are folks who won't hire Irish workers. Even this day and age."

"My Aunt amongst them. I apologize for her attitude," she replied. "Fortunately for you, for me, and for the house, Daddy and Mrs. Doyle are in charge of the hiring and the firing around here. Though, dear Aunt Winnie can certainly make one's life a little tougher, from time to time."

At that moment I lifted a gorgeous evening dress from the trunk. I was not sure if it was silk or satin, but it was cut in the latest modern tapered hourglass waist style with a plunging neckline and delicate beaded embroidery across the chest and skirt in a floral pattern.

"If you don't mind my saying so, this is the most beautiful dress I've ever seen," I said.

"Ah well, the Paris boutiques are so much more *chic* than anything one would find in New York."

Feeling a bit emboldened I responded. "Paris is on my list."

"Your list?" Saskia was genuinely puzzled.

I nodded. Before I could stop myself I blurted out, "I've plans to study medicine. I want to become a nurse, travel the world and help those who need it."

"Studying medicine, then?" Miss Rennard raised an eyebrow. "Aren't you bold?"

Not knowing if she was putting me in my place, I ducked my head.

But then Miss Rennard shared a mischievous smile.

"I like bold."

I stood there, holding her dresses in my arms. The wafts of Parisian perfumes, clove smoke, and just a tinge of sweat rose up to my nostrils and I imagined Miss Rennard's adventurous life in Paris. I found myself admiring this young woman.

"Anything else, Miss Rennard?"

Miss Rennard's smile exuded warmth. "Yes, I'd like to take a bath after dinner. It's my evening ritual. Nan Fitzgerald will know how I like things, so please do check in with her."

"Yes, Miss."

I exited the room as gracefully as I could manage, arms loaded down with dresses.

Somehow I managed the entire trip down through the servant wing to the laundry only dropping two slips and one petticoat. Feeling good about my accomplishment, I delivered the clothes to the laundry area where two older washerwomen were busy scrubbing sheets and linens. As mistress had instructed, I asked for Deirdre. Turned out she was an older laundress, with hands gnarled from years of garment work. At any rate, she relieved me of my burden.

After that, Peggy found me and asked, "Eve, would you give me a hand with the dusting?"

Of course, I agreed. Peggy and I carried the dusting tools into Mr. Rennard's study. It was a magnificent wood-paneled tribute to masculinity and its pursuits. Large buck heads with antlers were mounted facing one another from one side of the room to the other. One wall was entirely devoted to hunting weapons of all sorts: rifles, crossbows, pistols and more.

Smaller taxidermies were scattered around the room, some mounted in real-life poses. One very spry stuffed squirrel stood atop a stack of books. I accidentally touched the dead squirrel's fluffy tail, and shuddered.

"All of these poor dead animals. It's so awfully sad," I commented.

Peggy snorted. "City folk holiday in the countryside, then pride themselves in killing all sorts of innocent creatures."

I leaned in and inhaled the earthy, woodsy smell of the leather-bound books I'd been dusting. It was one of my favorite scents in all the world. As I ran my finger along some of the titles of the books I was dusting, I realized that the Rennards had quite the collection. I spotted Mary Shelley's "Frankenstein" and Hawthorne's "Scarlet Letter," and of course stacks of books on business and hunting, including several authored by Governor Roosevelt on hunting big game, both in the United States and abroad.

At that moment, Mr. Rennard entered, startling us.

Peggy curtseyed and said "We're just about done."

"No need to rush off," Mr. Rennard responded. He had seen me touching the books. "Ah, Miss Kelly, are you a reader as well?"

"Y-Yes, Mr. Rennard," I replied. "I adore reading. I am especially interested in medicine and the natural sciences."

Mr. Rennard considered my answer for a moment. "Well, here at Greythorne we value wisdom and knowledge highly, which you can perhaps see reflected in our little collection."

"It's very impressive. Perhaps one day I can mimic a fraction of your assembled works, sir."

"How kind of you, Miss Kelly." Mr. Rennard beamed. "Tell you what, you are welcome to borrow a book whenever you like. How does that sound?"

"Gosh," I replied, genuinely taken aback at the gesture. "That's very generous of you, sir. Thank you." I answered.

"Think nothing of it! Books are useless unless they are being read. Now, would one of you ladies run up and let my daughter know that I would like her to come meet me at the stables?" Rennard asked.

Peg and I glanced at each other and I nodded.

"Of course, sir. Thank you, very much, again!" I replied, hurrying off to find Miss Rennard.

Chapter 8

Paris Games, Hudson Rules

Saskia

The antique grandfather clock in the foyer chimed four times as I headed downstairs, and out the back door to the stables, filled with excitement. I'd had to select something from my closet from over a year ago, as everything I'd bought in Europe was being freshened up by the staff. Much as I was loathe to admit, it was actually rather nice to be back at home, with my own taste in the furnishings, and my favorite things around me. And I was delighted that even with all the pastry-sampling I'd done in Paris, I was able to still fit perfectly into my old dresses from last season. All in all, I was in an excellent mood.

Stepping outside the house, I paused and took in the beauty of our estate. The gardens were in the most gorgeous condition I had ever seen. Azaleas were just now coming into bloom, as were the lily of the valley and peonies. The dogwoods were also budding - when they were in full bloom it would be a magnificent array of snowy white petals that looked like fluffy clouds. Perfect box hedges, and a carpet of lush green lawn rounded out a strong sense of place and grandeur.

Father had poached Mr. Charles Platt who was much feted by

the Vanderbilts and their ilk, to come and design the formal gardens of Greythorne. Mr. Platt must be part wizard, as he and his team had down wonders for our little parkland. I was certain that when Father's guests would arrive, they would gasp at the grandness of the whole.

As I got close to the stables, Teddy caught up with me. Our steps crunched along the gravel path together.

"So how was Paris, really?" he asked.

"Paris was *merveilleux*," I shared.

He rolled his eyes at my French. *My brother can be such a peasant.*

"Were you able to have any fun, or did Aunt Winifred keep you under lock and key?" he joked.

"Well, she certainly tried to bore me to death...but as you know, I'm much better at sweet talking her than you are," I replied.

"Ha! Yes, true. Subtlety is not my strong suit," Teddy mused.

At that moment, my father swung open the stable door and gave me a hug. "Who were you sweet talking, Saskia?"

"Monsieur Vuitton, Father. He gave me this-" I lifted my gold fleur-de-lis necklace for Father to admire. "A token of his admiration."

He and Aunt Winifred had clearly been waiting impatiently inside. My Aunt looked like the cat that ate the canary - all of which gave me butterflies of excitement.

"Well done, darling. If anyone can charm people, it's you." Father paused to look at us all. "Well, this is a wonderful treat," he said. "Both my children are finally here with me, and my dear sister, too. Greythorne has been a cold and empty place with you gone, ladies."

Father rubbed his hands together with glee. "And, now time for the surprise!" Father announced. "Maxwell, bring him over -"

I gasped with delight as Maxwell led a magnificent chestnut stallion towards us. "Is that...?"

"It is, my dear! As you know, Mr. Waring had been drattedly difficult, but with the help of a new friend, one Mr. Robert Logan, I was able to persuade him to part with Devil's Own. The stallion is yours, my dear. A belated birthday gift. Do you like him?"

I hugged Father so hard, I practically squeezed the breath out of him. He laughed with delight at his success at surprising me.

"Here you go, Miss," said Maxwell. He handed me the reins, and I ran my hands over the horse's flanks and studied his skeletal and muscle structure. He really was a spectacular beast. I wished I had thought to put on riding attire, but it was so close to sunset, I didn't think I'd have enough time to ride.

"He's magnificent! Truly extraordinary. This is the best gift anyone has ever gotten me!"

"Even better than Monsieur Vuitton's jewels?" Father said, a playful tone in his voice.

"Of course!" I replied with a smile. I placed my hand the stallion's neck and scratched gently. The handsome Devil nickered, and leaned into my scratch. I could feel his muscles ripple beneath his warm and shiny coat. His horse smell was pleasing - a mix of oats and hay, leather and other earthy qualities.

"So, how does it feel, to be home from Europe?" Father asked.

"Wonderful, although I haven't really settled in yet. The journey was long and tiresome." I ran my hands along the horse's forelegs, assessing and appreciating the alignment of the bones and joints. The horse had extraordinary conformation.

"No doubt," Father responded.

"Truthfully, Father, I am looking forward to going back and spending more time abroad. My knowledge of art history has been greatly enhanced by my studies at the Louvre and other museums in Paris and beyond. And my French has really improved. Madame LaVoire would be so proud of me."

"I'm glad you found your time abroad so edifying," Father said.

Madame LaVoire, a *femme autoritaire*, had been my French tutor prior to my trip abroad. At one point, she had been so frustrated with my struggle to get the vowel sounds that she threw a piece of chalk across the room. Well, look at me now!

"I've been thinking, maybe on my next trip, I could spend some time in Florence..." I proposed. *No time like the present, to start planting seeds.* Devil's soft velvety nose nuzzled the palm of my hand.

Father stroked his beard, and contemplated me with a warm smile. It really is lovely to be home again...at least for moments like this.

"The horse was only the first surprise for you, my dear. As you know, I have my annual gathering of friends coming up soon."

"Yes, Father," I was a bit distracted, as I opened the horse's mouth and studied his ivory white teeth.

"Darling, I made sure he was fully evaluated before I purchased him," Father said, perhaps a little exasperated by my examination of his gift.

"I'm sure Father," I responded. "I just can't get over how gorgeous he is - it's hard to believe he's actually here."

"At any rate, what I wanted to share with you is that there is someone I especially want you to meet," Papa said.

Oh Lord, this was not at all what I wanted to hear. My stomach cramped and tightened. "Really Papa. And who would that be?" I asked sweetly.

Across from me, Aunt Winnie was watching me like a hawk. She seemed pleased with my response and nodded with a smile.

"It's the fellow I just mentioned, Robert Logan. The fellow who helped me procure Devil's Own here," Father beamed. "Intelligent, good humored and hard working. In a short time, he's become one of my most trusted business associates. Of all the eligible men, Robert is the best of the batch."

I needed to stop this before it got out of hand.

"Father, I came running home at your request, but I wasn't really done with being in Europe. I've heard of Mr. Logan from some of my friends in Paris who love to gossip about the society news from home. However, I've never met the man, and truthfully, I'm not ready to be engaged to anyone," I said hotly.

Father's brows knitted together and I saw his color darken. But really, what did he expect? He had ambushed me, in the stable of all places! He placed his hands on his hips, (never a good sign) and scowled at me.

"Happy as I was to gift you an entire year abroad to travel and learn, that time is now over. Indeed, some of my friends questioned my judgement in giving you such a long time away, but I wanted you to see a bit of the world, and develop a sense of yourself," Father said.

He placed an arm on my shoulder, which only served to make me squirm.

"You're of the age to get married. Many of my friends, with daughters your age, have already been blessed with grandchildren. I summoned you home because I believe that Robert is the perfect match for you, and perfect matches do not wait around indefinitely. He is charming and even-tempered. He is also on the younger end, and is a self-made success - something very rare," Papa continued.

Teddy chimed in. "Listen Saskia, you know my feelings on new money, but even I have to agree with Father: Logan is a good man. A gentleman, but a progressive, like you. He even thinks women should get suffrage..."

Aunt Winifred huffed to hear this bit of information.

"I think he would make a fine husband for you, and a great addition to the family," Teddy finished.

I started to squirm, and Devil's Own sensed my anxiety - he pawed the ground with one leg, his ears tilted back and he whinnied. Maxwell scurried forward and took the reins and guided the horse back to his stable.

"What if I don't want to be matched? By you or anyone else..." I blurted it out before I could stop myself.

Father's face grew red and fixed and he took his hand off my shoulder as though I had scalded him - not good at all.

Suddenly, he took the walking stick he'd been holding under his left arm, and snapped it in two with a ferocity that made me hold quite still.

The stable grew silent as the stablehands stopped their chores.

One of the stable boys in a corner gave me a terribly sympathetic look. Ugh! The last thing I wanted was a servant's pity.

"Now, look what you made me do..." Father chastised me. "It's a bitter truth that all of life's pleasures, great and small, can be stripped away... Everything you have is due to me. And what I have given, can also be taken away. In exchange for an extraordinary life, all I expect is your obedience and loyalty to our family."

He reached over to grip my wrist, and caused my skin to blanche under the pressure. "It would be a shame if I had to sell that horse..."

Across from me, Aunt Winnie desperately sent silent signals, trying to tell me to back off. Even Teddy shook his head in warning.

It was rare for Father to direct such anger towards me, and frankly I didn't care for it at all. However, it was clear that I needed to accept temporary defeat. So, I took a breath and turned my facial expression into something I hoped looked like submission. "Father, you misunderstood...I do very much appreciate your efforts on my behalf. I look forward to meeting Mr. Logan. I just ask that nothing is decided until I have made up my own mind."

Father released his grip, and flashed his million-dollar smile at me. "Well, that's excellent to hear! There, see, Teddy? An agreeable young woman, your sister has become."

Father beamed, proud as could be at my acquiescence. He turned back to me, grin plastered across his face. "As for Mr. Logan, he will be joining us for the annual Ambrose Hunt. I'm confident that once you meet him, you'll agree with me. I will expect your best behavior, and an open mind, Saskia."

Gosh-amighty! "Of course," I replied.

Teddy glanced at his pocket watch. "Dinner should be ready shortly."

I massaged my wrist. "Please excuse me, but all of the travel has affected my appetite. I think I'll head up to my room to get a full night's sleep."

Father looked at me for a moment, then nodded. "Of course," he announced.

"Thank you, Father," I said, doing my level best to sell the dutiful daughter routine. "For everything you have given me, and the care you have provided me over the years. Though I might not express it the way you wish, I am truly grateful."

Aunt Winifred frowned at me as I passed by. I'm sure she was disappointed in my behavior, but honestly, if she had at least given me some warning, I would have been better prepared to handle the situation. Sometimes my Aunt could be so exasperating.

I was angry at Teddy, too. He'd made no effort to forewarn me as to Father's plans for me. I knew that Teddy often felt like the runner-up in our family, so this opportunity for him to ally himself with Father in determining my future must have felt like a gift.

As I slinked away from the stable, a pit of dread opened within my stomach. I had vowed never to fall into the early marriage trap that had stripped so many women of bright, interesting futures. Women like my Aunt Winifred: married at eighteen, stuck with a dolt or someone cruel or neglectful, or self-centered and entitled, living a tiny life, only to end up eventually widowed and alone. Surely that would not be my fate?

No. I would convince Father that now was not the right time for me. I could see that based on his angry response a moment ago, getting him to change his mind was going to be a challenge. I had never heard or seen him be this determined about my future. For a moment, a sour taste rose in my mouth, but I shook it off.

After all, I'd been able to sweet talk my father, too, more than once...And maybe there were flaws in Mr. Logan that I could uncover and subtly reveal to my father, as though he had himself discovered them. *Men!* I sighed.

I consoled myself with the thought that Miss Kelly would be preparing my soak. I had plenty of time to figure out my next move. Didn't I?

Chapter 9

Drawn In

Eve

In the kitchen, I stood impatient, hopping from one foot to the other, as I filled a pail with hot water ladled from the giant iron kettle kept over the fireplace. It had been a long busy day, but I still felt full of energy and nervous anticipation at spending time with Miss Rennard.

Nan and Peggy came in, carrying their empty buckets. Meanwhile a handful of scullery maids were busy putting away the crockery under Mrs. Doyle's watchful eye.

"How's it getting on?" I asked the sisters.

"Ugh, the bath's still not full!" Nan said, glum as ever.

Peggy nudged her to cheer up. "Come on mopey, one more trip should do it." Then Peggy winked at me, "Honestly, I can't imagine why the Mistress wants to be in more hot water than she already is!"

Nan giggled.

"What do you mean?" I asked.

"Oh, I'll fill you in later," Peggy responded. "Let's get cracking. Sooner we're up there, sooner we're done."

With the bucket full, Peggy closed the tap and helped me haul it back down to the floor.

"Sure you can manage this one yerself?" Peggy asked with an eyebrow raised. "It should be the last trip."

"Don't underestimate me, Peg!" I grunted and did my best to hoist the two nearly-full buckets past my knees. Water sloshed, so I made do with small steps out the doorway and down the hall to the stairs.

I lugged the heavy load all the way upstairs and along the hallway, doing my best to avoid looking at walls filled with more dead beasties and dour ancestral paintings.

This time, the door to Teddy Jr's room was open. I couldn't help but be intrigued when I saw a large tool chest...

I looked around and saw no one; then I lowered the buckets and tiptoed inside.

Close up I could see that the tool box had drawers crammed with hacksaws, knives and skinning tools. A dead goose was resting on blood-stained newspapers on a large wood desk.

Ugh! What a foul thing to be doing in a bedroom...

I spotted a glass jar filled with cloudy greenish fluid. Something white floated in the murk. Without thinking, I gave the jar a gentle shake.

Animal eyeballs floated to the glass's surface. I shuddered and jumped away, only to SLAM into --

Teddy Jr.

Again.

"Jesus!"

"No, just me," he replied, amused. "Twice in one day - I'm beginning to think you fancy me."

I blushed beet red. "Sorry sir...I'm still learning my way around."

Teddy stared at me, unconvinced by my weak lie.

"Um, I'd best be going, your sister's waiting for her bath," as I headed for the door.

"Ah yes, my sister adores her bath," he said. I could hear him lock the door behind me as I rushed out and grabbed the buckets.

I made it to Miss Rennard's *ensuite* bathroom and poured the hot water into the tub. Peggy and Nan had laid out clean cotton towels and other items on a silk-upholstered divan. Steam rose in the air. I got the rest of the *ensuite* ready for Miss Rennard, following Nan's detailed instructions. It wasn't too complicated, really.

First, I made sure that the bedside area was ready for night-time, with a fresh carafe of water and a clean crystal glass. Pillows were freshly plumped and the bedcovers open and ready. After that, I made sure Miss Rennard's preferred French milled soaps (*ooh-la-la!*) were at the ready, near the white clawfoot tub. The bathroom itself was larger than any bedroom I'd ever slept in, with gray stone tiles on the floor. The elaborate crown moulding along the ceiling reminded me of an upside-down wedding cake.

An open bay window looked out over the grounds. A chill breeze blew into the bathroom, which would soon ruin all our efforts to bring hot water up. I went over to the window and latched it. As I looked outside, I spied the coachman, Maxwell. To my surprise, the man was gazing directly up at the window from a spot of shrubbery below. *What a strange and creepy fellow.* As I drew the curtains closed, he looked disappointed. *Well that was just too bad for him!*

I opened the bedroom door - "Miss Rennard, your bath is ready."

She emerged from her changing area, and entered wearing naught but a sheer silk robe of the softest shade of pink. Despite my attempts to avert my eyes, it was impossible not to notice that Miss Rennard was blessed with a stunning figure. This was the first time I had ever been in the presence of a young woman my age in a state of complete undress. I found myself irresistibly drawn to peeking at her gently rounded breasts and shapely hips...

No, no, no! I berated myself - *Stop it! What on earth is wrong with me?*

Miss Rennard leaned over the tub and touched the water with her fingers. "The perfect temperature, thank you, Eve. Would you be so kind?"

"Of course, Miss."

She stood in front of me and untied her robe, then began to shrug it off her shoulders. I held the robe and looked away, as she slid into the tub.

I hung the robe on a hanger and went to leave the bathroom. "Anything else, Miss?"

"Ah, Eve, not so fast. I'd like you to attend to me as I bathe. I have some lavender oil on the dresser beside the wash basin. It's a little bottle with purple flowers on it. Please bring it over."

"Yes, Miss." I scanned the various bottles on the dresser and spied it. As I handed the bottle to Miss Rennard our fingers grazed one another's, and I could not help but feel a tingle of excitement run through my body. *I really must stop blushing at every interaction with Miss Rennard,* I scolded myself.

"Usually one or two dropper fulls is enough," Miss Rennard said, as she opened the bottle and added the oil to her bath. A delicate sweet floral perfume filled the air, and the tub water turned a delicate shade of purple.

"That's a lovely scent," I said.

"I picked it up in Provence," she explained.

Of course you did.

"Here, Eve," Miss Rennard handed me a sea sponge. "It's difficult for me to reach between the shoulders. Be a dear, and sponge my back for me?"

"Of course, Miss," I said as I soaped up the sponge, dipped it into the hot tub and gently rubbed her back. Her skin was unblemished and gleamed like priceless alabaster under the light of the bathroom's two dim electric lamps.

She sighed with pleasure.

"You don't mind that I call you Eve, do you?" she asked.

"Not at all, Miss," I replied.

"And you needn't call me 'Miss Rennard' behind closed doors; you may call me Saskia," she said with a gentle smile.

"Yes, Miss - I mean, Saskia..." This was an unexpected turn of events. Normally, young women of Miss - I mean Saskia's - stature, did all they could to keep separate from the help. Even being addressed as "Miss Kelly" was a big improvement over the more common, "Girl!"

"Do you miss Paris?" I asked.

"I do. I had a unique measure of freedom there. Even under Aunt Winifred's watchful eyes," Saskia said.

We both giggled.

"I envy your life and your freedom," I blurted out before I could stop myself.

"It's just a gilded cage," she replied with a shake of her head. "While I do have some creature comforts, they come at a great cost. I'm expected to play the dutiful daughter, regardless of how I might feel about it," Saskia fretted.

"I suppose we all are," I responded. I understood all too well how a parent could control a young person's life.

"And soon, I fear, the role of obedient and pretty wife," she added. "My father can be loving and generous - but everything comes with strings attached."

"Parents have strange ways of showing their affection," I offered. I recalled Mr. Rennard generously offering me the free use of his library. Was there a string attached to that? I chided myself for being so naive.

Saskia sighed and changed subjects.

"Eve, I hope you don't think this is too personal - do you consider yourself a devout Catholic?"

"Not at all," I shook my head. "I mean of course when we worked in New York City, Ma made sure I attended Sunday School...but my family's beliefs go back to before the Church. Why do you ask?"

"Just wondering," she responded. She craned her neck left and right to relieve tension, and raised her arms up over her head in a great stretch. The action reminded me of the barn cat who used to sneak inside the Tarrytown Inn on cold winter nights and stretch out on a pillow by the fire. I swear, I could hear Saskia purr contentedly. Suds and small bubbles slid down Saskia's lithe form, around the gentle curve of her waist and tracing her spine to the water.

I was so distracted that I didn't see her reach out toward me. Her soapy, glistening hand grasped my wrist gently, and brought it to her face. Her lips were incredibly soft on the back of my rough, calloused hands.

My heart fairly pounded out of my chest. I drew back my hand and dropped the sponge. My voice quavered, "Will there be anything else Miss - Saskia?"

Saskia stood up from the tub and faced me. Water streamed down her body. It was like gazing upon the goddess Venus emerging from the ocean.

"Join me?"

I stood as still as a statue, struck with a heady mix of excitement and fear.

"Not sure what you mean?" I croaked.

"Allow me," Saskia reached over and turned me towards her. She began to unbutton my maid's uniform.

I reached for Saskia's hands. *This will not end well...*

Saskia paused and looked me in the eye. "Don't worry, I've locked the bedroom door." She swept one of my wayward curls back behind my ear, with a gentle touch. My innards turned to jelly.

I was utterly bewitched. I nodded yes while trembling. My clothes dropped to the floor.... The night was cool against my skin, but there was a softness to the air from the bath's steam and lavender scent. I expected to feel mortified at being so exposed, but instead I reveled in the freedom from confinement. So many thoughts raced through my mind...most strongly a sense of boundless joy for the first time from someone touching me and being attracted to me. It was a far cry from how I felt back at the Inn, when men like Owen had pinched or grabbed or leered at me.

Saskia kissed me on the side of my neck... She inhaled my scent. I shuddered with pleasure, tinged with a titch of terror. She grasped my hands and pulled me close. I slid into the tub, and we sat facing each other.

She leaned in and kissed my breasts, softly biting each nipple. "You are gorgeous," she murmured between nibbles.

I was amazed at how my body reacted with pleasure to her touch. It was as though Saskia had turned a secret key, and I was now unlocked and open. I moaned a little, and Saskia put a finger to my lips.

"Shhhhh..." she said. She pulled me towards her and kissed me on the lips. As my mouth opened, hungry, she used her tongue to caress mine...my heart raced inside my chest. She tasted like strawberries....

"Is this your first time?" she asked with a deep and husky warmth.

I nodded, but was afraid to make eye contact.

Saskia sensed my fear, and lifted my chin so that our eyes met. "You're in good hands," she whispered.

At this, her hands slid underwater, touching me in the most intimate way one could imagine. I leaned back in the tub, my eyes shut but my mouth remained wide open, breathing deeply, and exhaling uncontrollable gasps and groans of ecstasy as Saskia worked her magic on me.

Waves of intense pleasure washed over me. *Great goddess of compassion!* I opened my eyes and felt an almost electric vibration pass through my body - the bathroom lights started to flicker. The water in the tub rose up around me as though drawn to me, and that strange prickling sensation came back to my fingertips, racing up my forearms. I didn't know what was happening but I couldn't stop. As my body crescendoed with pleasure, the waters in the tub rose higher still, and then fell, cascading onto the tile floor. I felt utterly and completely alive.

Chapter 10

The Master And The Servant

Eve

I exited Saskia's suite, awash in a sea of turbulent and conflicting emotions. My body felt like it was floating on air, and the sweet scent of her lavender oil followed me everywhere. But at the same time, my mind and gut churned with anxiety over what had just transpired between us. With each step I took away from Saskia's door, the ecstasy diminished, and the nausea and worry increased. My stomach felt tight, and my hands would not stop trembling.

Before I exited the tub, Saskia had taken my hands and whispered in my ear, "Who are you, Eve Kelly?" And truly I did not know how to respond. Who was I? What was I? My head was swirling with a cacophony of thoughts. I tried to breathe deeply through my nose to calm myself as I tiptoed down the hallway. I prayed I wouldn't run into anyone as I was sure that my face would betray me and reveal the maelstrom of thoughts rattling around my head.

Most loud within my mind - did someone just make love to me? A woman? And not just any woman, but the lady of a prestigious household?! I had never imagined that touching someone and being touched could be pleasurable, especially not for the woman. In all that I had ever seen or read, the male was the one who "took his pleasure." There was never any discussion of women and their experiences. Most older women I knew seemed to just sigh and tut tut, rather than discuss romantic moments. Goodness knows my Ma had never breathed a word to me on the subject. A famous jape rose to my mind - the English mother who said to her daughter before her wedding night, "Hold your breath and think of the Empire!"

I'd often seen young women flutter about, dreaming of romantic moments with men - but that had never been in my mind. As a younger girl, hearing the chatter and banter of girls around their fancying of this man or that, I'd often worried then reassured myself with the thought that maybe I was just a late bloomer. I'd assumed that attraction to the opposite sex would eventually occur. But, now, for the first time I realized why it had never come to pass.

Truthfully, there'd been a few occasions where I'd had strong feelings of affection towards one young woman or another. I had just chalked it up to my being a caring person, or to those women being particularly kind to me.

As Ma had never discussed any of the facts of life with me, I had done some digging in various libraries, to at least find out some information on my own. Back in New York City, I'd had the chance to study Dr. William Acton's book "The Functions and Disorders of the Reproductive Organ." I had hid in the corrals on a couple of rainy weekend afternoons, covering the book with another title, in case someone stopped by and noticed. Thankfully no one had, as I would have been mortified.

At any rate, Dr Acton was considered a modern expert, and it was apparently a widely read book on sexual advice. The good doctor wrote something like "the majority of women are not very much troubled with sexual feelings of any kind." I had found that sentence strangely comforting to me; that I was not aberrant from other women in my lack of desire.

Then my mind flashed on to Henry James' work "The Bostonians" in which he described a "Boston Marriage" between two women. I understood that for a small number of very wealthy privileged women - women like Saskia Rennard - it was possible to establish a household with another woman and avoid the pitfalls of marriage to a man. Such women could be financially independent, and even pursue careers of their own. They did not need to bear children and were freed from the tedium of childrearing and homemaking. On the topic of physical love between these women, Mr. James had been mum.

In my wildest dreams, I'd never imagined that a stunning, breath-taking woman would take a romantic interest in me. The heat rose again in my body just at the thought. The lights overhead *flickered*; I took a deep breath through my nose again, to try and calm myself.

What on earth was causing the weird sensations in my body, and the strange effects on my surroundings? I was certain the water in the tub had risen and then fallen of its own accord. But it happened right at the same moment that the electric lamps had flickered on and off, rapidly. I felt as though I might be going mad, except that Saskia had also noticed the same strange phenomena. So I couldn't be going crazy, could I? Not if someone else saw what I saw?

As I tiptoed down the dark hallways, Greythorne seemed quite foreboding. Even the air felt oppressive, like a warm, moist blanket which threatened to suffocate me. I found myself nearly gasping for breath as I hurried on down the dark hall. *Pop, creeeaaaak, pop* - strange sounds emanated from the walls and made my skin jump. I passed by Teddy Junior's room. The light was on and I could hear a soft strange moaning sound from within. I scurried away. I didn't want to know what was going on in there, and I didn't want to be caught gawking either.

I finally made it to the servants' quarters, but as I rushed through the long corridor, I felt as though someone was creeping near me. The hair on my arms stood on end and goosebumps rose. I made it to the corner, and then turned right and raced down the long dark hall-way, when out of the shadows, my body slammed into...someone.

Ah!! I squeaked - and a pair of hands reached out to grab me. I feel myself go lightheaded and weak kneed.

A lantern rose up into my face - it was Isaiah. He chuckled as he let go of me. "We gave each other quite the shock! Are you alright, Miss Kelly?"

I was so relieved to see his friendly face. "I'm alright, just startled is all."

"You're out and about quite late," he commented.

"Yes," I sighed. "The chores, you know?"

At that moment, Bette appeared around the corner, lamp in hand. "What's the matter!?" she asked.

"Nothing," Isaiah replied. "We bumped into each other in the dark."

"Saskia kept me long after the bath, talking my head off about Paris and boys and jewelry..." I blurted out. I really wished I was a better liar....

Bette stared at me for a moment, then sniffed and nodded. "I'll be waiting outside, Isaiah," she said. With that Bette disappeared around the corner, and out of sight.

I shrugged at Isaiah. He smiled kindly at me, "Don't take it personally. My wife is that way with pretty much everyone, even me sometimes," he added with a twinkle in this eyes.

I smiled back at Isaiah. Before he left, he turned and looked at me, this time dead serious. "One piece of advice, Miss Kelly. Don't get too involved with the family. Remember who is master and who is servant. Nothing good comes from meddling in the family's affairs."

I was stunned. I felt my jaw drop as I floundered to respond. Did Isaiah somehow know what had just happened in Saskia's rooms?

"Y-Yes, Mr. Franklin," I managed. "I understand."

Isaiah looked at me with a bemused expression, then nodded once, and departed after his wife.

After he left, I sat on the floor of the corridor, my back resting against the wall. I was not yet ready to go to bed, and definitely not ready to talk to my mother.

Sweet goddess of mercy! What have I gotten myself into? All of the sudden, my life had become very, very complicated.

Chapter 11

A Lock

Saskia

What a magical night. I tied my robe around me. It had been a pity to leave the tub, but the water had grown cold and it was getting late.

Across from me, Eve finished buttoning up her uniform. Even from here, I could see her fingers trembling. *Poor thing,* I mused. Without thinking about it, my hand found the small manicure scissors in my robe's pocket.

"Here let me help you." I came over to Eve and stood behind her. As I tied her apron strings, I pretended to fumble the knot once. With Eve distracted, I quickly brought up the scissors and clipped a single, thick copper curl from her flaming mane. The hair and the scissors disappeared back into the robe, and I kissed her on the neck.

Eve sighed with pleasure. "Is this what Paris was like?" she asked.

"Yes... If you know what you're looking for," I replied.

And unfortunately, now that I was home, moments like this would be far and few between, and likely become impossible once I was married. Only ten days...

Eve kneeled down to clasp her shoe buckles. I studied her - she truly was such a gorgeous young woman. My bedroom clock struck the hour and she leapt up, her eyes darting to the clock hands.

"I have to go..."

I nodded and walked her to the door. I unlocked it and peeked outside - no one was near. "Go."

Eve slipped out and I caught one last sight of her bouncing red curls as she hurried down the hallway. I closed the door and went over to my dressing table. Once seated, I pulled my silver manicure scissors and her lock of hair from my robe's pocket. Inside the dressing table drawer lay a piece of velvet cloth which I retrieved to wipe my scissors clean. I measured and cut a length of yellow satin ribbon from my drawer, and tied it around Eve's hair with a perfect bow.

I tucked the scissors back into their small leather case and snapped it shut. Father had always taught me to take care of my tools.

Also inside my drawer was an olive green leather-bound case with brass studs and the familiar LV logo embossed. I undid the brass clasp. Inside were multiple locks of women's hair, each neatly tied with a satin bow. Monsieur Vuitton had done well in executing my design. He thought I was collecting jewelry, of course. In reality, it was for something far more valuable - my collection of treasured memories. Moments that I would likely never be able to revisit again, if Father's plans for me were successful.

I brought the lock of hair to my nose one last time to breathe in her scent. The hair was still damp, and in holding it I could recall every moment that had transpired that evening. I placed it carefully in its own unique slot, closed the case and slid it back inside my drawer, safe and sound. As I tucked the case away, I decided to stay focused on the moment, and the pleasures I had enjoyed and shared with the beautiful Miss Kelly....

I took a few moments to brush my hair as I looked at my reflection in the mirror. My time with Eve had left me with a rosy glow on my cheeks. I drew a lot of pleasure when I studied my face in the mirror.

My mother had blessed me with her beautiful facial symmetry and my father with his grey eyes and thick glossy hair.

Exhausted and totally satisfied, I climbed into my four-poster bed and curled up in a cozy position. In my mind's eye, I replayed the evening dalliance with Eve. I pictured the strange moment when sparks seemed to zing through the air and the water in the tub rose in a series of waves. She really was a mysterious and fascinating young woman. I looked forward to getting to know her better.

Chapter 12

Brotherly Love

Saskia

The sun rose over a dry and fresh spring morning. I popped out of bed excited for the day ahead. My brother and I had made a plan to go out together for a long ride and a hunt. It would be my first chance to really ride Devil, and I couldn't wait.

As for my brother, we hadn't had any time alone since I'd been back, and as much as I was loathe to admit it, I did miss Teddy's acerbic wit and boisterous demeanor while I was away.

I'd asked for Eve this morning but she hadn't been available--no doubt thanks to some assignment from Mrs. Doyle--so I put up with that sourpuss older Fitzgerald sister to assist me with dressing in my favorite cream-colored jodhpurs, houndstooth riding jacket and black riding boots. I strode out of the mansion towards the barn, contemplating how best to navigate the rocky shoals of our relationship with one another. Although we were siblings, we could hardly be more dissimilar, and the year spent apart might possibly widened that rift.

Frankly, the two of us shared little common interests. The very things that draw me to Europe--travel, business, opera, ballet, politics, the arts--Teddy found either dull, tedious, or both. He was not much of a reader either, which of course frustrated Father who took great pride in his vast library. Worst of all, my brother lacked social graces, oftentimes being far too direct and rude, in settings where a little tact would serve him better. My girlfriends had often been wounded by his casual rudeness, so I didn't include him anymore on my social forays away from Greythorne.

Teddy's rudeness and inability to delicately navigate social settings worried my father most of all. Whenever Teddy really crossed the line, Father would declare that he, "Was not building a successful business empire only to have it run it into the ground by his son behaving like a brash, uncompromising brute."

But who says it should be Teddy? I often mused about that while on the Continent. *Who is to say that I could not run a successful business empire myself?*

Teddy spotted a patch of mud and knelt down to scoop up some in his hands, which he then proceeded to rub across his face, neck and hands to disguise his appearance and scent from potential prey. He smeared even more on his breeches and jacket. *Oh, the poor laundresses!* The image of him covering himself was too comical, and I couldn't contain a giggle.

It was just as Aunt Winnie had said - the boy still loved to play in the mud. Although, for Teddy, this was not playtime, but instead quite serious.

"Having fun?" I asked as I approached Teddy. He stood up with a grin and reached out a mud-filled hand to me. "Want some?"

"I'm good, thanks," I replied. "Unlike you, I prefer to keep myself as neat and tidy as possible."

"Suit yourself," he shrugged. "But I've found using mud to really help. Perhaps we might put a wager on who is more successful today?"

I knew I was at a disadvantage, since Teddy's favorite pastimes were hunting and collecting trophies. While I'd been gone for a year, he no doubt had been sharpening his skillset. Nevertheless, I wanted to be in his good graces. Thankfully, I also adored riding and hunting, so it was no hardship for me to spend time with him in these pursuits.

"I'm willing, if you are. What do you propose?" I asked.

Some of my fondest memories were of the two of us out on the estate, joking, riding and chatting, as we stalked prey. This felt very much like our old way of being, and I was glad we could settle back into our relationship as though no time had passed by.

"Whoever bags the most ducks today, gets firsts dibs on telling the cook which recipe to prepare?"

"Sounds good," I said. Frankly, I would be happy to let him win, as he was a far more sensitive person than I was, and little things could set him off. It didn't matter to me if Bette made *canard l'orange* or *confit* or any other wonder - it was all delicious.

More important, our stablehands brought out our horses and I sighed with pleasure at the gloriousness of my new stead, Devil's Own. I reached into my jacket pocket and pulled out a chunk of raw carrot. His soft velvety muzzle tickled the palm of my hand while he used his teeth to take the carrot. The stablehand gave me a boost onto my saddle.

Maxwell brought out two of our favorite golden retrievers, Jasper and Jed. Chosen from a litter of prize winners a couple of years ago, they were sweet and funny. Most important, they used a very soft mouth grip when actually retrieving during a hunt.

Teddy whistled to the dogs as Maxwell let them off their leashes. They came bounding up to us, barking with big happy toothy grins. Devil snorted and pricked his ears back, when Jed galumphed a little too close for his comfort. I reached down and gave Devil a rub on the side of his neck, and spoke softly to him. "Easy, big boy. Easy." He relaxed within a few moments, which warmed my heart.

Ah well, it really does feel good to spend some time with my brother. Perhaps I could persuade him to be more supportive of my desire for independence. If Teddy would stand strong beside me, it would be much easier to convince Father that it was unnecessary to force my hand in marriage.

Devil was in his element, his nostrils flaring, and his head proud and high as we cantered next to Teddy and his horse. Teddy knew every trail like the back of his own hand, and so I let him guide us towards our fresh water pond which lay southward near the center of the estate. Jasper and Jed ran ahead, barking every once in a while for the joy of the hunt. The fresh water was the best area to hunt deer and mallards. The deer often came to the pond to quench their thirst. And of course, the ducks loved to build nests, and fish for worms and other tidbits in the mud beneath the water's surface. The birds' spring migration was happening at the moment, so the timing was perfect.

"Let's tie up over here," Teddy said, as he wheeled his horse over to a thicket of young saplings. We hopped down and after tying up the horses, took our guns, bags of powder and shot, and a picnic basket on a short walk through some shrubbery. Jasper and Jed ambled along beside us.

I sensed a joyful lightness at being back here on our family's estate. The grounds were beautiful, the air was fresh, and I did not need to concern myself with impressing anyone or making unnecessary small talk. While I did enjoy the pleasures of a big city, the countryside made me feel right at home and quite content.

"I built a new duck blind, just this past fall," Teddy said, pointing to a well disguised A-frame shelter just ahead in a cove at the entrance to the pond. He'd done a good job; the grasses and reeds were well woven on the wood frame, and Teddy had been smart about it. Instead of stripping all the vegetation right beside the blind, which would have made concealment impossible, he'd obviously taken the time and effort to bring over the plant material from elsewhere. It would provide excellent concealment from the flocks flying overhead.

"It held up well over the winter," I said, being complimentary whenever I could to butter him up a bit. "As have you. Looks like you shot up nearly a foot since I went away. But you'll always be my little brother, Ted."

I had meant that endearingly, but my brother scowled in response.

"Just like father and Aunt Winnie are always reminding me.

Always little. Always a kid," he replied. "We'll see how you all feel after the Hunt."

I decided to change the subject. "So Teddy, be honest with me. How was it being here with Father while I was gone?" I asked as we took our seats inside and got comfortable.

Teddy shrugged, as he loaded his gun with his precise combination of powder and shot.

"Not great, but not horrible either. You know Father," he sighed."He always has to have his way in things, and he insisted that I accompany him on multiple business trips to all sorts of backwaters. And even though I did my best to please him and follow his rules, he refuses to acknowledge it. But nothing would stop him from bragging endlessly to his friends and business associates about how wonderful his daughter is...'The jewel in the family crown,' " Teddy said, aping Father's baritone and pomposity.

"Oh, Teddy, aren't you exaggerating a bit?" I asked, kindly as I could. "I mean, Father takes you everywhere because he clearly sees *you* as the future of the family."

Teddy looked at me, and shook his head. "He doesn't care about me or respect me, not the way he adores you," he said. I opened my mouth to respond, but he raised his hand to stop me. "Don't bother, Saskia. I know it's true, and there's no point in you denying it."

I put a hand on his shoulder, and said, "I'm really sorry Teddy. Try not to let Father get to you. He really is from another time, and can be cruel and critical of both of us," I said.

"I suppose," Teddy said. "Do you want me to load yours as well?" Teddy asked.

"Sure," I replied. I watched my brother as he carefully loaded my shotgun then laid it down beside me. I picked it up and began to study the scenery, sighting along the double barrel. No birds yet, but a beautiful pale blue sky with only the thinnest layer of clouds stretched out overhead. A small breeze blew across us, but I trusted Teddy to use the appropriate shot ratio for the wind.

Teddy hummed to himself as he rummaged through his hunting

pockets to find his duck whistle. He brought it up to his lips and gave it a few good quacks. We waited quietly for a few moments, before we heard in the far distance, responding quacks.

We smiled at each other and raised our shotguns to our shoulders, getting ready.

"So how was Paris?" Teddy asked. "Are the Parisian women as beautiful as one might expect?"

"More beautiful by far," I replied. "Every shade of hair, every tone of complexion, and all better dressed than any Dutchess County heiress could ever hope to be."

Up against the clear blue sky, we saw a small formation of birds approach. Their telltale quacks gave both of us that thrill of antici- pating the shoot. We placed our fingers on the triggers of our guns, and spoke quietly.

"Any *special* friends?" Teddy asked, without a trace of judgement.

In that moment, I felt a deep sense of love for my brother. Despite his shortcomings, he accepted me for who I am, as I did with him.

"Yes, actually," I said in a whisper. "A lovely friend named Isabel- la." I hesitated for a moment, then said, "I'm really quite nervous about this Logan fellow."

Teddy kept his eye on the gun sight, but grunted in agreement. "I know you are," he replied. "But, in all honesty, he really isn't an unpleasant person, at least from the little time I spent with him."

"Cold comfort," I replied. "At least my potential future husband 'isn't unpleasant.'"

"Oh come now, Saskia," Teddy hissed. "What have you got to worry about? Father won't let his jewel of a daughter languish in some unhappy marriage. Look, Logan is a self-made man who is worth a lot of money. If we bring him into our family and portfolio, we can always push him back out later if he proves to be anything other than a good husband and honest dealer. You'll never have to work, never know the pressures of economics and commerce. After you pop out a couple of kids, you will be able to travel and shop and play to your heart's delight."

"Oh, I'm so glad I get to be the downpayment in the Rennard-Logan merger. Not that what I want out of life matters, anyway," I said, so irritated at my brother that I forgot to whisper. The ducks on the pond snapped their heads in our direction.

"Are you joking?! You always get what you want!" My brother bellowed. His loud voice made the ducks erupt in a chaotic, splashy scramble, quacking furiously. They took off above us, and flew overhead. We quickly lay back and each fired our shotguns. The birds squawked and dove in different directions away from the sound, but both of us hit a few birds.

The awkward moment still in mind, Teddy avoided talking to me, and instead commanded the dogs to "Go retrieve!" Jasper and Jed took off, plunging into the pond, swimming out to where the ducks we'd hit were floating. We sat quietly and watched them. Jed grabbed three and Jasper snagged two more, then they paddled back to us, proud of their hard work. They were back in mere moments, gently laying the ducks at our feet.

We both laughed as we watched the hounds try to shake the water and mud off, and Teddy piped up, "Saskia, I'm sorry for what I said before. You shouldn't have to marry anyone you don't want to. I can't go against Father too strongly, but I will do what I can to help. Just promise me one thing."

"What's that?"

"Promise you'll meet Logan and give him a chance. A fair chance," Teddy said, an expression of seriousness settling across his brow. "And think about the world we live in, and how people like us must navigate through it before you make any rash decisions. What do you say?"

"Deal," I replied. "It looks like you bagged three, and I only two, so congratulations."

We clinked our bottles of cider and drank. It was delicious. Jed and Jasper lay on the ground beside Teddy, tongues lolling.

Suddenly, Teddy put down his bottle, and quietly lifted up his shotgun. I turned to see what he had spotted. It was a doe, who had just emerged from some bushes and was busy nibbling on grass. Before I could stop him, Teddy cocked the gun, then fired. The deer was struck, but since we were using birdshot, it would only cause her pain. She screeched from the shot hitting her left hip, then lay on the ground panting and crying.

I rushed out of the blind and pulled my bowie knife out as I reached the poor thing. I came up behind it, took hold of her head, and quickly slashed the deer's throat open. I held it against me while it bled out. Its eyes, at first frantic and darting, gradually stilled and rolled back to stare at me accusingly. The deer's hide was warm, and a grassy earthy aroma tinged with the iron smell of blood, mingled in my nostrils.

Teddy came up to me a few moments later. "Jed bumped into me as I lined up the shot," he said a bit defensive.

I bit my tongue, as I realized I couldn't say anything critical without hurting his feelings. So I pivoted, and instead reassured him. "Of course, Teddy." I stood up and Teddy pointed at me and laughed.

"Now who's the one covered in blood?" he said. "You'll need to get cleaned up before your friends arrive for your little tea party," he added.

"Ugh," I replied. My hands and the sleeves of my jacket were sodden with the doe's crimson lifeblood.

"It's okay," Teddy said. "You go ahead and I'll take care of dressing the deer and bringing it back."

"Thanks," I said. I turned away and headed back to Devil, shotgun in hand, while my brother sliced the deer open and removed the intestines with skilled efficiency.

Chapter 13

Whispers In Velvet

Eve

Mrs. Doyle had assigned me the task of making sure the west wing's sunroom and adjacent powder room were ready for company. Apparently, a few of Saskia's socialite friends had been invited to come over for afternoon tea. According to Saskia, she'd been pretty much coerced by her Aunt Winifred to start participating in the local social scene. *The pressures of being rich!*

Both spaces had clearly been decorated with identical intention by the late Mrs. Rennard - may her soul rest in peace - with delicate floral wallpaper, white rattan chairs with matching floral cushions that sat around a large beautifully carved wood dining table with floral details on its solid legs. Dusky purple and pink hued wool rugs underfoot. Electric lights designed to look like candelabras flickered from their wall mounts. Three of the room's walls had large picture windows that opened up to vistas of the estate's manicured gardens, forest and lawn.

The decidedly feminine touches made the space one of my favorite parts of Greythorne to spend time in - even as a mere house-maid. It was a rather nice change from dead animals frowning down upon me. After finishing the dusting, wiping down the tables, and making sure there were no cobwebs hiding anywhere, I headed into the powder room with a bouquet of fresh cut delphiniums in hand.

The powder room carried the same theme of femininity, with a brighter floral wallpaper and large windows bringing in lots of natural light. As I placed the blooms into a blue porcelain oriental vase, the door cracked open, and I heard a whispered "Eve..."

Surprised at the sound, I looked in the mirror and saw Saskia slip inside the room behind me. She flashed a devilish smile, and held a finger to her lips as she locked the door behind her. Somehow, she was even more stunning than usual, in a high necked rose-colored bodice with full puffy sleeves, and a charcoal grey full flowing skirt. The tapered waistline accentuated Saskia's hourglass figure.

"How fortunate to find you here," she said. Saskia put her arms around me, and brought her soft lips to mine. Her ambrosial lavender scent caressed me as I inhaled. I surrendered to her tender, deep kiss. My heart shuddered in my chest as passion swept over me and I wrapped Saskia's lithe form within my own arms. I ran my rough fingers through her shimmering locks, only to find them slightly damp.

Our lips eventually parted, as we came up for air, and I beheld the vision of my affection. With her gorgeous glossy honey-colored hair, sparkling gray eyes, pink rosebud lips and sharp wit, Saskia was so beautiful that each time I was in her presence, it seemed as though I'd been carried away into a most magnificent dream.

"Your hair's wet," I noted, as I moved a lock of hair that had fallen forward across her face. "You've had a bath..." I managed not to voice a disappointed 'without me,' though I felt that through and through. My only hope was that it did not show on my face.

"Ah well, I had to scrub myself half to death, after going hunting with my brother," Saskia said. She took my hand in hers and gave each knuckle a tender kiss. I loved that she did not criticize my calloused hands or bitten nails. Heat rose up within me despite my best efforts to stay composed. Saskia could arouse me with just a look or gentle touch. Her mischievous smile returned before she contin-ued, "But if you are not otherwise engaged later, I think today might be a two-bath kind of day."

"Perhaps," I replied, doing my best to mimic her confident coquet-tishness. Sometimes over the last few weeks, the mistress had pretended to be disinterested in my affection, only to surprise me with a passionate kiss or unexpected invitation to her chambers. I intensely disliked the push-and-pull of things, and struggled not to let it wound me. In contrast, the on-and-off-again seemed to drive her wild.

Saskia was about to respond, when there was a sharp rap on the door. We quickly separated.

"Miss Kelly? Are you in there?" Mrs. Doyle asked.

"Yes ma'm! I'll be right out, just finishing up," I said.

Saskia smirked.

"Please be quick about it," Mrs. Doyle said. "Miss Rennard's guests will be arriving within the next thirty minutes and I need your help with bringing out the tea *accoutrement*." I could hear Mrs. Doyle turn and walk away, her heels clicking as she went.

Saskia sighed.

Deep down, I longed for constancy in a world where nothing seemed reliable. Saskia's caginess was like a constant pebble in my shoe, keeping me uncomfortable and off kilter. I decided to change the subject, "Are you looking forward to seeing your friends, despite your Aunt?"

Saskia shrugged. "I do wish Aunt Winnie would find other hobbies rather than meddling in my social life. And really, after a year abroad, I'm not sure how much we'll have in common. Most of them are the daughters of Father's rich friends, whom I know from finishing classes or time at the girls' academy. Some of us were not on the best of terms, even before I'd left. Ah, well you'd best get going, my dear. Let us halt this moment until later, yes?"

"As you wish, Miss Rennard," I replied, curtsying lower than I normally would.

That really seemed to get her going, because before I was able to reach the door handle she had once again snaked her graceful arms around me and drawn me into another kiss. "Aren't you cheeky?" she laughed.

Goodness, how was I going to get anything done?

I nodded and opened the door to survey the area, then bustled out and made a beeline to the kitchen area. Saskia would remain behind for a few moments to make sure we weren't seen together.

Bette could do wonders with a bit of flour, butter and sugar and the bounty of berries from the hot house. The kitchen smelled like a posh bakery. As we left the kitchen, Nan and I carried trays laden with floral china pots filled with steaming hot tea. Meanwhile Frances and Peggy brought the tiered tea trays, filled with freshly baked blueberry scones, clotted cream, Bette's home-made strawberry jam, and an assortment of mouth-watering fruity tarts. My friends and I had decided to divide the tasks; I would be responsible for serving the hot tea.

As we approached the sunroom, I could hear women's voices chatting and laughing. Saskia sat at the head of the table, regaling three of her friends who sat around the table, with stories from her time abroad. We entered carefully and placed the trays on the sideboards.

The three young women seemed close to Saskia's age and wealth. Well, I amended, I could only guess at their wealth based on their very expensive silk dresses, gaudy and opulent jewelry, and of course, the dismissive looks they gave Nan, Peg and I when we entered the room.

To Saskia's left was a rather plain young woman with narrow features, large bulging brown eyes and mouse-brown hair. Her clothes and jewelry however, were anything but drab - she wore a modern, perfectly tailored crisp ivory shirt waist and flax linen skirt, with a highly polished, enormous pearl necklace and matching teardrop pearl earrings. As I poured Miss Mousy some tea, I caught a whiff of maple syrup wafting from her.

On Saskia's right was a bold raven-haired beauty, with dark almond-shaped eyes, an olive complexion, and a rather generous bosom. Unlike the others, she wore a dress with a plunging decolletage, which was apparently most distracting to Saskia. I immediately took a strong dislike to Miss Well-Endowed.

She looked familiar to me, although at first I couldn't place her. Miss Well-Endowed was also quite touchy-feely with Saskia, holding her hand, and bold enough to move that wayward lock of hair from Saskia's face with a light touch and a giggle. I found myself clenching my jaw in irritation.

Across from Saskia, a wide-eyed young woman perked up as we entered. "Oh thank goodness! I'm practically starving to death!" She feigned exhaustion by bringing her forearm to her head, looking up to the ceiling in mock despair. She wore a brightly colored ruffled, layered and puffy sleeved purple dress which made her look as though she were a human wedding cake.

Miss Well-Endowed snapped at Miss Cake. "Oh, Candace for heaven's sakes! I watched you eat four entire chocolate bars on the ride over here! You're going to get larger than Greythorne if you don't watch yourself!"

What an awful thing to say! I started to recognize who these women were! I'd never been one to read the society pages until I'd met Saskia. And then of course, I'd been studying them in the little free time I had, to understand more about the world she floated in. Miss Mousy was the one-and-only *Gloria Carnavoy*, future heiress to an enormous family fortune. made by her Father. Mr. Carnavoy was considered utterly ruthless by his employees and competitors, at least in the news articles I had read.

I realized I had seen Miss Well-Endowed in society page photographs, so it was fascinating to see her in real life. She was Mrs. Antonia Caldwell-Merriweather, apparently the daughter of a Spanish princess who'd married into a Boston Brahmin family. The grainy black and white photos in the society pages had not done her justice. If I remembered correctly, she was herself recently married to one of the most eligible bachelors in the Northeast; a Mr. Charles Merriweather, whose family were newspaper titans.

As for poor Miss Cake, she was actually Miss Candace Entwhistle, of the Philadelphia Entwhistles, who were old-time candy and chocolate makers. Miss Entwhistle blushed but ignored the slight from her supposed chum. "Saskia, dear, you must tell us all about the gay young men who chased after you in Paris! Let us live vicariously through your adventures."

Saskia delicately buttered her scone, as she gave Miss Candace a smile and a wink. "Let's just say I was *extrêmement* occupied with various potential courters in Paris," she replied.

"From what I have heard lately, it's not just young men *en vacance* in Paris who are interested in you Saskia," said Miss Mousy quite cheekily, "I've heard whispers that you're on Mister Robert Logan's dance card."

Ugh! I cringed, but did my best to hide my reaction by turning quickly to the sideboard to retrieve the cream and sugar. I don't think anyone noticed.

To my relief, Saskia dismissed the comment. "Oh, Gloria, that's just the rumor mill! Never even met the chap. I've barely gotten back from France, and I'm still settling in."

"Well, " Gloria pressed on, disregarding Saskia's clear desire to avoid the conversation. "My cousin Owen told me that the very handsome Mr. Logan will be heading this way to pay you a visit in the near future."

At her mention of the name Owen, I inadvertently shuddered, as I recalled the dreadful young man who assaulted me back at the Inn. Anyone with that unfortunate name, reminded me of the past. Surely this couldn't be the same individual...

"Is that so?" Saskia replied with a disinterested tone. "Owen...who?"

"You, girl," Gloria waved at me.

105

"Yes, mistress?" I said in my best imitation of polite deference. "Can I get you anything?"

"Sugar," was all she said before turning back to Saskia to say, "My cousin Owen *Turner*."

Feckin' hell! It was the same loathsome toady who'd repeatedly harassed me at the Inn.

Gloria continued, oblivious, "You'll remember him; he told me he just saw you down in Tarrytown a few weeks ago."

"Oh yes, I do recall," Saskia said, fiddling with her teaspoon. "I was only there for a brief moment on my way back home."

"How much sugar Miss?" I deliberately interrupted, as I proffered the sugar bowl and silver tongs, wanting very much to redirect Gloria's attention.

"Two lumps please," she replied.

Saskia shot me a quick, grateful glance, thanking me for the interruption. "Anyway, what about *your* dance card, Gloria? I'm sure there are lots of interested fellows trying to snag some of your attention."

Gloria sighed dramatically. "One wishes so, but you know my father, the *great* Andrew Carnavoy. No one's good enough for Papa. He's such a stick-in-the-mud! He won't let me go anywhere without being supervised by my brother James, or cousin Owen. Papa wouldn't let me near any of the winter dances last year without a male escort! Even the Vanderbilts! He doesn't seem to trust any men at all, no matter how cultured or proper they might be."

Based on my personal experience, Mr. Carnavoy was probably quite smart and wise to think so. Of course I kept my thoughts to myself and simply continued my work, using silver tongs to lower a sugar cube into Saskia's teacup. She looked up and flashed me a most seductive smile. I blushed at the attention, and fumbled the tongs for a moment, dropping them with a clatter onto the floor.

"So sorry!" I exclaimed.

"Clumsy girl!" Gloria chided. I bit my tongue as Peggy ducked down and retrieved them for me quick as a wink. I whispered a

"Thanks, Peg," as I retreated up against the wall with Frances and Nan.

"Ah well, I suppose it's hard to find decent help this far away from the city," Gloria said, obviously thinking that she was being quite charitable. "It's a pity that all you have on hand are these dreadfully lazy, thieving Irish *bridgets*."

At that comment, my face flushed red with anger and I had to bite my tongue to stop from blurting out a response. Nan rolled her eyes at Peggy and I. Saskia glanced at me, then quickly looked away.

In a flash, my anger was replaced with disappointment that Saskia didn't say something to take Miss Carnavoy down a peg or two. Instead, the ladies continued to gossip and enjoy their tea.

As if things could not get worse, Mrs. Caldwell-Merriweather leaned in towards Saskia, her ample decolletage raised up in a most coquettish manner.

"Oh, Gloria. Our dear Saskia has no time for boys. She's busy traveling the world." She placed her bejeweled hand upon Saskia's forearm, lingering far too long. "Besides, a gentleman caller would seriously eat into her riding and hunting time. Isn't that right, Saskia?" I could feel the slow burn of anger in my gut, so I changed my focus to watching Frances and Nan replenish the rapidly emptying tiered tea trays with more baked goods.

"You know me too well, Antonia," Saskia grinned. "Guilty as charged: I do like a good hunt."

"Darling Saskia, you must come stay with me at our country estate," Antonia purred, with the tone of a cat lapping up cream. "It's been *far too long* since we've had any time together."

Saskia pulled her hand away and replied with a slight edge in her voice, "But Antonia dear, I presume you must be far too busy for company, now that you're setting up your new home with Charles. You'd made that quite clear last year, as I was about to sail to London."

"Ah well, it was only that I was doing all I could to help Charles in the beginning..." she replied, a touch hurt.

To my delight, Saskia did not back off. "I doubt he wishes to share your attention so early in your married life together."

Saskia turned her focus to the tray of pastries, and selected a small ruby red fruit tart, while Antonia's eyes narrowed. Saskia's eyes found mine. *Goodness, what this woman can do with a look.* My cheeks flushed red and Miss Antonia noticed. She looked me up and down as though examining a painting for its flaws, and then cocked her head at Saskia, a sly expression crossing her face.

"Not at all dear, you misunderstood me," Antonia responded. "Charles travels for work quite often and it gets dreadfully lonesome in that big house up in Newport. If you come for a few days, I can take you to the beach and out boating on the river."

And then, Antonia Caldwell-Merriweather winked at me. *At me!*

Oh gosh almighty! Could she possibly know that Saskia and I were...

And was she suggesting a secret liaison with Saskia?

Had they been together in the past?

My mind flashed on unwanted images of Saskia lavishing attention on Miss Antonia's bosoms. A wave of noxious jealousy rose up within me. How dare that woman flirt with the woman I was.....?! Actually what could I even call it? Romancing? Courting? I blushed bright red as I tried to think of an appropriate adjective to describe what was happening between Saskia and I. Stop it! I told myself, this was not the time or the place....

Miss Candace who seemed naively oblivious to any of the underlying tension, piped in with, "Antonia, I know you just adore Saskia, as we all do, of course! But even if she is too busy, Gloria and I would love to come spend time at the new mansion." She continued, her mouth forming a tiny pout. "By the way, I think Gloria must be right about Mr. Logan. Since you've returned, the charming man has ceased to respond to any of my invitations - even for the most elegant society events! Are you really not interested in him? If so, you should let him know so that he can cut bait and fish in other waters. It's been quite frustrating!"

"I shall be glad to do so, when I make his acquaintance," Saskia replied smoothly.

Finally, to my relief, the ladies rose up to take a stroll in the gardens. Once they departed, we began to gather up all the crockery and serving ware. Peggy snorted as we headed down the hall, each lugging heavy trays. "The nerve of them, calling us lazy. I'd love to see any of them put in the kind of day's work that we do day in and out."

I nodded, my mind preoccupied with worry about the present and the future. Robert Logan and the wealthy guests would be arriving in the next few days for Mr. Rennard's annual retreat. Was he really intending to propose to Saskia? Would she say yes? What would happen to me, to us....? Each night I found myself wishing I could slow time down... And then during the day, I wished time would fly faster and faster still....Either way, I had no peace.

Chapter 14

An Unquenchable Thirst

Eve

Since that first magical evening with Saskia, I had been on call almost every night, to attend to her bath. Each time had flown by in a blur of exquisite touch and emotion. I would leave her rooms feeling emotionally and physically more fulfilled than I could have ever imagined. And yet, each time I exited her room, my heart would begin to race within my chest with fear, and I dreaded the next day which dragged on endlessly.

My body, now awakened, seemed to have a mind of its own. At inopportune moments during the day, I would feel heat and sexual tension rise up from my core. I would be struck by an intensely deep sense of desire, a yearning to be touched and given sweet release. I had even locked myself in a bathroom stall, with a clean cloth wedged between my teeth, and touched myself for at least momentary relief.

But tonight Saskia had been in a mood. Snippy and withdrawn, quick to enter and exit her bath with no fanfare, and definitely no lovemaking. When I tried to talk with her, she had snapped at me, and so I exited her room with a sigh and not a little frustration. I did have compassion for her; tomorrow, the guests would be arriving for the fancy gathering, including her suitor, Mr. Logan.

And, of course, with Saskia's future up in the air, I felt a new sense of fear about my own. Would she end up marrying Mr. Logan? And what would become of our dalliance? I knew Saskia hoped that she would be able to put the suitor off, and convince her father to let her travel once again. I hoped so, too, for her sake, and just as selfishly for my own.

With the abrupt, 'No, not tonight, Eve,' still ringing in my ears, I stepped out into the darkened hallway to sneak back to our room, albeit earlier than usual. I felt as though eyes were watching me, and I was self-conscious at all times within the mansion. It was stressful and exhausting. Even my sleep was fitful and restless. Ma had taken to staring at me, too. I felt as though I were a butterfly stuck with a pin under a magnifying glass. Weakly I flitted down the dark hall, anxious to get to bed.

Luck, it seemed, was not with me, as I ran into two of the scullery maids, Edna and Maude. Just this morning, I'd accidentally overhead the same two gossips complain to each other that I was "a lazy favorite" of Miss Rennard's. It was awful to realize that some of the staff resented me for the "special attention" I was receiving. Peggy had come to my defense, insisting that taking care of any one of the Rennard family was more than a full-time job, and that I could hardly be lazy, when I was at Miss Rennard's beck and call. Peggy was a great source of support and comfort, although of course she had no idea that there was more going on behind closed doors. I had paused, then entered the kitchen pretending to not have heard a thing, so I ignored Maude and Edna sneering at me as I passed them by.

Once down the grand staircase and into the servant's wing, I smoothed down my apron and made sure my uniform was neat before entering our room. I opened the door, and had to squint in the darkness. *Ma must be asleep.* I sighed with relief.

Suddenly, a hand reached out of the darkness, and grabbed my shoulder. I was so startled that a wave of silvery energy rippled through my body, and I accidentally flung someone across the room, their back striking a wall. I wilted to the ground from the sapped energy, and that strange pins and needles sensation returned, prickling my fingers and toes.

"Holy hell!" I said.

A lamp snicked on and Ma sat up from the floor, her hair and nightdress in disarray.

I recovered my senses, "I am so sorry! Ma - are you alright? Did you get hurt?"

Ma released a deep breath and stood up. With wild eyes she regarded me fearfully. "I'm fine."

"I'm so sorry. I don't know why..." I dropped my face into my hands.

Ma started to pace in front of me.

"This is bad. Very bad," Ma said.

I stood and grabbed my mother's hands. "What do you mean?! What aren't you telling me?"

"Enough. We'll not speak any more of this. Your father's last words were for me to keep you safe, and damnit Eve, I am going to do that whether ye like it or not."

At the mention of my father, my thoughts drifted backward—first to the awful darkness and acrid stench of steerage on the passage over, then to our small cabin deep in the snowy New York winter. My eyes unfocused and images raced in front of my vision -

I see my Da fly across the room, his head striking a corner of the stone fireplace. He's slid to the floor, a pool of blood forming beneath him. "Aaaahhhh!" A scream fills the air. I see my Ma, so much younger, raise bloody hands in the air, my Da laying on the floor in front of her...Ma cradling his head in her lap.

A sense of horror flowed through me, deeper than anything I had ever felt. I let go of Ma's hands.

"Holy hell....... I killed Da!" I hunched over and hyperventilated. Tears rolled down my face as I rocked back and forth. The acidic tang of panic flowed through me. "I'm a *monster!*" Waves of overwhelming nausea hit. I ran to the chamber pot and threw up.

Ma, tentative, came over. She gently held my hair back away

from my face, until the dry heaves ended. I sat up and wiped my face with my apron.

"T'was an accident. You're not a monster. Let's just forget this. Now Eve, please."

"Not until I get some answers. You've kept me like an ostrich with my head in the sand!"

"I've *protected* you!" she snapped. "And frankly this is why I've told you over and over to keep your head down, and your hands busy," Ma retorted.

"You didn't protect me! You *smothered* me," I was so thwarted by her.

Ma pulled herself together. It seemed like she regretted telling me as much as she had. My suspicion was confirmed, when she turned to me and declared "We'll not talk of this again."

In utter frustration, I rose up and headed to the door.

"Where are you going?!" Ma asked.

"To get some air!" I shouted, as I slammed the door shut behind me.

I ran down the hallway to the servants' kitchen, eyes teary and heart pounding. I burst in but stopped short when I discovered Isaiah watching his wife with adoring eyes, as Bette finished tidying the kitchen.

"Oh! You're still working?" I asked - immediately embarrassed by how obvious my question was.

Isaiah was kind in his response. "My wife is a perfectionist."

"Aright, old man - I'm almost done," Bette smiled at her husband. "Something you need, Miss Kelly?"

"Just some tea. Show me where it's kept, and I'll manage. I need to clear my head. Oh and please, just call me Eve."

Bette opened the cupboard on the left wall. "Here you go, Eve: mugs are here, and the tins hold all sorts of tea."

I came over and pulled down a mug. "Would you like some?" I asked.

Isaiah looked at Bette, then stared at me, and nodded okay. "Sure."

Secretly, I hoped this meant her icy facade was starting to melt. Dina was so lovely, and so was Isaiah - I felt sure Bette must have some of that same warmth deep down. I retrieved two more mugs, as Bette wiped down the counters.

"What's troubling you?" he asked.

"It's been a very long day..." was all I could muster to say.

Bette barked a laugh. "Aren't they all?!" she responded. "Especially with the fancy muckity-mucks coming."

The kettle whistled, and I poured hot water over the tea.

"How long have you been here?" I asked, as I handed them the steaming mugs, then took a seat.

"We came over 25 years ago, with Miss Helen Burnside from Terrebonne Parish, Louisiana. Mr. Rennard's late wife. You've probably seen her portraits - her daughter looks much like her," Isaiah explained. Meanwhile, Bette kept her own counsel and mostly glared at me as she sipped her tea.

"What's it been like...working here?"

Bette and Isaiah shared a look. Isaiah responded, "Mr. Rennard pays on time, and has never abused myself nor the missus. Our hard work is rewarded, more handsomely than most might expect."

"Mind you, we don't sleep here," Bette added.

"Mr. Rennard gave us a bit of land on a corner of the estate. We built a small cottage and raised our son, Nathaniel. Now he has a good job in New York City," Isaiah said with pride.

Bette sighed. It seemed to me that she must miss her son a great deal.

"The Rennards have given us more than most folks like us get for being the help," Isaiah added.

With that, we sat for a few minutes and sipped the tea as it cooled. The warm tea felt and tasted so very comforting, and I sensed myself being able to relax a bit. Isaiah made small talk about our emigration from Ireland and our time in New York while Bette nodded and made small noises of agreement.

Finally, Isaiah finished his tea and stood. Bette followed suit.

They quickly washed and dried their mugs. "We'd best head out," Bette said sharply.

A flood of fear returned as they exited. I raised my hand and chewed on my index fingernail as I pondered the night's events. I delayed as long as I could, until my tea was bone cold, before rinsing the mug and creeping back to our room. Thankfully, Ma was asleep, so I silently changed into my bedclothes and climbed into my cot.

After tossing and turning much of the night, I finally fell into a deep slumber. The next thing I knew the sun was streaming in through the window, and I could hear a clatter of noise and activity outside.

I sat up and was relieved to see that Ma had already left our room. With all the extra pressure on us with the guests arriving, I had no desire to face Ma's wrath or discuss last night's events. I hurried through getting dressed and ready for the day. I selected a freshly pressed uniform and as usual made sure that everything in the room was tidy and neat.

I headed down the hallway and as I got near to the Fitzgerald sisters' room I heard giggles and laughter from within. The sounds warmed my heart.

I knocked on the door. "It's me. Eve."

From inside Peggy called, "Come in!"

I opened the door and entered. Inside the large bedroom, Peggy, Nan and presumably their youngest sister Frances, all rushed around to complete the finishing touches on their uniforms. Although we had not met when she arrived yesterday, I felt like I already knew Frances after hearing her sisters talk about her nonstop since I'd arrived. She was slim, frizzy and freckled, with a fizzy disposition more like Peg than Nan.

"Are you lot ready?" I asked with a grin.

"No, not at all. We're going to be late, and Mrs. Doyle will be murdering us," Nan said with her usual pessimism.

Peggy, busy tucking France's frizzy hair under the maid's cap, retorted. "Stop being so mopey, Nan. Frances, this is Eve Kelly."

Impatient, Frances pulled away from her sister's fussing to shake my hands. "Hello, Eve, it's grand to meet you!" Her eyes were lit up with a playful joy.

"You, too."

"You're lucky, Eve," Nan said. "Getting tomorrow off with everyone else. Not sure how we drew the short straw."

"I suppose so," I sighed. "Though it's just a trip to Poughkeepsie with my Ma."

Peggy threw her hands up in the air. "Jesus Christ! Franny, would you ever hold still for more than a moment?!"

Frances giggled. "You know the answer is no, never!"

Nan looked at her little sister's overall presentation and commented, "I guess it's as good as it'll ever get."

I looked at the three sisters and shared, "You're lucky to have each other."

Peggy piped up. "You only say that 'cause you don't have to share a room with the two of 'em!"

"Not sure I wouldn't be willing to trade with you, Peg....try spending a night or two with my Mother..." I half-heartedly joked.

Peggy considered; "Fair go, it's not a very tempting offer." We laughed and commiserated on our way out the servants' entrance to the grounds.

Outside, I took a deep breath. The morning air felt fresh and clear. I felt lighter than I had last night, at least for the moment. The other servants were streaming towards the front of the house to welcome the arriving very important guests. Isaiah was in his best butler uniform and even Maxwell looked as though he'd made a bit of an effort to wrangle a comb through his hair and look less disheveled.

As I passed the barn, a flash of silver glinted from inside. I paused to take a peek. Overnight, several silver metal face masks had been hung on an inside wall. The black void of the empty eye holes sent chills running down my spine. I shook off the feeling and caught up with my friends, as we headed around to the front of the mansion. We were all wishing for an easy time with these new arrivals, and I secretly added to myself the hope that Saskia would be capable of dispatching Mr. Logan from Greythorne with no personal cost.

Next to the barn stood a few large oak trees. A handful of ravens soared down to the lower branches. They croaked and flapped their wings as they settled. It felt to me like a warning. I paused for a moment to make eye contact with one of the birds, but Peg called my name, so I hurried ahead. I strode by as quick as my uniform's heavy skirts would allow.

I recalled the ravens swooping around us at Tarrytown Inn, and how Ma had been frightened. Ma never talked to me about the old times and old ways, and now, more than ever, I wondered why. Short-tempered at the best of times, Ma made it clear that there were certain subjects that were off limits. My father, Sean, our family history, our past in Ireland before coming to America - all were mysteries. Getting answers out of my mother, was as difficult as coercing a pig to fly.

In front of Greythorne, the servants were quickly assembling by category and department. Mrs. Doyle held court to ensure that everyone was in line and presentable. We hastily joined in, just in time to have her scrutinize our outfits. She pointed to my apron which apparently had a twisted strap, and frowned at poor Franny whose frizzy hair was protruding from under her hair covering. Peggy and Nan quickly helped to push the wayward curls back underneath. At that moment, we heard the clatter of hoofs approaching.

We all gazed up the path to see a stream of carriages arrive to the estate. Meanwhile the Rennards descended down the stairs to welcome the guests. I caught a quick glimpse of Saskia, and my heart fairly leapt into my throat at her radiance. Ma noticed me gawking at her, and elbowed me firmly. I lowered my eyes and took up a respect-ful, and what I hoped would be a deferential, posture as the guests arrived. *Please make the time fly by*, I prayed to whatever spirits might be able to assist.

Chapter 15

Unwelcome Arrivals

Saskia

Under a bluebird sky, we stepped out of the front portico of our home and down the steps to await our guests as they slowly arrived in separate carriages, each pulled by pairs of elegant horses, finally rolling to a stop before us.

One of the new girls, a young freckled teen, blurted out "Ooh, this is so grand!" Mrs. Doyle gave her a glare that would peel paint. The young girl looked mortified and snapped her jaw shut.

Aunt Winifred was wearing another of her gawd-awful stuffed bird hats (this time a bird of paradise with gold and green plumage whose feathers were spread out as though ready to take flight) and a poofy, lacy, over-the-top Victorian black wool gown which made her look both frumpy and slightly clownish.

On the other hand, my brother cut a sharp figure in a well-tailored navy suit. He'd had his fair hair and mustache trimmed and pomaded. I marveled at how the lanky teen of a year ago had grown up while I was away. Turns out, he could be quite handsome and charming when he put his mind to it, and wasn't covered in mud and deer blood. Of course, for today he was on his best behavior.

Father was clearly in his element - wearing a custom tailored tweed suit, he really was such a dapper and handsome man. A strong wave of pride washed over me in appreciation of how hard he worked, and how much he had accomplished for Teddy and me.

The first of the five male guests arrived in a very elegant carriage. A tall, canny man in his mid-fifties burst out the carriage door, in a charcoal pin-striped suit. Servants hustled to unload his luggage from the back of the carriage, as the impatient man made his way towards us.

Father greeted him bombastically, "Welcome back to Greythorne, Andy! You already know my son, Theodore Jr., but please meet my sister, Mrs. Winifred Price, and my daughter, Saskia."

I smiled coolly at our guest as Andrew Carnavoy - head of the vaunted Carnavoy lumber and shipping empire, and wealthiest man in Dutchess County - stared down at me, his eyes tracing the outline of my curves. The man was as subtle as a toppling tree trunk.

"Miss Rennard, charmed I'm sure," said Mr. Carnavoy. "Gloria speaks highly of you," he added, his eyes lingering on my chest.

"Pish posh!" Chimed in Aunt Winifred, desperate to peel the man's gaze from my figure. "Such formalities really aren't necessary, Theo. It is wonderful to meet you, Mr. Carnavoy. Please, call me Winnie."

She thrust her hand forward, snapping Mr. Carnavoy out of his reverie. Graciously, he took her hand in his, and laid a gentle peck on the back of her gray lace gloves.

"Charmed, Winnie. Miss Saskia."

I studied the man's features. Despite being in his fifties, he radiated good health. He was tall, wiry framed, with bristling beetle eyebrows, dark brown eyes and luxurious brown hair worn with a side part. He had a neatly trimmed mustache, but was otherwise clean shaven. Father had told me that he was a timber and shipping titan with homes in New England and New York City. I'd heard that in his youth he'd been quite the lumberjack. He offered me a calloused hardened hand, and I was impressed. Some of these men had never done an honest day of work in their lives - their hands were as soft as a newborn baby's.

As Carnavoy approached Father, he joked. "I brought my lucky hunting knife."

Father put a friendly arm around Carnavoy. "I anticipate an excellent hunt - so make sure your blade is well honed."

Carnavoy replied with a snigger, "Oh, it's wicked sharp." I tried hard not to roll my eyes, but really, *men!*

Having now met Carnavoy, I mused that his daughter Gloria must take after her mother's side of the family. Unlike her *pater familias*, she had been mousy and dull. I watched as Mr. Carnavoy made his way down the line.

Next up, exiting in a slow, ungainly manner from his carriage, was James Whitaker. I believe he was in his late forties, quite short, stout and bewhiskered. He had attempted to cover his balding pate with a comb over of greasy strands, to ill effect. A tobacco baron from South Carolina, when he smiled at me, I caught sight of unpleasantly yellowed teeth. As Father introduced him to me, Mr. Whitaker leaned in, and I was forced to bring my perfumed handkerchief to my nose, to block the reek of stale tobacco wafting off the man. His kiss upon my glove almost made me nauseous. How on earth could Father tolerate the man's stench? I supposed money can be quite the salve.

A handsome young man, clearly the infamous Robert Logan, quickly stepped in, forcing Whitaker to back off. Logan was in his early 30s, smooth but cocky, and as Father had shared with me, a powerful young steel baron from Pittsburgh. He was dressed impeccably from head to toe with the finest tailoring in an elegant pin striped charcoal wool suit, and shiny black leather derby shoes. He had broad shoulders, was easily over six-feet-tall, and had gorgeous thick brown hair, a chiseled jaw with dimples as he smiled. His tie matched the azure blue of his eyes. He even smelled good - hints of leather, wool, spice and bourbon. No wonder the girls had been buzzing about him in Paris.

As Whitaker retreated, and Logan grasped my hands, I gulped a breath of fresh air.

"I see that meeting me has almost taken your breath away," he winked - he knew full well what had caused my almost asphyxiation. "Ah, Miss Rennard, you are a vision for my travel weary eyes. Robert Logan, at your service."

"Mr. Logan! A pleasure to meet you." He really was quite easy on the eyes, and I could see why Father had favored him. I leaned in and whispered, "Thank you for rescuing me."

He smiled, "Whitaker can be quite...aromatic. Please call me Robert."

Before I could respond, Father came over and clapped a hand on Robert's shoulder. "So glad you're here, *and* that you two have finally met!"

"The pleasure is all mine," Robert replied with a warm smile. "Theodore, what a lovely home you have here. I have never seen a setting more idyllic nor a family more charming."

"Oh, Robert, come now with the show of manners. Greythorne is at your disposal and we are thrilled you could make time for our little ritual," Father replied. And then, Father couldn't resist adding "Saskia has been looking forward to your arrival, haven't you my dear?"

"Of course!" I heard myself say with perhaps a bit too much forced enthusiasm. In truth, I was pleasantly surprised with how handsome he turned out to be. So far his quick wit had charmed me (the barest amount, surely) and I was at least curious to learn more about him. Hopefully my time with him over the next few days would not be too dull.

Across from me, as the guests passed by, the servants all curtseyed and bowed. Eve kept her eyes downcast. Was it a sign of respect or to avert making eye contact with me? I wondered. *It was probably for the best*, I sighed to myself.

I recognized Emil Henry from the moment he emerged from his lavish burgundy carriage. He was in his 40s, cunning and persuasive,

Haitian-born, and an exceedingly rare Black titan. According to Teddy, Monsieur Henry was wealthy from sugar and rum trade. While not tall, he carried himself in a stately manner. His suit was of the moment, and his salt and pepper hair made him look distinguished. He stopped in front of Aunt Winifred, and I almost giggled as he took Winnie's hand and brought the back of it to his lips for a kiss. Aunt Winnie blanched and Teddy made a bit of a sour face. Aunt Winnie was torn between being mortified and flattered at the male attention, even from an unwanted direction.

With that he pivoted and went over to Eve. "*Ma chérie*, you are so very lovely," he said with a resonant French Creole accent. He took her hand without hesitation and brought it to his lips. I had to hand it to him, the man had excellent taste. *How impertinent, and yet impressive.* Here was a fellow who did as he pleased, and *knew* that he could get away with it because of his wealth and power.

Eve blushed, as she would.

Last to arrive was Mr. Winslow Hardwick. He was in his 50s, tall and domineering, grey and humorless. The most interesting thing about him was the vintage Indian short bow he carefully unloaded from his carriage. I heard Teddy ask him about it, and he replied, "My grandpappy won it in battle against the Red Sticks back at Fort Mims."

A cotton baron from Mississippi, Mr. Hardwick apparently had a strongly negative attitude towards Monsieur Henry. Like me he had seen Monsieur Henry's presumption. "What in tarnation?!" Hardwick said under his breath, in his Southern twang.

Mrs. Doyle, who never missed a beat, stepped out of line between Monsieur Henry and Eve. "Welcome sir. I must ask the staff to return to their stations." Her voice had that edge of steel that made one want to immediately obey. But not Emil; the man reluctantly dropped Eve's hand, amused. "*Mais oui!* Don't let me delay you."

Emil pivoted and came directly over to me, then proceeded to do the same with my hand.

"*Bienvenue chez nous*," I offered.

"Mademoiselle Saskia, mèsi pou ospitalite ou."

I stared at the man - the words he uttered sounded like French's distant cousin in my ears.

"Fransè mwen an byen diferan de Ewopeyen yo.." he said smiling. I looked at him bewildered - what?

"Pardon?" I replied.

"My dear, I said my French is quite different from the Europeans," he translated.

"Yes, of course," I replied, not wishing to look ignorant.

After that, Father and Teddy escorted the men up the steps.

I watched Eve and the other servants head back to their stations. She gave me a quick glance, and then was gone. I turned to follow our guests up the stairs. It would be a long few days.

Chapter 16

Unwanted Touch

Eve

The morning passed in a clatter of chaos as Mrs. Doyle had us all running to and fro to make sure each of the guests was helped in their unpacking and settling in. We'd been told we'd have the entire Saturday off as recompense for the extra labor, which gave us something to look forward to. Still, for the moment we were scurrying to do all of Mrs. Doyle's bidding.

Even though each of the men had their own valet, Mrs. Doyle insisted that we assist in whatever manner each guest required. One crystal decanter of Mr. Rennard's best bourbon for Mr. Whitaker. Extra blankets and a roaring fire (despite the warm day) for Mr. Carnavoy. An extra basin and water ewer for Mr. Henry for his ablutions.

Once the men were settled, we hurried down to the kitchen to aid Bette and her scullery team, Maude and Edna, in finishing preparatory touches for the luncheon service. We tried to avoid bumping into one another in our haste. Edna especially had a nasty tendency to poke one foot out and try to trip me as I walked by.

Luckily Peggy spotted Edna try this loathsome trick, and pulled me back at the last moment. I resisted the urge to tell her off or stomp hard on her foot. After all, I didn't want trouble. At any rate, Mrs. Doyle sent us into the pantry, to pull out platters for Bette to place the meats on.

Peggy and I had barely had a moment to chat in the hustle-bustle.

"Phew! Thanks Peg!" I said, as we had the room to ourselves.

"Bloody Edna!" Peggy said, shaking her head. "She's a bad 'un."

"No joke," I said. "But thanks just the same for looking out for me."

"Ah, to be sure you'd do the same for me," she said. She climbed up a small wooden ladder, and started to lower the large platters down to me. Each one was white porcelain with the Rennard family crest emblazoned in the center of the dish. *Subtlety itself.* "You and your Ma are bloody lucky to have tomorrow off. Be sure I canna understand why almost everyone has a free Saturday - except for us. Mrs. Doyle insisted that we poor unfortunate Fitzgerald sisters will nae get a day off til Sunday..."

"Well, at least you get the Lord's Day," I teased, as I took each dish and added it to the stack on the counter. "We'll be here and working our fingers to the bone, no doubt."

"So what'll you do tomorrow?" she asked.

"Ma and I will head to Poughkeepsie for a bit of shopping and to get some lunch. Time for someone else to wait on *us* for a change," I said.

"Do you think Miss Saskia will be willing to spare you for 24 hours?" Peggy teased.

My heart skipped a beat, but I did my best to keep a straight face.

Fortunately, at that moment, Isaiah struck a fancy brass gong in the foyer. We hurried out of the pantry, platters in hand. In the kitchen, Mrs. Doyle had us put the platters down, and pick up our first appetizer trays to circulate. We bustled into the foyer, as the Rennards and their guests emerged from their rooms, each dressed in tweedy country attire, laughing and conversing.

Saskia was breathtaking in a coral satin dress, again modeling the modern Gibson Girl look with the closely tailored fabric showing off her gorgeous figure. My eyes widened a bit, but I caught Peggy flashing a look at me, and so I winked at her and shrugged, quickly changing my facial expression to a more neutral composition.

Robert Logan caught up to Saskia as they came down the stairs. He took her by the elbow, and she flashed him a brilliant smile. My stomach clenched and a most unpleasant sensation of jealousy rose up inside me. I had never envied anyone as badly as I envied Mr. Logan. I marveled at his freedom to flirt and charm with the object of my affection, with little to no concern of what others might think.

Peg, Nan and I were laden with platters of h'ors d'oeuvres. I had a platter of canapés - some sort of caviar, on a wee bit of cream, atop little mini toasties. They were quite the success, as were the oysters Rockefeller, and little ham and cheese croquettes that Nan and Peg carried about. Meanwhile Isaiah carried a tray of glasses filled with sherry for the guests to enjoy. We circulated as the Rennards and their guests chatted and mingled.

At one point, Mr. Rennard cleared his throat and the level of conversation died down. "Welcome gentlemen! It is excellent to see you all. This is the seventh year of The Ambrose Hunt, and I expect it to be our best weekend yet. As you know it is named after my dear father, Ambrose, who had the wisdom and the foresight to establish the family business here in New York nearly fifty years ago. Please raise your glasses in a toast to my father, Ambrose, may he rest in peace."

"Here, here!" The men replied as they each raised their glass.

"Merci, Theodore, I am so very delighted to be here as your guest this year," Monsieur Henry added.

Hardwick glowered at the Haitian, who simply ignored him.

Mr. Rennard signaled to me, and I came over and offered canapés to him and Mr. Logan. As they reached from the tray, Mr. Rennard leaned in and nudged Mr. Logan, "Not disappointed, I hope?"

Mr. Logan shook his head. "God no. Your daughter is fabulous, Theo."

I prayed that my face remained entirely neutral, because inside I could feel my gut churn with envy and frustration.

"Happy to hear it. I hate dealing with that cheapskate Carnegie!" Mr. Rennard responded.

Mr. Logan laughed. "Hopefully that will no longer be a problem for you."

I worked my way across the room towards Saskia, just as Aunt Winifred approached her and I proffered up my tray. Saskia refused to meet my eye, and so I cast my gaze downward as her aunt took a canapé. After popping it into her mouth, she leaned in to whisper through a mouthful of crumbs to her niece, "Well, girl, what do you think of your Father's pick?"

"Does it matter?" Saskia responded, tartly. Did she glance at me, then? It was so brief, so hard to tell.

"It does to me," her Aunt replied, as she waved me away. Though I wished to hear what Saskia had to say, I instead pivoted and caught up to Nan, whose platter was also nearly empty. She took a moment from serving the guests to warn me with a quick whisper, "Watch out for that fellow, Whitaker. He reeks to high heaven."

"Oh saints," I replied. She quickly dodged away, but sadly the warning came too late. I could smell Whitaker as he approached me from behind. He snagged a canapé from my tray and shoveled it into his mouth. I offered him a napkin to clean his food-filled whiskers, while my eyes teared up from the stench.

"Thank you m'dear." Whitaker said as he wiped his mouth. "You are a sight for sore eyes," he said, once he finished swallowing. "How lucky of Theodore to have you."

I smiled politely and replied, "I consider myself most fortunate to be working at Greythorne."

Aunt Winifred who wanted another nibble, overheard and chimed in, "Indeed you are!" That woman had a way of being utterly irksome. I'm sure she wanted all of us to grovel at her feet in gratitude for our jobs. It was a lot of nerve coming from a woman who would be destitute if not for her family's largesse.

Teddy Jr. and Mr. Carnavoy came by and helped themselves to the hors d'oeuvres. Carnavoy eyed me as though I were on the menu, and I involuntarily shuddered. Sounding quite irritated, he asked Teddy, "What's Emil doing here? A Haitian? In Greythorne? Ambrose must be spinning in his grave."

Teddy shrugged and replied, "Father is color-blind when it comes to money."

I looked up to see Saskia watch me from across the room. All of the sudden, a hand GROPED my rear and then -

PINCHED HARD.

"Oh!" I uttered, surprised. My vision grew blurry, a buzzing sound grew inside my head, and my fingertips tingled. The lights in the room suddenly flickered.

Mr. Rennard and the guests looked up at the lights frowning. Nan looked at me with a mix of horror and pity, as she'd apparently seen who'd groped me. Before I could blink, Saskia arrived at my side. She placed a hand on my forearm in a calming gesture and whispered in my ear, "Just breathe."

Her touch calmed me down so that I could see clearly again. Meanwhile, Saskia flashed a gracious smile and spoke to Mr. Carnavoy (apparently my assailant), who stood directly behind me. "Mr. Carnavoy - has Father shown you his collection of hunting rifles?"

"The legendary Armory of Theodore Rennard? A pity to say, no, not yet. I've heard tell though," he replied.

Saskia guided the man past me out of the foyer and into the study.

As I regained my composure, I caught Nan giving me a most sympathetic look. I shrugged. My rear stung, but not as much as my dignity. At least the lout had been shuffled off by Saskia. Clearly money did not equate to class.

Pretty quickly after that my tray was empty, so we gathered up the used glasses and plates and carried them back to the kitchen. Ma was working alongside Edna, Bette, ensuring that the kitchen team had all of the dishes and sundry items needed to serve the next meal.

"How did it go?" Bette asked.

"The food was gobbled up," I replied and smiled at Bette. I was still trying to get on her good side - if indeed she had one.

"Eve might need a little salve on her rear after the groping she got," Nan half-joked as she dropped off her tray.

Oh God no. I shook my head at Nan.

"Ooh that sounds awful," Frances commented with wide eyes from behind a stack of dishes. I saw Edna and Maude exchange snide looks of joy at my discomfort.

Ma looked up, her eyes were flinty. "Who was it?" Ma asked.

"Ma, it's okay," I said

"No, it isn't."

"Please Ma, don't make a fuss."

Nan whispered to me, "Sorry I mentioned it."

Mrs. Doyle who'd apparently also heard Nan's comments much to my chagrin, came over and looked me in the eye. "Eve, why don't you do a quick tidy of the sitting rooms, somewhere the men aren't for right now?"

"Yes, Mrs. Doyle. Thank you."

As I gave my tray to Franny, Bette commented, "She's fresh meat to that lot, and they can smell it."

Mrs. Doyle replied crisply, "Not if I can help it."

Ma shared a look of gratitude with the elder servant, then turned to me, "Off you go, Eve."

I rubbed the sore spot on my bottom, as I exited the kitchen and headed to the west wing sitting rooms and study. I hoped that no one had noticed that my reaction to being groped happened at the same moment as the lights flickering, but I wasn't entirely sure. Teddy Rennard had given me a very quizzical look.

I popped into the study to fluff the pillows and make sure the room was in order. As I leant over the sofa to position the cushions I heard a sudden *click*. I fairly jumped out of my skin, terrified that it might be one of the men.

To my relief, it was Saskia. She entered and locked the door. "I wanted to check on you, especially after I saw that horrible man grab you."

"I'm fine, *Miss*," I snipped.

But Saskia would not take a hint. She placed her palm on my cheek, which made me squirm.

"*Miss*?! What's bothering you?"

I focused all my attention on wiping a few bits of invisible dust off the oak bureau.

"Nothing at all, Miss," I reply as blandly as possible. "You and Mr. Logan seem to like one another well enough..."

I saw Saskia stiffen. She narrowed her eyes as she considered her response. "You do know I have to play the game, right?" She asked, eyes shimmering in earnestness. " That I can't summarily dismiss Robert out of hand. My father would explode with anger. I am doing my best to play the cards I'm dealt."

I turned and faced Saskia, letting go of my jealousy. "Yes, of course," I replied with chagrin, taking a moment to realize how much pressure she was under. "I admit I'm a bit of jealous of the freedom he has to court you in public without a care in the world."

She opened her arms and embraced me. I wanted so badly to melt into her, but -

"What if someone comes in?" I asked, nervous.

"Don't worry, I locked the door," she said with that mischievous smile of hers, and then leaned in with a passionate kiss. Her lips parted like velvet rose petals. Our tongues entwined, and she reached down with her right hand inside my uniform to play with my breast. I groaned as the heat rose in my body in response to her touch... We slid over to the couch and for the next several minutes we were swept up again in our desire for each other. This time, we both kept our clothes on, but it was easy enough to lift up our skirts and use our hands to pleasure each other while kissing. My body arched up at the same moment as hers - we both moaned as our bodies shuddered in waves. Afterwards we relaxed, and she held me loosely in her arms.

"I'm still holding out hope that after this weekend is over, I can convince my father to allow me to go back to Paris, or maybe Florence or London. You would come with me, of course. Wouldn't it be nice if we could do that?" Saskia pondered.

For a moment, I gave myself permission to imagine what it might be like to leave my Ma, and live my own life, follow my own dreams. The possibility was thrilling... I could see the world, especially Italy and France, but perhaps also return to Ireland. I had far-fetched dreams that one day I would be able to go back and connect with my family who still remained in and around Dublin. Perhaps I would even have the opportunity to study nursing in Europe - I'd heard the Sorbonne in Paris was a mecca for the study of medicine. Maybe I could learn French...

"Yes, it would be incredible," I replied.

Saskia kissed me - it was only a few minutes after we had just made love, but the fire in my body rose up again as if it had not just been sated. Perhaps my life could take an unexpected turn for the better? A new freedom of possibility, unlike anything I'd ever known, spread out before me. At the same time, I had never been so afraid of my uncertain future.

Chapter 17

Request Denied

Saskia

God *this woman feels good.* We kissed long and deep. There was definitely an additional frisson of deliciousness by doing so in Father's study. All around us the sounds of others in the house (wood creaking, feet stepping, muffled conversation floating through walls) were so loud in the silence of our kiss. And there, in the back of my mind, a tiny ball of worry - *what if Father finds out?* I decided to redirect my imagination away from that potential horror.

These moments with Eve made me think back to Paris, to lazy afternoons spent in the arms of Isabel, in her private chambers. What I would give to go back to Europe....and the possibility of bringing this delicious creature with me? *I simply must!* After all, Isabel had regrettably moved on, though not necessarily to greener pastures. Her parents had strongly persuaded her to consider the Comte Montdidier as a possible *époux*. At the end, we had a sad parting and I threw her farewell note in a fireplace: "Dear Saskia, I adore you, but as much as I would wish otherwise, my parents have left me no option but to marry Herve. Farewell, *ma cherie.*"

As Eve nibbled on my left ear, sending a gentle pulse of electricity up and down my spine, my mind turned to my own potential husband, Robert. Much to my surprise, he was most charming, and quite handsome. If he really were as modern as Teddy says, then perhaps a life with him might not be as oppressive as a typical marriage? What if he was actually skilled as a lover, too? If not, I could certainly show him the ropes.

But then what of Eve? I really did dislike the thought of letting her go. And, I suspected that the current of electricity that sped through me when we kissed, was only the surface of a very deep well of talent. There was something special about Eve. Something I couldn't quite put my finger on just yet.

Perhaps I could even navigate a future in which Eve remained my personal maid, provided I perform adequately as Robert's wife? My mind swirled at the possibilities.

Then again, Robert was from Pittsburgh and the thought of living *there* of all places...ugh.

I sighed, and she asked "Penny for your thoughts?"

"I'm supposed to go to Manhattan for a girls' night tomorrow, while the men have some private time. I'm meeting Gloria and Candace there, but I am not in the mood for any of it."

"I'm heading to Poughkeepsie with Ma for the night," Eve said. She didn't sound particularly enthusiastic, which wasn't surprising to me. From the little I'd observed of the two of them together, it was obvious her relationship with her mother was a prickly one. I pictured Mrs. Kelly finding us in here, and was torn between horror and amusement at imagining her face. Perhaps it was unwise for me to picture such things. I took a deep breath and wrapped my arms tightly around Eve's midsection, causing her to exhale sharply.

The lights flickered, just barely. *There it is again. How peculiar.*

Jiggle, creak, rattle. Eve and I both fairly leapt off the couch as someone outside tried to open the door to the study.

Eve's eyes were wide with fear as she hastily adjusted her uniform.

"Hallo!" Teddy called from outside the door. "Saskia, are you in here?"

"One moment, *cher frère*," I called as Eve and I made sure we both looked presentable. I fixed my hair as best I could, and Eve smoothed down her uniform. "It will be okay," I whispered to her. "My brother won't say anything and my father is clueless..." She nodded, but her cheeks were still almost as red as her hair.

I walked over and unlocked the door, as Eve followed behind carrying her pail of cleaning supplies.

As the door swung open, I was met with my brother and Father waiting outside. "Sorry, Father, I had developed a headache and needed a quiet room to recuperate."

"I trust you feel better now?" He asked, a frown of concern crossing his face.

"Yes, much, thank goodness," I replied.

Teddy looked from me to Eve and back. A wicked smile grew on his face.

Don't you dare... I glared at him.

"Miss Kelly, thank you for your efforts these past few days. Are you enjoying the library?" Father asked quite kindly.

"Very much sir, thank you," she said in a flustered manner, as she went past me and hurried out the door.

"Quite a nervous little thing, isn't she?" Father observed as Eve rushed off.

"I quite like her," I said as blandly as possible.

Father and Teddy entered the room, and Teddy whispered in my ear, "I bet you do, dear sister."

With that obnoxious leer on his face, Teddy really was irritating. I stepped hard enough on his toes to cause his smirk to disappear.

"It's dinner time in a moment," Father pointed out. "I have taken the liberty of ensuring that Robert is seated next to you, and that Mr. Whitaker is downwind from all of us," he winked. "And I instructed Isaiah to open the windows throughout."

"I appreciate that, Father," I replied. "I'll be right there, just need to freshen up."

Dinner was excellent, at least as far as the food was concerned. Bette really was a marvel in the kitchen. The meal began with more oysters, this time raw and served over ice. Bette made a delightful vinaigrette that perfectly balanced the sweetness of the oyster with a delicate acidity. After the oysters, came a delicious beef consommé redolent with herbs and a splash of French cognac. Then the mains - turbot in lobster sauce, canard à la Rouennaise and roasted saddles of spring lamb. All served with whipped potatoes, peas, and other vegetables from our greenhouse. The men oohed and aahed as the other servants placed the dishes in front of us with a flourish.

After half a dozen courses, and nearly as many glasses of wine, it was finally time for dessert. The servants served us slices of cake as we finished our drinks. It was a gorgeous *charlotte rousse*, one of my all-time favorites. Laced with whiskey and studded with raspberries, the ladyfingers delicate and perfectly framing the custard within. Everyone was wowed by the presentation, except perhaps for that stick-in-the-mud Hardwick, who was thin as a rail and looked as though he lived on oats and dry tack.

Robert and I had chatted throughout the meal, mostly about horses. He was quite the horseman himself, and had taken to building and owning a stable of race horses outside of Pittsburgh.

"So what do you think of Devil's Own," he asked, as we sipped some port.

"He's gorgeous," I replied. "His speed and smooth gallop are an absolute wonder. I think he is the most extraordinary horse I have ever had the privilege to ride."

"He'll also be very valuable for breeding purposes...his sires and dams were all multi-award winners," Robert pointed out.

My stomach tightened at the mention of breeding horses. I really didn't want the conversation to steer too much towards marriage and family. Fortunately, the arrival of our cake slices took care of my worries.

Robert dropped all interest in conversation once the morsel was delivered in front of him. He practically salivated and rubbed his hands together, then forgot his manners and took a taste before the rest of the table had been served. Father was busy lighting Teddy's pipe, but Aunt Winifred caught the *faux pas* and her eyes narrowed in response. For some reason, it made me like him more.

"Gosh this is excellent," he said, after his first bite. "I might want to steal your cook away from your father," he said jokingly.

"Many have tried...but fortunately for my father, she won't budge," I said.

Monsieur Henry -"Call me Emil" himself - sat across from me. He was actually quite a fun dinner companion, with a roguish sense of humor. "Robert, a French-trained cook will always be superior to a local American one. But perhaps in Pittsburgh such people are harder to find?" He smiled as he delivered the slight dig.

Now I know folks from the East Coast tended to be snooty about anything west of the Appalachians. Having been there once with Father long ago, my impression of 'Steel City' was that it was a rough and tumble backwater.

"You're not wrong," Robert replied. "My serving staff are Amish."

"Amish?" asked Mr. Henry. "I am not familiar with these people."

"They are also known as the Pennsylvania Dutch."

"Ah, Dutch," said Emil. "So your cooks offer you pickled herring every morning?"

At this James Whitaker guffawed, then said, "Wouldn't expect someone like you to know that the Amish ain't Dutch. They're *German*s living in the Keystone State. 'German' in German is 'Deutch.'"

Emil smiled, despite Whitaker's condescension, no doubt used to suffering such treatment. The man chuckled as he dipped his head in feigned respect to Whitaker. "Ah Monsieur, thank you for helping me learn something new about this magnificent country."

Whitaker eyed Emil suspiciously, not sure if he was being ribbed or respected. I covered my smile with a quick dab of my napkin.

Emil turned his attention back to Robert. "But, Monsieur Logan, German cooking?! Sausages and cabbage for dinner? I'm sure that would get tiresome very quickly."

"Ah, but you have you never had a dutch apple pancake, then. Quite delicious," Robert replied. He looked down at his disappearing dessert, "Although perhaps not as delicate as this..."

Emil flashed his brilliant white teeth in a smile, then pushed back his chair a little to stand. He raised his glass in a toast to Father. "Theodore, *merci beaucoup* for the delicious meal. Compliments to your chef! Please everyone join me in a toast of thanks to our generous host."

All around the table the men paused and raised their glasses. As usual, the Southerners, Whitaker and Hardwick, glared at the Haitian, annoyed by his apparent lack of submissiveness.

"Thank you, Emil! Thank you gentlemen..." Father replied as he raised his glass in response. Eyes having met, we tipped back our cups.

As Emil sat down, Whitaker stood up with a flourish and produced a cigar box in his hands. "Perhaps it's time for us to all enjoy some fine Virginia *seegars* after dinner this evening..."

Father, who loved fine tobacco, smiled warmly at Whitaker.

"Perfect timing. Gentlemen, if you are all done, let's adjourn to my study for further conversation and a smoke."

With a general scraping of chairs, the men arose from the table.

Feeling a bit impetuous and emboldened by my wine consumption, I found myself approaching Father. "I would very much like to join you all this evening."

Before Father could respond, Teddy blurted out, "That's totally inappropriate, Saskia."

Aunt Winnie, her face somewhat red after all the food and alcohol she had imbibed, snapped at me. "Have you learned nothing from me, my dear?! Tobacco is the realm of men, as is your Father's study. Neither are at all suitable for a young lady."

I could tell that Father was conflicted between pride in my boldness, and discomfort at my modern attitude. "I'm afraid your aunt and your brother are right," he responded. "Plus I promise you'll have ample opportunity, after you return from your overnight to Manhattan, to chat with Robert and our other guests. Now, run along for your nightly bath, my dear." With that, Father and Teddy caught up with the guests.

I despised being patronized. My jaw clenched in anger, but before I could leave, Robert took my hand and faced me quite earnestly. "In my home I believe that women should be included in every activity, should their heart desire it. Perhaps we can smoke together another time, Miss Saskia."

I smiled weakly in response, trying to compose myself, although inside I was fuming. "I appreciate it," I replied.

I spotted one of the Fitzgerald sisters and waved her over. "Could you please tell Miss Kelly to prepare my bath. I will be heading up shortly."

"Yes, Miss," she bobbed and replied.

I sighed and tried to shake off my annoyance and frustration. I really had no desire to go to Manhattan tomorrow just to be with Candace and Gloria...*ugh!* And I realized I would need to spend a little time one-on-one with Father as soon as the weekend was over... things were not heading in the direction I wished them to.

Part Three

Chapter 18

The Unholy Ritual

Eve

The evening seemed endless. I'd been busy serving earlier in the dining room, only to be repeatedly irritated as I watched Saskia flirt with Robert over dinner and dessert. She reached over with her long tapered fingers, and gently swept back a wave of his hair, in the same way that she had done with me. Recognizing the gesture made me feel cheap and used. *I've been such a fool.* Why on earth did I think that someone of Saskia's position would choose to be with the likes of me, when she could have any man, any woman she wanted?

I left immediately after Saskia tried to invite herself to join the men. I wondered why she would want to be part of their after-dinner conversation, when they all seemed either deadly boring or relentlessly leery to me. All except for Monsieur Henry, whose subtle way of needling the other guests was very amusing to watch.

After that I pivoted into the kitchen for the rest of the night, working with the other scullery maids, helping with the crockery - washing, cleaning, putting it all away. All under the watchful eye of Ma and Bette, which meant that Maude and Edna kept their mouths shut and focused on the work at hand, thank goodness.

Finally, it looked like the guests were done with dessert. Peggy set down a tray full of dirty dishes near the basin and came over. Ma was working with Maude to put away the clean crockery in the pantry.

Edna came over to me. "Hey Eve, Mrs. Doyle wants you to do a quick check of Mr. Rennard's study before the men return there."

I glanced at the kitchen clock. "I need to start Miss Rennard's bath."

In her usual snide way, Edna said, "Well, they've just started dessert, so you should be able to fluff the room, and not miss out on Miss Saskia's special bath time, dearie."

Edna clearly enjoyed getting a rise out of me, so I took a deep breath and walked out without another word.

I headed directly to Mr. Rennard's study, duster, cleaning rags and pan in hand. Inside, I quickly fluffed the pillows, then pulled out my duster up to remove some cobwebs that I'd spotted on the face of one of the enormous mounted deer heads.

Holy hell! The deer's eyes SHIFTED and FROWNED, and its mouth GRIMACED at me.

I jumped away only to bump into a ceramic horse statue.

CRASH!

The horse figurine shattered as it hit the floor. *Damnation!*

I rushed and knelt down to quickly sweep up the pieces when I heard men's voices approach.

Oh no! I scanned the room to find a suitable hiding place. There! I raced to a large oak wardrobe, and pulled the doors open. Besides some hunting paraphernalia, there was enough room for me and my cleaning supplies. I barely managed to climb in and close the doors as the men entered.

I sat folded up tight, my left eye pressed up against a thin crack between the two doors, as the men smoked and talked to each other. The heavy burgundy brocade curtains were pulled back by silver tassels, and the windows were open. A steady stream of cigar smoke flowed out into the evening air. These wealthy men were much like puffed up peacocks, strutting to show off their plumage. And much like peahens, we women were very much in second class, useful only for providing certain services...The time ticked by so slowly. I didn't think this day could possibly get any worse.

Suddenly, Mr. Rennard nodded at his son. Teddy rose up and went over to one of the bookcases. He presses his fingertips on a little corner of wood. A section of shelving swings open to reveal a secret cabinet within.

Teddy reached inside and retrieved a white goblet. *Is that ivory?* I wondered, seeing the brilliant white vessel. But when Teddy held the object up for all in the room to see, I realized what it was.

A skull! A human skull...

My mind could scarcely believe it. A *skull* mounted onto a base. I bit my knuckles to stay quiet...

I focused my gaze until there was no doubt in my mind : the eye sockets glittered with dark stones, perhaps obsidian? It sat on a base made from some type of animal horn - an unholy goblet.

The men rose, and a seriousness settled over the room. Even more frightening - none of the men were disturbed by the sight of this horrific chalice. Emil's eyes gleamed and he cracked a wide smile. Teddy whispered into Robert's ear. He nodded as Teddy placed the goblet on table.

Mr. Rennard went to his wall of weapons and pulled down a Bowie knife, the sort of blade hunters would use to field dress an animal before bringing it home. The metal flashed brightly in the evening light. Teddy opened a crystal decanter and poured some red wine into the open top of the skull goblet.

The men watched in silent reverence, as Mr. Rennard drew the blade across the palm of his hand. At first I wondered if the edge was dull, since he made no grimace or sound. But when the blood ran, dark and fast, I knew it was no false weapon. He made a fist and droplets of blood trickled into the goblet. He then tied his palm with a kerchief, and turned to his son, who held his own palm outstretched, eyes wide in excitement. Mr. Rennard slashed into Teddy's palm - my skin crawled as I saw Teddy grin. He, just as his

Father had, squeezed his hand into a fist and let blood drip into the goblet.

The strange ritual continued as each man offered his palm for Mr. Rennard to slash, then drip blood into the cup. When it was Monsieur Henry's turn, I could swear he smirked, while the Southerners both blanched and elbowed one another. Mr. Rennard glowered at them and they held still. Their blood mingled in the goblet.

Mr. Rennard raised the chalice as the men bowed their heads. An unholy bishop, he chanted in Latin. "Repeat after me - *Hoc sacramentum sanguine fratrum.*"

"*Hoc sacramentum sanguine fratrum,*" the men replied in unison.

"*Qui nos prodit, in extremis laborabit,*" Mr. Rennard continued.

"*Qui nos prodit, in extremis laborabit,*" they replied.

"In this sacrament we are bound as blood brothers. Anyone who would betray us will endure unending suffering," said Mr. Rennard as he lifted up the chalice. Then, as if knocking back a slug of whiskey, Mr. Rennard tipped the skull backward and drank, then lowered the cup. Blood and wine stained his whiskers.

My stomach heaved.

Each man in turn, sipped from the same bloody goblet; even Mr. Hardwick and Mr. Whitaker, who looked as though they might vomit.

Just as it seemed like the evening was getting to its end, my left leg started to fall asleep. I had horrible pins and needles and felt forced to wiggle it -

!*CREEAK*...

Damnation! The wardrobe's old wood was moving underneath me. I held my breath, and shrank back as Teddy turned to stare at the wardrobe. After what seemed an eternity, he relaxed and returned to the conversation. The men finished their cigars and exited, except for Monsieur Henry with Teddy.

"One moment, Teddy." Emil pulled a glass vial from a waistcoat pocket. He poured the goblet's crimson remnants into the container, then stoppered it. "In my culture, blood is sacred," he said.

144

Finally, the two men left, and I heaved an enormous sigh of relief. As I tiptoed out of the study, the mansion felt eerie, the hallways long, dark and windy. Dark oil portraits of Rennard family members glared down at me from the walls. I swear I felt all of their beady eyes upon my skin, and I shuddered to think at the history of this family.

My first stop - to warn the Fitzgerald sisters. Impatient, I flung the door open. Peggy, Nan and Frances were getting ready for bed. Peggy's thick long blonde hair was only partially plaited. Nan was in a state of half undress, and Frances' face was wet with washing.

"Girls!" I was so wound up, I could barely utter more than a single word.

"Gosh Eve, catch your breath, you poor thing. Franny, get her some water," Peggy ordered. She pulled me over and sat me down in a chair. Meanwhile, Frances dried her face and hands, then poured me a glass of water from the bedside urn. I took a few sips, closed my eyes, and focused on my breath again for a few moments to calm down.

I opened my eyes. I was still so frazzled it was hard to string my thoughts together. "I'm not sure if you'll believe me..." I started.

Frances giggled. "Was it Miss Saskia and Mr. Robert?"

"Franny!" Nan scolded her little sister. Nan sat next to me, and took my left hand in hers. "Take your time..."

I took a deep breath and began to describe everything I'd seen. Peggy quickly plaited her hair, while Nan and Frances just sat listening. Frances' eyes were as huge as dinner plates.

After I finished, Nan turned on Peggy. "And *you* thought working for the Rennards would be the best thing to ever happen to us!" Nan accused.

Peggy bristled. "How was I supposed to know? The pay is so good. Our room and food are better than anywhere we've been. Even the uniforms are nicer than the usual homespun."

"Well, now we know why they pay so damned well," Nan asserted.

"Hold on a minute, Nan. Aye, I ken these are creepy rich men doing strange stuff. But they're not bothering us. These jobs aren't that easy to come by. It's not as if there are families like the Rennards on every corner. Besides, if we leave without proper notice, it might be hard for us to get any work at all. I say we stay, at least finish out the season and leave on proper terms. Summer soon, and that's a good time for job hunting, aye?"

Nan frowned and put her hands on her hips.

Franny looked from sister to sister, not sure what to do.

"I'm going to go talk to my Ma," I said. As I headed out the door, I could hear the sisters raise their voices and argue with one another. I sighed and turned down the hallway, only to bump into that creepy awful Maxwell.

"Gah!" I shrieked.

The crude little man grabbed me by the shoulders. "What's got you in such a state, eh Miss Kelly?" he asked as he leaned in, his whiskers way too close to my face for my comfort.

"Let go for goodness's sake!" I snapped as my skin prickled with electricity.

All of the sudden, his eyes widened and his walrus whiskers stood on end - he let go in a hurry, as if he'd gotten stung by touching me. He backed off, and I pushed past him. No time for niceties now.

I hurried inside our room. Ma was sitting at the small table, in her nightgown, brushing out her auburn hair. More and more streaks of gray had appeared lately. "What's happened?" she asked.

Where do I begin? "Ma, you were right about the rich being... peculiar." I described what I'd seen in the study between the Rennard men and their guests.

"Feckin' hell!" Ma's face went through rapid emotions - confusion, fear, and finally settling on anger. She folded her arms, slitted her eyes and pursed her lips at me. "I told you this place would be trouble!" she accused.

"I know, I know," I said to placate her.

"Well we can't just up and leave," Ma strode back and forth across

146

the room as she thought out loud. "The Rennards would not take kindly to us leaving them in the lurch."

I nodded. "I told the Fitzgerald sisters about it, too."

At that Ma grew angrier. She looked me in the eye. "You went to the Fitzgerald sisters first?!"

Ouch. She was right - I had thought of them, before I'd thought of warning her. Still it would hardly do to confirm her observation. "Really Ma, it didn't mean anything. I just passed their room first."

Ma held my gaze for a moment and I saw her expression darken.

"Be that as it may, we can't be responsible for them," Ma said, doubting my veracity.

Impatient, I headed back to the door. "I need to go see Saskia."

"What? Now?! Have you gone mad?" Ma snapped.

"Ma - she's been away for a whole year. There's no way she could know about what her father and brother are up to," I replied, trying to keep my voice neutral. "Besides, she's told me she wants to depart from Greythorne. Perhaps we can continue in the role of servants with her as she travels abroad again..."

Ma stared at me. "That girl's got a hold on you."

"That's ridiculous!" I snapped back.

"Is it? Seems like you'd choose that pretentious princess over your own flesh and blood!" Ma roared.

Anger surged through me, as I responded, "Like you wouldn't be happy to wash your hands of me!"

All at once, Ma's hair rose all above her head - like a porcupine's quills. Her eyes bulged in fear, and a high pitched *crack* pierced the air. She clutched the Celtic pendant at her throat and held it up - both of us could see a thin crevice ripple across the pearl at its center.

"The pearl..." I trailed off. My mind turned inward and a memory came back to me, unbidden.

Ma carries me up the steps of a rustic cabin in the woods. She's wearing all black: mourning clothes. It must be right after Da died. The door opens and an older woman, with grey curly hair and bright blue eyes, invites us in. Ma calls her Fiona.

The next thing I remember, I am on the floor, looking up at the thatched ceiling. Dried plants and strange animal bones hang from the rafters amid cobwebs galore.

"It's not the wee one's fault..." says Fiona in a deep Irish brogue.

"Will you help or no?" Ma snapped.

"Tsk." Fiona scatters a handful of runes, crystals and animal knuckle bones across the floor, then kneels and draws a strange star shape in chalk on the wood floor all around me.

Fiona lights some herbs on fire and the air grows thick with haze and she begins to chant:

"From the points of the star, from the powers of the Morrigan, hold the child fast, safe shall she be, bind the powers and hold the key.

Strong be the powers of the Morrigan. Capture the light and hold the key, so that this babe, blessed will be. Fierce be the powers of the Morrigan."

I felt a shimmer pass through me. A soft opalescent light rises from me, up and up from the center of my chest into the air above. Fiona waves her hands gently, and the light shrinks into a small hard pearl which she captures and presses into a Celtic shield pendant. She hands the pendant to Ma who puts it on a chain around her neck.

"Will she be...normal?" Ma asks.

Fiona snorts.

"You know what I mean," Ma says.

"Her gifts are held back, inside the pearl. At least, they will be until she comes of age. Moira, you must prepare her," Fiona responds. "You must teach her about your legacy. If not, the consequences..."

"Eve, lass, do you hear me?" Ma reached for me as my mind snapped back into the present.

Her touch proved to be the final straw. A surge of rage swept through me and I screamed at her. The air between us seemed to ripple. Our water basin and ewer crashed to the floor, the doors to the bureau flew open, and our books and bedside things scattered in a flurry around the room as though a tornado had plucked them up and flung them higgledy-piggledy.

As the emotions left me, my knees buckled and I fell to the floor. My mind became filled with foggy mist, my eyes were out of focus and I was exhausted. I lay there for several moments, before I began to revive. I sat up and looked for my mother, who sat on the floor against the wall, watching me. For the first time in my life, she looked small and frightened and frail.

"You were supposed to teach me!" I say quietly as I rise up to my feet. "Instead you kept me weak and ignorant..."

"D'ya think it was easy for me lass, alone in the world, a widow with a wee bairn, with nothing at all after Sean died...?" The fire in her eyes sparked as she retorted, "I did the best I could!"

I shook my head. What else was there to say? I turned away, left her sitting on the floor, calling after me, and exited the room, closing the door behind me.

I headed down the corridor and up the stairs to Saskia's chambers. As I climbed I thought about Ma's accusation that Saskia would know what her father and brother were up to. I fervently hoped my mother was wrong, and that Saskia would be as appalled as I was.

Mercifully, no one was about as I snuck from the servants' wing, up the servants' staircase, careful to avoid the noisy third step. The hallway leading to the bedrooms seemed darker than on previous nights. The faint waft of dinner and tobacco smoke hung in the air. Every fifteen feet, the mist was highlighted by the dimmed electric lights in a pale and sickly yellow.

As I turned the final corner, something struck the back of my head hard. My vision clouded over and the last thing I recalled was falling to the carpeted floor.

Chapter 19

Dreams Crushed

Saskia

I'd been grumpy, to say the least, as the evening had not gone as planned. First Father and Teddy shot down my attempts at joining them in the study. How criminal of me to want to be part of their conversation with our guests. I loathed it when Father and his friends treated me like a decorative item instead of as an intelligent human being fully capable of holding my own. True, I didn't have the business acumen of someone like a Hetty Green, whom I had recently read in the Wall Street Journal was now worth about $60 million dollars. But I was well read, and could hold my own in conversation, debate, and negotiation with any man or woman.

And then, for whatever reason, Eve had decided not to come to my boudoir tonight. Maybe she hadn't liked watching Robert flirt with me, but the silly thing needed to understand (as I had already established) that I had to at least entertain the thought, if only to keep the peace with my father until these guests left.

After all that, I'd had to make do with washing my own back after the Fitzgerald sisters finished lugging up the hot water. It had been most annoying and tiresome.

It was difficult to fall asleep, with my mind aswirl. Finally I did, but the rest was anything but comfortable.

After far too short a time, I woke with a start upon hearing a loud *thump* and whispers outside my door. Mystified, I got up and wrapped my silk robe over my negligee and went to the door.

There, in the hallway, Teddy and Maxwell were struggling together to carry a giant trunk past my bedroom door, heading to the stairs.

"What in God's name is going on?" I asked.

"No time to chat at the moment, Saskia. Go ask Father," Teddy huffed as the two men wrestled the trunk down the back stairs.

"Very well," I replied. My curiosity was peaked. Perhaps Father just wanted one of his strange taxidermied animals from the attic to show off to his friends. *Men.* I sighed.

I went back to my room to grab my slippers and then came down the main stairs. On my way across the foyer I came across Eve's mother, Moira who had emerged from the servants' quarters. She was in quite a state, with her hair up under a nightcap, wearing a rather ratty old robe over her nightgown.

"Where's my daughter?" she snapped at me, rudely.

What's gotten into everyone tonight? I wondered.

"I have no idea," I replied. "Last I saw her, she was clearing trays of dishes away from the dining room. Haven't seen her since."

"You're a hoor and a bloody liar," she snapped at me, her Irish brogue stronger than ever. "Stay away from my daughter, you miscreant!"

"What the devil are you talking about?" I said, aghast. How dare she!

At that moment, Bette stuck her head out from around the corner. "Mrs. Kelly," she called. "You're looking for Eve? She's in the kitchen. Follow me. I will take you to her."

Bette's head whipped around the corner and I heard the stairs creak under her weight as she descended. Mrs. Kelly held my gaze a moment more, unafraid and unbothered that she had just accosted the maiden of the house that employs her.

"When my father hears about this..." I begin, but before I could threaten her, Mrs. Kelly turned and hurried after Bette around the corner and down the stairs, without offering me the slightest apology.

I stood for a moment. Had Eve told her mother about our trysts? No, it was impossible. Eve would never admit that, especially not to her prudish, conservative mother. After all, Eve had shared with me that everything she knew about the human body and its incredible potential came out of medical books. Medical books! Incredible. I was glad that I had Aunt Winifred for that conversation, awkward as it was.

Had we been overheard? Discovered? I shook my head - I had been certain we had been discrete. God, how I missed Paris, where I didn't have to give a lick about any of this nonsense.

I gathered my wits about me, and decided to follow Mrs. Kelly in her search for her daughter. After all, I'd been told that Eve had gone to bed with a bad headache. Clearly that was not true, and why on earth would Eve lie and not come to me?

As Mrs. Kelly entered the kitchen I followed at a discreet distance. I heard Bette's voice call out from inside, "Mrs. Kelly, your daughter's in the cellar!"

I quietly tiptoed to the doorway to watch the mother-daughter reunion. Inside the kitchen, Bette was nowhere to be seen, but the door to the cellar was open. Mrs. Kelly glanced over and noted that the oil lantern was not on the hook. Clutching the odd pendant in a pale fist, she entered the dark stairwell, calling for Eve.

"Eve!" She rasped, half yelling and half whispering. She took a tentative step down the old steps. Cool air from below rustled her dress and frazzled hair. "Eve, come now."

As soon as Mrs. Kelly had gone inside, Bette emerged from hiding behind the door and slammed the door shut.

I gasped!

Bette bolted the door. Judging by the sounds of thudding and yelling behind the door, she must have knocked poor Mrs. Kelly down some steps. I giggled at the sounds - after all, the woman had been insufferably rude to me, just moments earlier.

"Who's there?" Bette spun around.

I stepped forward but then my father appeared behind me and lay a comforting hand on my shoulder. "Just me and Saskia, Bette. All that business taken care of?"

"Yes Mr. Rennard," Bette replied. She gave me an indecipherable look, then turned back to her chores.

"What's going on?!" I asked.

"Come with me, dear." Father took me by my arm and led me away from the kitchen. "We have much to discuss."

Chapter 20

Chains In The Dark

Eve

I stirred from the blanket calm of unconsciousness into a panic-inducing pitch darkness, my body folded over on itself in an unnatural position. My neck and shoulder bore the brunt of my weight, and I realized I was upside-down, with my legs pressing upon my upper body. I tried to move my arms and legs but hit solid walls on every side. A box? It smelled of Saskia's french lavender oil and dust. My mind reeled at the possibility I had been stuffed into a too-small coffin. I could scarcely breathe and felt groggy.

My body bounced along as though on a lame horse, and then suddenly I was dropped hard onto a floor. I began to panic - my heart pounded in my chest, my skin tightened with goosebumps, the hair on my head prickled with electricity.

"Bloody hell!" said a man's voice.

"Quit complaining and unlock it!" I recognized the second voice as Teddy Jr. I shuddered as a metal clasp turned and the lid opened above me. After the darkness, the light shining in my eyes was almost unbearable. I scrunched my eyes closed. My heart calmed a bit now that I could breathe freely.

"Ah, Miss Eve - good evening," Teddy said.

I gingerly opened my eyes to find Teddy's face was so close, I could see the stubble on his cheeks, and smelled his breath; a sweet and sour smell of strong alcohol and tobacco. I cringed, then felt the cold prick of a sharp blade against the skin of my throat. "Not a peep out of you," Teddy said. I was too stunned to even attempt to speak.

Teddy pulled me up and as I looked down I realized I had been locked in one of Saskia's enormous trunks. I stepped out of the box, then swayed on my feet, still wobbly. My eyes went in and out of focus. My brain felt like it was pounding inside of my skull. They had brought me inside the barn. Harsh yellow light from oil lanterns cast shadows around the space. The silver masks on the walls glinted in the lantern light. Their open mouths looked as though they were mocking me. My neck had a painful crick that made it hard for me to turn my head.

Teddy removed his blade from my throat, only to instead raise a pistol aimed at my heart. The hunting hounds slavered and drooled in their cages, their gold eyes evaluating me as potential prey.

"Get it open!" Teddy snapped at Maxwell.

Maxwell nodded, then scurried over to the center of the barn floor. He swept some hay off the wood floor, until a trap door with a heavy brass ring appeared. He knelt down and lifted the door up. *KA-CHINK! KA-CHINK!* Down below, I could hear the rattle of a heavy chain.

A wailing sound floated up from below, sending shivers up my spine.

Maxwell climbed down a few steps and disappeared from my view. I heard him snap, "Shut the hell up! No one can hear you, so save your breath."

"Franny, shhhh," a woman whispered.

Sweet mother of mercy!!! Were the Fitzgerald sisters down there?

"Let's go," Teddy said. He pulled on my arm, and brought my face close to his. Suddenly, he opened his mouth, and his pink slimy tongue licked my left cheek slowly, as though I were a lollipop. I cringed in disgust.

"Been wanting to do that since I first laid eyes on you. I half expected you to taste of cabbage and taters," Teddy said as he snickered.

My eyes came into focus, a rush of energy flowed through my body, and that strange prickling sensation returned to my fingers and toes. A silver ripple burst out of my chest. The air between me and Teddy seemed to vibrate, and Teddy stumbled backwards, away from me and into a workbench littered with tools and buckets.

"What the hell!" Teddy's arms and legs flailed. He lost his balance and fell to the barn floor. Maxwell stared at me as Teddy scrambled back up, brushing the straw from his clothing.

A wave of exhaustion swept over me, causing my knees to buckle. I felt as feeble as an old crone. Teddy scrambled over and grabbed me by my arms, squeezing hard.

"You're hurting me," I whispered.

Teddy leaned in. "Don't kid yourself about my sister. To her, you're just the latest in a long line of ignorant playthings."

"I'm as much a person as you -" I replied, mustering as much pride as I could under the circumstances.

"Ha!" Teddy barked. "Are you mad?"

I was bone weary. A lightheadedness took over, and I fell into a deep tunnel of darkness, without a sound.

KA-CHINK! KA-CHINK! KA-CHINK!

I shook my head - what was that horrid sound? I slowly opened my eyes, vision blurry in the dim light.

"Eve, can you hear me luv?" Peggy asked. "We're in a pit...all chained up."

What!? I shook my head and tried to get my eyes to focus, only to see Nan, Peggy and Frances, in a near-dark, windowless space, all chained to a wall, each with heavy cuffs on their wrists. *Oh my God!* My mind swirled in a sea of panic. I could feel my heart beat pick up speed and a cold sweat broke out all over my body, making me shudder in the dankness of the clammy, chilly subterranean room. The air smelt dank and moldy, mixed with sour notes of sweat and fear.

I nodded as I tried to sit up. "Yes...I'm awake," I said. Everything was blurry and the dim lantern light was not very helpful. The back of my head seemed to throb in rhythm with every beat of my heart.

"We're in deep trouble, girly," Peggy said.

KA-CHINK! KA-CHINK!

I turned my head and realized Nan was the source of that clanking sound. Her feet pressed against the wall, she was pulling hard on her chain over and over again, using her bodyweight to tug. Her attempts to break free had only resulted in bloody, chafed wrists. Although the ground was just compacted dirt, the walls were reinforced with thick rough hewn planks of wood. There were no sounds from outside or from above - only the desperate sounds of our own breath and Franny's whimpering filled my ears.

I tried to touch the back of my head with my hands, but discovered my wrists were trapped in the same style of iron handcuffs, attached to a length of thick and heavy chain mounted to a heavy iron ring set into the wall. "My head is killing me," I said.

"I think you got hit on the back of the head," Peggy said. "Turn around a bit and let me take a better look." I obliged as best I could, swinging the chain over to one side. "You've definitely bled back there, but it looks like it's dry now."

I groaned; my head ached, my heart ached, my wrists burned, and my body felt bruised all over. Despite the shackles and my splitting headache, I managed to stand up, and swayed for a moment. An overwhelming wave of nausea swelled up from my gut, and I vomited into a corner.

"There's a pail of water to your left," Nan said, in her always-practical manner.

I crawled over to the pail. Mercifully, the chain my arms were bound with had enough slack for me to gulp a few handfuls of the foul-tasting water. It was not the freshest, but at that moment it tasted sweet in my sour mouth. I splashed a little water on my face, hoping it would make me feel more myself. I sat back down against a wall and looked over at my fellow prisoners.

Poor Frances wept quietly, as she rocked back and forth in an almost-fetal pose. Peggy and Nan were on either side of their sister, as close as their chains would allow.

"How long have I been out?" I asked.

"A few hours," said Peggy. "I wish we'd listened to you last night..."

Nan sighed. "There's no point in regretting the past. We just need to get on, and figure out how to be gone from this blasted place," she said.

Steps echoed down from above - the thud of footsteps, followed by a rasping metal sound. Dust and dirt rained down on us, falling between the slatted boards of the barn floor. The trap door above lifted up, and daylight poured in, striking my eyes with a burning intensity. I winced and turned my face away. Nan gasped, and I heard Peggy utter an invective.

Maxwell clomped down the steps, followed by Isaiah. Both men carried pistols. Isaiah was in black tie and tails, while Maxwell was dressed in his Sunday best: a faded brown suit with a yellowed shirt showing underneath. Maxwell had even waxed his whiskers and combed his hair - a rare occurrence, given that I'd never seen him do either since we arrived at Greythorne.

Frances's whimpering grew louder as the men descended to the bottom. Maxwell walked over to Frances and prodded her with his boot. "Stop your bloody whining," he said as he pulled out a ring of keys.

She gulped and grew quiet. Maxwell unlocked the chain from her handcuffs so that she was no longer anchored to the wall. Franny's hands, however, were still bound by the heavy iron manacles. "Come on then, up you go!" Maxwell pushed her towards the ladder where Isaiah waited, calm as a cucumber.

"Watch your step, Miss," Isaiah said, as he guided Frances up the stairs. I glanced up and saw Teddy leaning in from the opening at the top of the cellar. He was freshly groomed and pomaded, and appeared to be in traditional hunting attire with a black jacket, cream riding pants and shiny black leather boots clad to protect his lower leg. A brown leather riding crop hung from a leather cord on his wrist. A bowie knife was strapped to his thigh.

Maxwell made his way around and unlocked the chains from each of our handcuffs, one-by-one before shoving us towards the ladder. "Let's move it!" he said.

I watched as Peggy and Nan followed their sister up into the blinding light above.

After my chain was removed, I walked to the base of the ladder. Isaiah helped me get started on the ladder without a word. I looked at him with profound sadness, but he would scarcely meet my accusing gaze. "You told me Mr. Rennard never harmed anyone," I said.

Isaiah's brown eyes were deep but firm as he clarified in his deep baritone voice, "I said he's never harmed *us*." Isaiah leaned in, and in a whisper said, "And I also told you to keep your nose out of the family's personal business, but we both know how well you heeded that piece of advice, Miss Eve."

I sighed as I climbed up the stairs, moving as quickly as my exhausted mind and stiff body would allow.

Teddy had his pistol on the Fitzgerald sisters as I emerged from below into the now sunlit barn. Isaiah clambered up last.

"All right ladies, after me please," Teddy said. We looked at one another in dismay as we exited the barn. An early morning mist swirled above the ground, and the air was cool and still. I stumbled along, struggling to find my balance, my vision still blurry. A warm and clammy hand pushed me from behind, lingering just a moment too long on the small of my back - it was Maxwell, urging me on. "Keep moving!" He moved over to Frances and gave her a shove as well.

Isaiah approached and rasped in my ear, "You'd best cooperate." I glared at him, a burning anger growing in my chest. Teddy led us past the barn, and through a dense strand of maple trees to a pretty glade, at the entrance to Greythorne's forest trails. In front of us a picnic table awaited, with a pitcher of water, some scones and fresh fruit. We looked at the spread, bewildered.

"Take a seat. We're going to remove your handcuffs," Teddy said. We did as we were told, unsure what was going to happen next. Maxwell unlocked our handcuffs, one by one, and we rubbed our wrists. Peg wrapped her arms around Frances, trying her best to comfort her. As Nan's manacles fell away, Maxwell nodded at her raw, chafed wrists. "Made a bit of a mess of yourself," he observed. "Not the smartest of the batch, I see."

Teddy trained his gun on each of us girls in a sequence, going from me to Peg, to Nan, to Frances, then back to me. With his spare hand he reached into his jacket pocket and retrieved a hand rolled cigarette and a match. He popped it into his mouth, then lit it with a match struck against the picnic table. He breathed in the acrid tobacco smoke and exhaled with pleasure, spewing a thick gray cloud into the air. "Help yourselves. Eat something," Teddy said.

We hesitated, but then Isaiah reached over, grabbed a scone and took a bite. "It's okay. Bette baked these fresh today," he said, as he wiped the crumbs off his lips. "Blueberry - my favorite," he added. Maxwell reached over and grabbed a fistful of hot-house blueberries.

We looked at each other, shrugged. I realized I was ravenous - so we tucked into the breakfast. For the next several minutes, we quietly ate and drank. I began to recover from my withered state; my eyesight improved and the fog in my head cleared out. *But why were they doing this?*

"I don't get it...what do they want?" Frances whispered, as if reading my mind.

"Nothing good," Nan said, glowering at Teddy.

As we finished our allotted food, Teddy savored one last drag on the cigarette, dropped it and crushed it with his boot heel. He looked up at us. "Alright ladies. Feeling a bit better? That's good; well-fed game provides the best sport. It's time for you to head into the woods.

I'll begin counting down from thirty. If I see you after the count is over, I will shoot. If you can successfully hide, you may survive today's hunt."

"A *hunt?!*" said Nan. Peggy grabbed Nan's hand, and I grabbed Franny's, as her face blanched pale in terror.

Teddy looked at us with disdain. "Calm down, girls. If you panic you're less likely to make smart decisions. An even temper combined with your relative youth, and who knows? Maybe you'll survive the day. Some of the older codgers tire out pretty quick, so bear that in mind. Should you manage to outlast the hunters for a full twenty-four hours, we will give you a nice bit of cash and a train ticket out of Poughkeepsie to the destination of your choice. Quite generous of Father, really, when you think about it."

We looked at each other, utterly bewildered by this crazy situation.

"No questions? Wonderful. In that case, let us begin. Thirty. Twenty-nine. Twenty-eight..." Teddy started counting down. I took one look at his face then -

"We need to go!" I yelled as I reached for Franny's wrist and began to pull her deep into the woods, Peggy and Nan following right behind me. We started to run along a narrow game path which lead deeper into the still-dark woods. The sun hadn't yet crested the small hill to our east, and so a bitter mist clung to the dead leaves of the forest floor. The trees were tightly knit with thick and thorny underbrush preventing us from leaving the path. In the distance, a high stone wall sat, nearly completely obscured by brambles.

"We need to get off the path - it will be too easy to follow us," I said. I turned to my left, away from the mansion, and began to push my way through, my clothes and hair getting snagged on wayward branches.

"She's right," Nan said, and she followed right behind me. Tears streamed down Nan's face. Her vision obscured, she tripped over a tree root. "Aaaah!"

161

I turned back to help. Franny and Peggy gathered around her. "Are you hurt?" I asked.

"Twisted me ankle," said Nan. She wiped the tears from her eyes with her dress sleeve.

"Come on sis, we need to keep moving," Peggy said. She and Franny each took an arm and lifted Nan up.

"Do any of you know these woods?" I asked.

"No, it's part of the Rennards' estate but we don't usually walk here," said Peggy.

As if things weren't bad enough, Franny started to blubber and hyperventilate. Peggy pulled her to a stop, and slapped her hard on the face.

"Ow!" Franny cried. Franny's eyes widened and her left cheek grew red with the handprint of her sister visible on the skin.

"Shhh! Get a hold of yourself! You'll lead the bastards to us if you don't hush!" Peggy hissed, eyes narrowed. "You can cry later."

Franny nodded, gulped and took deep breaths. She rubbed her cheek with her left hand.

"Does the stone wall surround the entire estate?" I asked, as I turned in a slow circle looking as far out as possible.

"I think so," said Peggy.

My mind flashed back to when we first arrived at Greythorne. I remembered sitting on top of the carriage with Ma, mind and heart filled with excitement and anticipation, as we rolled over a little bridge that spanned a babbling brook... *God what on earth was happening with Ma!* I shook my head - no time to think of my mother now.

"Hold on - there's a creek that runs through. I saw it when we first arrived. Maybe there's a way out along the water," I said.

Nan, thoughtful, responded, "Makes sense."

"Let's reach the stone wall, then follow it until we find the creek," I urged. The sisters nodded in agreement. We took off again, this time focused with a plan, feeling a tiny sliver of hope, despite the dire circumstances.

Chapter 21

Take A Stand

Saskia

The grandfather clock downstairs chimed eight bells, as I stood at my bedroom window, gazing out at the mist swirling over our land. I felt as insubstantial as the haze itself; my future slipping out of my control by forces beyond my power.

I brought my right hand up to my nose and inhaled; between my fingers was the fiery lock of Eve Kelly's hair. Father had shattered my plans last night, thanks in large part to my own personal Judas, Teddy. I had gritted my teeth in frustration when Father had brought me to his study after that strange altercation with Mrs. Kelly.

In a nutshell, Father made it clear that he knew I had been "having some private fun" with Eve. After that revelation given to him by my jerk of a brother, Father had ordered the immediate removal of both the Kellys from our property. He had instructed the staff to make sure they were escorted to the Poughkeepsie train station with fare and wages. I knew there was an early train time from to New York City this morning, so by now they would be long gone....I sighed. Not even a chance to say farewell. Such a pity.

Outside, the stablehands were busily leading the horses through the mist. The animals were gorgeously curry-combed with gleaming coats and glossy manes, all bridled and saddled for Father, Teddy and their guests to go hunting. Father's chestnut stallion, Samson, stood a good hand taller than the other beasts. His eyes roamed and his nostrils blew hot steam into the chilly morning air.

Our servants were trickling out of the property and walking down the gravel road to enjoy their day off. It was Father's custom each year during the hunt to give the staff a full 24 hours of the weekend off (as gratitude for all their hard work). It was strange to admit, but for the first time I found myself envying the simplicity of their tiny, little lives. Most of them had never traveled abroad or been in any grand salons, or parties or soirées...perhaps their ignorance was blissful. Unfortunately, I had tasted freedom, and its loss was a bitter pill for me to swallow now.

The other thing my father had impressed upon me last night was the "undeniable fact" that my time as a single woman was rapidly drawing to a close. I was expected to take Robert's proposal seriously; and if I didn't choose him, I'd likely have even less attractive options presented to me. Most of the men my age in Father's circle, had been born into it, and so had an irritating level of pomposity and grandiosity. For men like that, it was clear that I was supposed to be ever so grateful to have their attention, rather than having them making an effort to pursue and court me.

I contemplated Robert now, as he and the other guests began to emerge outside. He cut a splendid figure in his tailored black hunting jacket, tan riding pants and black leather riding boots. He pulled a carrot out of his pocket and offered it to his horse, who snapped it up in the blink of an eye. Robert certainly seemed thoughtful and far more progressive than Father. And he was definitely attractive...I caressed the lock of hair with my fingers as I pondered my future.

Tap, tap!

"Come in," I said. I tucked the hair away in a pocket.

Aunt Winifred bustled in, dressed in her tweedy traveling clothes and sensible walking shoes. "I'm heading out, my dear," she said. "Off to visit the Turners in Hyde Park for the weekend...."

"Lucky you,"I said with a sour tone.

"Why aren't you ready? Aren't you going to New York City with Andy's daughter Gloria?"

"I'm not in the mood to go anywhere," I snapped.

"Be that as it may, your friends will be waiting for you. What on earth's the matter with you?" She asked.

"Father is commanding me to marry Robert," I replied.

Aunt Winnie gave me a strange look. "Ah, so you're pouting..."

"I am not pouting!" I bit back, annoyed that she could so easily read my mood.

"Oh, I see, my mistake...Never mind."

Though not invited to take a seat, my Aunt nevertheless plopped herself down on the end of my pale pink damask chaise lounge, her weight causing the other end to rise up a bit. "Oh!" she said startled, then pushed her undercarriage back to a more stable position.

Okay, so this was not going to be as brief a chat as I'd hoped. I pulled out my chair, and sat facing her, my hands in my lap, exuding the patience I did not actually feel.

She gazed at me for a moment, then followed with, "You and I are more alike than you realize."

I tilted my head trying to imagine in what possible ways that could be true.

"I wasn't always an old fuddy duddy," she said.

"I'm sure you weren't," I lied. I couldn't possibly imagine my Aunt as a young woman out on the town, but I had been taught to respect my elders, and butter them up whenever appropriate.

Aunt Winnie leaned forward as though to whisper a secret to me, even though there was no one who could possibly hear us. "I did have a little fling before my father, that is your grandfather, Ambrose, made clear whom I was to marry." She sighed and her eyes grew a little misty. This was a different side of my Aunt, who usually had a biting retort on the tip of her tongue.

"Oh Auntie, do tell," I said, actually interested for once.

"Well, it was a while ago and I don't wish to bore you, but suffice to say our family would never have approved. In fact, it took me a while to accept the reality of our role as women in the family. We Rennard women can be quite headstrong, as you know. Nevertheless, your grandfather used me as a bargaining chip to help build his empire. I had to marry Walter Price of the Poughkeepsie Prices, whom he had personally selected. It was never what I wanted," she added.

My eyebrows raised at hearing this for the first time. "But you loved Uncle Walter," I said.

"Ah well, over time, I made my peace with the situation. Appearances are just that. You cannot possibly know what goes on behind closed doors for any married couple. I was at least fortunate that Walter was kind and not cruel, and gave me a little freedom. And, at any rate, when he died you were just a child," she said. She gave me an awkward pat on the back of my hand.

"In hindsight, now as an old woman, I do still have regrets. The times are different now than 40 years ago...perhaps my best advice to you is to not make the same mistakes as me," Aunt Winnie added, looking directly at me with her clear blue eyes. With that message delivered, she rose up awkwardly, bustled out and shut the door firmly behind her.

I sat stunned for a few moments. I was sad for myself and for my Aunt - both of us not seen as more than property to be used by the men in the family for their own benefit. Of course, Father would argue that he was doing this all for me - to give me financial security and protect our social status. The money was of course something I did not wish to give up, but did I really care about the gossips, or about pleasing a man, even a pleasant handsome one?

Aunt Winnie was right. I still had time to assert myself and not meekly submit to Father's wishes. I leapt into action. I pulled out my riding gear, tossed off my dress and kicked off my slippers... Perhaps, I could show the men a thing or two about my capabilities as an equestrienne and hunter. After all, why should men have all the fun?

Now dressed to ride, in my favorite tan jodhpurs, white blouse and navy riding jacket, I exited my room and quietly walked down the back service stairs. I reached the ground floor and went into Father's study. I knew exactly what I wanted - so it only took a moment for a me to choose the Winchester and a box of bullets. I exited and turned the corner, only to bump into a stray young stable-hand, whose name I believe was Bert.

"Sorry, Miss," the young lad began, doffing his cap in a sign of respect. All of sixteen- or seventeen-years-old, his Adam's apple bobbed nervously up and down, somewhat distracting me, as Bert cast his gaze downward. Pimples marred his face and the first wisps of facial hair darkened his cheeks and chin.

"No need to be sorry," I replied. "Please go and saddle up my horse, Devil's Own, and bring him to the rear courtyard for me."

"Umm, Miss, I'm supposed to be leaving for the weekend," he hemmed and hawed. "Mr. Rennard insisted we all be gone by 9," he said, his brown eyes begging for permission to leave.

"No doubt if you are quick about it, you'll be on your way shortly after you've completed this one simple task," I replied. I stared at him with my frostiest gaze. He reddened, and lowered his eyes again. "Of course, Miss. Right away," he said, then turned to scurry off to the stables. *If only all men were as pliable.*

I followed him out the side door, and walked quietly towards the front portico, so that I could watch Father and his little group of friends embark. I stood behind a corner column, able to see without being seen. I knew if Teddy or Father saw me, they would put a rapid stop to my plans.

Aunt Winifred emerged down the front steps, trailed by an unhappy servant struggling with a mountain of luggage. It looked as though she'd packed enough dresses to last a month, though it would only be a short two-night stay.

Meanwhile, all of the hunters gathered in their tailored black coats, ivory pants and gleaming riding boots. The stable hands had done wonders with the horses. They stood proud, heads high, their bright metal bridles glinting in the morning light. The men didn't look too bad either; Robert was undoubtedly the most handsome, but Emil looked very elegant in his hunting clothes, his mahogany skin contrasting with the cream color of his breeches, white shirt and black frock jacket. And of course, Andy Carnavoy wore a very expensive tailored ebony riding coat with charcoal velvet lapels, and matching tall riding boots so shiny and new I could have used them as a mirror.

As hunt-master, Father was quite dashing in his traditional scarlet riding coat. He had a bowie knife strapped to his thigh, a crossbow and bolts in a quiver slung across his back. He had been on a crossbow kick since before I left for Paris, eschewing the power of a pistol or a rifle for the silence and precision of the archaic weapon. It required more stealth and accuracy, but could also be a more merciful death if the bolt struck the animal directly into the heart. He spotted my Aunt, and walked over to her as she prepared to climb into her carriage.

"Ready for battle eh, Theodore?" Aunt Winnie said slyly.

"I like to be ready for anything," Father replied.

Aunt Winnie gave Father a gentle elbow to his ribs. "Be careful - some of those wild animals have claws."

Father chuckled and offered his hand for her to settle into the carriage. She leaned out the window and said, "See you soon, little brother."

"Safe travels." Father closed the carriage door, and the drover picked up the reins and coaxed the horses into a trot. "Give my regards to the Turners. Tell William it is a shame he couldn't join our hunt this year."

Father pivoted and headed over to his stallion, Samson. The beast chomped on its bit and danced around, as the stablehand tried his best to keep it steady. Father mounted the stallion without need for a step, and sat tall. In spite of our differences, moments like this made me very proud to be Theodore Rennard's daughter. Especially when I saw the portly Mr. Whitaker's ungainly efforts to mount his steed. A stablehand had to place his hands under Mr. Whitaker's large behind and shove him up onto the horse. I stifled a giggle.

"Why, good morning," said a voice to my right, nearly sending me out of my skin in surprise. I turned to find Robert standing behind me, a warm smile on his face. "Whitaker is a bit of an ass, I agree."

"More than a bit, actually," I replied with a grin. Robert laughed, then glanced at my attire and gave me a knowing look. "You look both lovely and formidable, Miss Rennard."

"Thank you," I replied in a whisper. If Robert called too much attention to me, my hopes of joining the hunt would be dashed. I was sure that I was about to be outed. "But please, call me Saskia."

"Of course," Robert replied, matching my tone. He reached into his jacket and pulled out a silk sky blue handkerchief. It was embroidered with his initials. "Would you be so kind as to hold this for me, while I ride?" he asked.

A bold move. I brought it up to my nose and inhaled. "Caswell-Massey No. 6; one of my favorites," I said.

"You have quite a refined sense of smell," Robert said, looking quite impressed.

"Ah well, it's one of Father's favorite colognes," I explained. "But, as you can see from my attire, I plan on going for a ride, too."

"I hadn't realized hunting was another of your hobbies," he started.

"Mother died when I was quite young, so I was raised to appreciate the more masculine pursuits of riding and hunting. You'll find my pianoforte skills a bit wanting though," I added with what I hoped was a flirtatious expression.

"Well," he began, flashing a brilliant smile, "We are peas in a pod. I have recently acquired some excellent hunting ground adjacent to my own estate. Nothing so grand as your father's, I'm sure, but I would very much enjoy the opportunity to ride and hunt with you one day, Miss Saskia," he said. "Will you be joining us today? I hadn't realized your father had anointed you into his august hunting company yet."

"Father and Teddy wouldn't want me to show them up in front of you and the other gentlemen," I said as convincingly as I could manage. "I'm just off for a ride in the countryside. No need to bother my father with such details, mind you, Robert."

Robert offered up a beautiful, radiant smile. A genuine smile, in a handsome face.

"I admire your independent spirit." At that he grasped my leather-clad hand, brought it to his mouth, and kissed my glove gently. I deliberately tucked his handkerchief close to my chest, which he certainly appreciated. With the barest of winks, he took his leave of me and headed over to join the rest of the men. As he strode away, I was left with a lingering feeling of pleasure over the warmth of his company.

I had to admit, Father really had done a good job in selecting Robert - there was much about him that was pleasing, not least of which was his open mindedness and messaging to me that with him I would not lose all of my freedoms.

Bette circulated amongst the men, carrying a silver tray with small glasses of hot spiced punch. Each man reached down to take a cup, while Teddy rode out of the stable on his thoroughbred, carrying a hessian sack. Like my father, he cut a dashing figure in his black frock coat and tan breeches. Teddy adored his horse, Cerberus, who like my brother had an air of unpredictability to him. Teddy rode up to each of the men, and handed over a silver face mask.

"When we enter the woods, make sure to wear your masks," Father said in a loud enough tone for all to hear. I didn't really under-stand the point of the masks. To me it seemed like they'd be dread-fully uncomfortable to wear, and obstruct the rider's peripheral vision...but perhaps that was part of the challenge.

Maxwell brought over the hounds, holding on to their leashes for dear life. They were excited and agitated. They lived for the hunt - when they could be free to roam in the woods and follow the scent of their prey. Maxwell waved a bit of cloth for the dogs to sniff. What could their quarry be? Likely it was fox scat or some other unpleasantness. They certainly seemed to like it - their eyes rolled, jowls drooled, and legs pawed the ground.

Bette brought my father his glass. Father leaned down and whispered something to Bette.

She grimaced, then nodded. I smiled. How very like Father to give poor Bette yet another task to do, despite the woman being ready to put her feet up.

Father lifted his glass up high and raised his voice. "Welcome to our annual Ambrose Hunt. Work together, follow the hounds, and take your prize! To a glorious hunt!"

The men raised their cups in unison and replied, "To a glorious hunt!" They downed their drinks.

Father flung his glass to the ground away from the horses - it shattered. The men followed suit. Father lifted up the hunting horn from the chain on his belt, and blew a long wailing note. Maxwell released the hounds and they took off, curving into the woods. Teddy spurred his horse forward and called out, "This way gents!"

A cacophony of men's voices and dogs barking rose up into the air, as they all took off after my brother.

I turned away and spotted Bert walking towards me with Devil's Own, saddled and impatient to get going. What a glorious animal - his silver livery sparkled against his dark glossy coat.

The lad gave me a quick boost, and I swung my right leg up and over. Once seated on my horse, I gathered the reins and wheeled him to the far left onto a narrow bridle path into the woods, one of my favorite riding trails. I gave my darling Devil a light squeeze with my thighs, and he sped up into a canter. The wind blew across my face, and the mist swirled below us, the green perfume of the forest rising up in my nostrils. I was determined to outdo the men at their hunt, and flush out a fox with my own skill, before they got to it. I knew that only by beating the men at their own game, would I be given a seat at the table and more power to decide my own future. In the meantime, I never grew tired of the thrill of riding a magnificent horse out into the woods.

Chapter 22

The Morrigan Awakens

Eve

A piercing horn blast shattered the early-morning stillness of the forest, sending all manner of small birds and furry creatures scattering through the underbrush. The sound stopped us in our tracks. Faint bays and howls of dogs and men whooping penetrated the forest.

"Jesus, Mary and Joseph!" exclaimed Nan.

The sisters and I gazed at one another with wild eyes and pounding hearts. A stabbing stitch in my side made it hard for me to breathe. Our plan was to stay off the trails as much as possible to reduce the chance of our being spotted, but a low lying soft mist still swirled at our feet and made it hard to see the ground below. We resumed our trek, pushing hard and as fast as possible through knee-high black and thorny buckthorn scrub, amidst a thick canopy of towering elms and beech trees. Unfortunately, every few steps I had to stop and yank a snagged fold of my skirt off the brambles and thorns.

Suddenly, a raven croaked loudly and landed on a branch directly in front of me. I glanced up and it croaked again, flapped its wings impatiently. On second glance, I was stunned by its unique appearance. Where every raven I'd ever seen before had pitch black eyes, this bird's were eery blue. It bore its beady eyes into my own and focused so intently on me that I stopped mid-stride. Tiny prickly sensations traveled up and down the tips of my fingers and toes as it opened its beak to croak.

But rather than an avian cry, I could swear I heard Ma's voice coming from the animal's own throat. "Eve," it said.

I stared dumbly at it, sure I had misheard.

"Eve, it's me. I don't have time to explain, but brace yourself."

"Ma?!" I yelped, incredulous. "What in the blazes is going on?"

"No time!" the Moira-bird cawed. "I'm going to crush the pearl. To unbind you..." The prickling sensation increased in intensity and traveled up into my hands and feet. What on earth did she mean? Pinpricks coursed through me, and soon I was feeling them all over my body. What was happening?

Peggy looked back to see that I was no longer moving forward and keeping up with them. "Oy, Eve, are you okay?" Peggy asked, watching me with bewilderment. Nan and Frances paused and turned back to see what had alarmed their sister.

I didn't have time to respond. I focused on the raven and felt my mind stretch and expand towards it.

My vision altered as my mind began to soar. Suddenly I found myself perched on a branch looking down at...me! Somehow, I was the bird itself, looking out into the forest, feeling the wind rustle through my feathers. Gods, what a sensation! I watched my hair begin to float, and my human body rise up from the ground, my arms soaring upwards, and my back arching. A bright silver light radiated from Eve-the-person, as I hovered in the air, hair standing on end as if I had touched a raw electrical socket.

The world looked and smelled and sounded so different in my little bird body. Brilliant hues of blue, green and red filled my sight. I smelled the scent of field mice, heard the chitter of a black squirrel, and with a precise and sharp focus saw it glance at me, then scamper down the tree trunk. The wind tickled me, beckoned me on as if whispering,

"Come on, fly." In the distance to my right, I could see the little water-fall sparkle as water flowed into the creek below. Ahead of my floating Eve body stood the three sisters, their mouths agape.

"Holy Mary, mother of God!" Nan said, crossing herself.

I could hear Ma's voice in my head, reciting a prayer in old Gaelic. Out of the dim recesses of my early childhood, I realized I understood the words she uttered. It had been years since I'd heard the old language, but those childhood memories were now clear and bright in my mind.

Ma invoked the Morrigan, with the following entreaty.

"Mighty Morrigan, I call to thee.

We are facing the unknown, and your children need the Sisters Three.

Open your wings, fierce, shining, and black as night.

Shield us from this threat, so we can join our energies together and as one, fight back in your honor."

Suddenly, a sucking whooshing sensation grabbed hold of me, as I pulled away from the bird and back into my human form. I came back down to the ground, hair swirling around my head. Every inch of my human frame vibrated with energy and clarity of purpose. My skin felt aflame, but not painfully so. As if I burned with possibility.

Frances, Peggy and Nan gathered around me.

"Jumpin' Jehosephat! You were floating, Eve! Yer eyes shot sparks," Franny said.

"Shhh... Give her some breathing room!" said Nan.

Peggy leaned down and offered me a hand up. "Are you alright?"

I clasped her hand and pulled myself together. I rose up, a bit wobbly in the knees, but feeling confident and radiating a new sense of self.

"I don't understand what's happening to me, but we don't have time," I said.

Baa-roo! The hunting horn's cry pierced the air; this time much closer. We could hear horse hooves and men's voices, now just on the other side of the gully.

"We need to split up - I'll divert them while you keep heading towards the creek," I said.

"Are you mad?" Peggy asked. "They'll catch you and kill you, Eve!

"Not mad at all," I said. "You need to trust me. Take your sisters and run. The creek is over that way," I pointed. "Can't be more than quarter mile away. I'll find you. Go!"

The sisters hesitated, but I waved them off. They turned in the direction I'd pointed, and ran off, Nan limping a bit, but determined not to slow things down.

I sat crosslegged behind some shrubs, and focused on the same nearby raven. I entered the raven's mind as it rose up. Again, the sensation of tiny needles prickling my hands and feet rose up within me as my mind traveled....

I flapped my wings to hover in place as I cast my eyes around the forest below. The stench of dog and male acrid body odor rose up into my nostrils, and I rotated to focus on the dogs and two hunters on their horses. They were racing towards my friends; I had to do something!

They needed a distraction. I angled my head downwards and soared directly in front of the leading dogs, croaking loudly, and concentrating harder than I had ever done before. I pushed out mentally towards the dogs, feeling for the same tingling energy I had felt when entering the mind of the raven. They responded with confusion at first, but I pressed harder: calmed my breathing and focused my energy as much as I could. To my surprise and relief, the dogs responded by skidding to a stop, eyes glued to me in my raven body. They changed course to follow me in raven form as I flew in the opposite direction from my fleeing friends. The horses and men were only fifty or hundred yards behind the lead hounds.

I relaxed my mental hold on the bird and felt it slip away into the sky. That same strange whooshing and sucking motion dimmed my vision, until within a heart beat, I returned to my body. I rose up to stand, only to discover that I felt shaky. A blanket of fatigue momentarily weighed down heavily on my mind. My eyesight needed a moment to adjust - for now I could barely focus beyond my hand.

BLAM! The crack of a pistol followed by the whistle of a bullet that whizzed past my right ear, striking a nearby tree. *Sweet mother of mercy!* The impact sent splinters flying. A few hit me in the face, causing pinpoint stabbing pain.

I jumped to my left and turned around. A mounted hunter with a silver mask rode towards me, smoking pistol in one hand, reins in the other. Rennard Sr. rode beside him, on his enormous beast of a horse, Samson. Even though he was wearing a silver mask, his scarlet jacket was clear as day. Rennard held his crossbow with one hand, his body seated high and forward on his saddle, leaning towards me.

The second hunter raised his arm and fired his pistol again. This time the shot was low, plinking off a boulder a few paces away from me, sending a spray of rock dust into the air. My wobbliness subsided, *thanks be to the goddess!* and I launched into a sprint.

After a few seconds, I took a quick glance back over my shoulder. Rennard had slowed his horse to aim his crossbow. He fired a bolt directly at me. I tacked to the right, and the bolt flew so close to me, the wind rushed by. I darted to the left intending to dive into a high green shrub for cover.

Rennard took the reins between his teeth and used both hands to reload his crossbow. If I hadn't been the target, I would have been impressed - instead I was terrified. He recalibrated and fired again, too fast and too accurate for me to escape being struck.

An intense searing pain ripped through my left shoulder, as the bolt punched through the thickest part of the muscle. I screamed and clutched my shoulder. The bolt held fast, the arrow head pierced through the front of my shoulder. Blood spilled down my sleeve - a wet heat. The pain was so intense, I could scarcely concentrate. Still, I knew I had no choice but to turn and face them. What else could I do?

The hunting dogs approached, gold eyes gleaming in the dappled light of the forest. Their interest in the raven had waned and now they descended upon me with jowls bouncing and spittle flying in every direction. I locked eyes with the lead hound, and took a deep breath to calm myself. Pins and needles began to radiate from my fingertips...

Reaching out with my mind, I experienced the dog's emotions of hunger, excitement and confusion. I closed my eyes and pushed hard at him. "Attack the men and their beasts."

He paused, then -

To my relief, he whipped around and began to snarl and snap at the two hunters' horses, the rest of the pack following suit. Unaccustomed to having dogs snap and bite at their legs, the horses began to whinny and buck, their eyes rolling in terror.

Rennard held on for dear life, clutching the reins tightly and gripping the horse's flanks with his thighs. But the second hunter was less fortunate. He cried out as he fell off his bucking horse. The mask fell, revealing the face of Mr. Carnavoy. As he lay on the ground, he pulled a pistol out from a holster and aimed it at me. His facial expression of cold hatred was a shock to see.

For years as a servant, I'd been used to being pinched or ogled or groped by men while I tried to just do my job. Ma had told me to just keep my head down; that it was just men being men, and that there was nought a woman could do. But this level of hatred and violence was entirely new and terrifying.

I inhaled, then thrust my consciousness into Carnavoy's bucking horse, who was terrified of the dogs snapping at him with bared teeth.

Colors changed - the red of Rennard's coat turned to a dark grey. A sharp pain stabbed my left foreleg as a dog's teeth clamped on. Screeching with a long high-pitched whinny, I rose up on my hind legs. I reached up high into the sky, waving my forelegs fast and hard, until the hound released his grip on me. Then my forelegs came thundering back down, the right hoof striking the man under me. Splat! It had hit him in the head so hard it crushed under my hoof like an overripe melon. I panicked, eyes whirling, nostrils flaring, and tore off into the forest, with one final cry calling for my fellow horses to follow me into the woods.

Exhausted, I let go of the animals. I heard a whoosh, blinked, and found myself looking out of my own eyes once again.

Rennard cried out, "Oh my God! Andy!" as he lost control of his horse and got pulled away. He shrieked as he disappeared, "What the hell have you done? You're a goddamn witch!"

Ha! You have no idea. Any euphoria at what I had just done would have to wait, however, because as soon as I came back to myself, I was overwhelmed with a wave of exhaustion and pain from my shoulder. I collapsed onto all fours and remained there for a moment, at least until I could gather up my strength. The damp earth felt good between my fingers as I dug them into the soil. The soil helped to ground me.

With the men gone and a moment to myself, I took mental inventory of my body. The pain in my shoulder seared as though a red hot poker had been thrust through the muscle. I pulled myself up and staggered into the woods, clutching the bolt that protruded from my shoulder. I headed in the direction of the Fitzgerald sisters, determined to reach them before the hunters.

Chapter 23

Feathers & Blood

Eve

After running for what felt like an eternity (but was likely just a few minutes) with no sign of the creek or the sisters, I ducked under some underbrush, and sat criss-cross on the damp ground. The gray sky seemed to be settling lower over the landscape, and the air smelt of rain. Nearby a trumpet vine with orange flowers grew up the side of a maple tree. But I could find no joy or beauty in it. There was a slight breeze, but the flowers, sodden from the previous night, sagged down dreary and unmoving. The wet air weighed upon me like a carpet of gloom. I needed a moment or two to think over everything that had just happened.

A pit of sorrow settled deep in my gut. I hadn't meant for Mr. Carnavoy to die, I just wanted to stop him. And of course, trying to control a scared stallion when I had no idea what I was doing...

What I needed was to find Ma. I couldn't go back to the house, but she was able to reach me with that raven, so maybe... I looked around and spied a tiny, red-throated hummingbird zipping in and out of the orange blooms above me. *Could I do it,* I wondered? I focused my eyes on the bird and began to reach out to it. Those telltale prickles rose up in my fingertips, so I knew I was on the right path. I took a breath and mentally *pushed*.

The world was suddenly bathed in shades of purple, red and blue that I had never seen before. A rapid-fire heartbeat thundered in my ears. I flitted up and down and around...I could sense the little bird's confusion, so I tried to soothe it and direct it. After a few moments of resisting, the little bird gave in, and I did a little spin in the air to look for Greythorne. I realized I was a good mile or so northeast of the mansion, deep in the woods. I rose above the forest canopy, and was struck by just how vast the Rennard estate really was. It seemed larger than even New York's Central Park, although maybe I was a bit distorted by scale as I was in such a tiny little creature.

When I saw the mansion, I pushed again, and I zipped forward at an almost unimaginable speed. I had no idea hummingbirds could be so fast! I flew past tree branches so quickly they were a blur. My eyes kept being drawn to red, pink and violet flowers and the sweet smell of sugar and pollen in the air. I felt a strong craving for sugar, but I forced myself to stay focused on the building.

In my present size, Greythorne was a dark gray monolith of cold stone that soared high up beyond my ability to comprehend. I flitted up to Saskia's windows on the left wing second floor. Her bedroom window was open as usual, thank goodness, so I flew inside and made a circle of her quarters. There was no sign of her. With one part of my mind, I wondered if she knew about the hunt? Did she know what her father and brother were doing?

I shook my little bird head which made my flight zigzag erratically and careen sideways. I took a deep breath to calm myself. I hadn't seen her with the men, and she was not at all like them - she couldn't possibly be. Maybe I could find her? Maybe I could get myself and the Fitzgerald sisters and Ma, and we could escape from here and leave all of this behind? Thoughts raced through my head, competing with the wild thundering of the hummingbird's tiny, ceaseless heart.

I flew out of Saskia's room, down the hallway, then downstairs. The dull faded floral wallpaper, the dim lighting, the dead animals everywhere - it all combined into a menacing, dark and foreboding place that gave me the shivers. I flew down to the foyer area and along a hallway decorated with mounted white-tailed deer heads, turkey with their tail feathers fanned out, geese and pheasants posed in flight or perched on branches with wings outstretched.

Suddenly, the study door swung open and dread filled my tiny bird body. Bette emerged from the study and came my way. Sweet mother of mercy! I didn't want her to see me or chase me out, so I zipped in between two pheasants posed on a small branch, and perched to join them. I tried as hard as possible not to move a muscle. I had to look as though I were dead and stuffed like everything else in here. She walked past me without a glance at first, but after a few steps she hesitated. I held still, my heart racing inside my ribcage so fast it was an almost constant percussive vibration. She paused and looked around, head tilted, for a few extremely long moments. She felt something was off as she scanned the various taxidermies around the room. When her eyes landed on me, even for just a moment, I almost broke.

But her gaze swept past me and my two pheasant friends, then she shook her head, chuckled, and continued down the hall. I released a quiet chirp after she turned the corner. I followed her as she headed to the kitchen, and slid through just before the door swung closed.

I flitted a good distance behind Bette in the kitchen. Once inside, I perched behind a large copper stock pot, hanging from a hook above the countertop.

The kitchen was silent as a tomb. With the staff on holiday, the usual hustle and bustle of scullery maids and other kitchen denizens was silenced. The white tiled room felt cold and sterile. Bette's favorite machete and other butchering knives glinted in the morning light.

Bette made a beeline for the cellar door, grabbed a key and unlocked it. As the door swung open, I saw Ma, looking fierce. She held a wine bottle up in the air like a club, ready to strike.

When Ma saw that it was Bette, she lowered her arm. "Oh! Blessed be!" Ma said. "I was ready to fight my way out."

"There's no need for that," Bette said.

I watched Ma put the bottle down. As she looked up, Bette pulled some sort of shooting iron out of her apron pocket, and aimed it at Ma. What on earth?! I was so stunned, my control over this little bird body faltered. Eve, pull yourself together!

Bette waved the pistol at Ma, indicating the cellar. "Let's head back down the stairs... Mr. Rennard's orders," *she said.*

"Bette! How can you help these monsters?" *Ma said, then moved a step forward.*

"Never you mind my reasons," *she replied, then pointed the pistol at my mother's head.* "Don't even think about it."

Ma nodded and turned to head downstairs. Bette followed a step behind. I flitted in behind Bette, biding my time. With a sinking sensation, I realized there was very little I could do to save my mother, in my present form as a tiny bird. I berated myself - I should have chosen a raven or another raptor. At least then I'd have the ability to attack.

"Listen Bette, we're both mothers. Can't we help each other?" *Ma asked.*

Bette laughed, bitter. "Why would I help you? If the shoe were on the other foot, would you help me or my husband? You've not said more than three words to me in all the weeks you've been here."

Bette wasn't wrong - Ma had kept to herself and not made an effort to get to know Bette or Isaiah.

"I just don't understand what could make you behave this way," *Ma said, as she descended slowly down the steps, completely unlike her usual brisk gait. She was trying to slow things down as much as possible.*

"You think you're entitled to hear my story. You think I owe you that, and then you'll understand. You're not worth me wasting my breath on you. Not you, nor that nasty bit of a daughter, creepin' around with Miss Saskia after hours..." *Bette said.*

Ma's face grew red with unspoken anger.

As they reached the bottom step, Bette cocked the pistol and said "You don't get it...the Rennards' power is bigger than you know." *She waved the pistol to move Ma ahead.* "Keep movin'."

I flew into Bette's face, chittering and darting in and out around her eyes.

With her free hand, Bette swatted me. I spun off towards the kitchen window, tumbling end over end before remembering to let the little bird recover and take care of the flying part.

"You bloody scut!" Ma yelled as she rushed towards Bette, something green and sharp glinting in her hand.

Bette pulled the trigger. BLAM!

At the same moment, Ma swung at Bette with a large shard of bottle glass. As she surged forward, Ma brought that arm around, aimed straight at Bette's throat. Bette's eyes went wide, as Ma's slash sailed past with no resistance.

At first, it seemed Ma had missed. But as thick red blood began to spurt out of Bette's neck, I knew Ma had hit the carotid artery. Bette collapsed on the steps below me. She gasped and clawed at her neck, making an inarticulate "ack" sound.

A cloud of white gun smoke and the acrid smell of gunpowder filled the space between me and Ma, so I couldn't see her. I darted through it, my eyes burning, only to find Ma collapsed on the tile floor. Her eyes were closed. She winced and sucked air through gritted teeth. Blood blossomed across her torso, turning the gray uniform black in the low light.

No, no, NO, NO! I smelt the distinct iron of spilled blood, my eyes darting to and fro, trying to take it all in. My little heart beat so fast I was sure it would fly out of my chest at any moment.

I flew in front of her and opened my beak, clicking and peeping loud as I could until I figured out how to speak normally. "Ma! Oh, goodness, Ma, it's me."

Ma's eyes opened, and she stared at me bewildered for a few beats, then smiled with warm recognition. She realized that I had shape shifted into the body of the small bird. Tiny silvery wisps of energy floated out of her, as she lowered herself down to lean against the bottom step.

"Eve," Ma whispered. She coughed hard, and spat blood out of her

mouth. *"I'm glad you're here. After your Da died, I was so afraid...I was determined to keep your magic bound. It was a mistake. I should have prepared you, rather than push away the old ways."*

"Ma, I understand." She reached up one hand and I rested my tiny claws on her index finger.

"You were right to want to help the Fitzgeralds. You were right to want more for your life than servitude," said Ma. She inhaled a ragged breath, determined to continue. *"Eve, you are kind, you are capable, and you are magical. These things together mean that you will not only survive, but thrive. Go live your life the way you want to,"* said Ma. It was more than she had ever said to me at once in my entire life.

"Ma, please hold on. I'll come back and help you."

Ma drew a raspy breath and shook her head. *"I'm hurt, and you've got to do everything you can to escape. Don't let yourself be caged again, Eve."*

I dug deep inside and uttered the following prayer to the Morrigan for my Ma to be protected until I could return: *"Great Queen, grant my mother your sheltering protection and warm embrace. Sustain her in her hour of need as proof of your greatness. Restore all that is weary within us, and help us to heal our bodies and our minds."*

Ma's eyes brimmed with tears as she lifted me up to fly off. *"Let your powers flow and soar."*

Sad and exhausted beyond words, my mind released the hummingbird. The now familiar swooshing sound roared in my ears and my vision faded to darkness. It was as though I were in a dark tunnel for the next several moments. I groaned and opened my eyes, only to find my human form curled up in a fetal pose on the forest floor. Tears spilled down my face as I lay amidst the tree roots. I was totally spent from the magical energies which had coursed through me.

What if I couldn't get back to Ma in time? I could scarcely imagine what life would be like without her - assuming I survived the day. No matter how angry she made me, how frustrated I was in our relationship, I knew in my heart that she loved me, and that the two of us were woven together by our blood, our history, and our shared experiences. The sharp fear of loss struck hard at me, but I drew a deep breath and filled my senses with the rich fertile loamy soil beneath me. Mother Earth helped to comfort me with the steadiness of nature all around me. I had prayed to the Morrigan - not for my own benefit, but for my mother's salvation - and now I had to have faith that I would have the courage and strength to face what lay ahead.

The shoulder pain that had been ignored while I focused on Ma, came back now with a vengeance. It was a throbbing nauseating sensation, making it hard for me to concentrate. The crossbow bolt was still trapped in the muscles of my left shoulder. The bleeding had almost completely stopped. Worried about the damage, I moved my left elbow and wiggled my fingers. Thank goodness the nerves and muscles hadn't been completely destroyed by the bolt. It was a lucky break.

I realized I had no better options, so I gritted my teeth and snapped off the arrow head with my right hand, then reached behind and pulled the shaft out in one smooth motion. Despite the excruciating pain, I was able to get the bolt out without making a single sound.

I knew what I needed to do next. I rose up, tore a piece of my skirt and bound my shoulder, then headed out to help my mother and rescue my friends.

Chapter 24

Witness To A Crime

Saskia

O nce Devil and I were deep within the woods, I slowed him to an easy trot so we could both catch our breath. I inhaled the delicious scent of the forest. It must have rained in the night, because the dead leaves and soil were wet and loamy. The birdsong of the finches and sparrows suddenly subsided, and I began to hear men's voices. Whose they were, I could not tell, but since I hadn't spotted any game yet, I wheeled around and decided to follow them.

I made sure to trail well behind them so they wouldn't see me - at least, not until I wanted them to.

I came to a fork in the trail, and headed left up a steep hill to get to one of my favorite lookouts on our estate. The trail was lined with "Snow Queen" hydrangea, a dark green tall shrub that had been one of my mother's favorites; I loved it as well. With spring in the air, the soft white clusters of petals waved gently in the breeze. The skies threatened rain, but for now at least it was dry and cool.

To my right was a large ravine. I heard men's voices and hoofs coming up behind me. I wasn't ready to be seen so I quickly dismounted Devil, and pulled him off trail and into a thicket. I tied him to a branch, then crept back towards the side of the trail. Three horses approached; Samson with Father astride, a chestnut Hanoverian mare ridden by Robert, and a petite but fiery grey Arabian ridden by Emil. I ducked beneath some bushes, as the men trotted up the trail.

I overheard Father say, "I finally got control over building the final trunk of the Philadelphia to Pittsburgh line..."

"I bet that required some palm greasing," Robert commented.

"Cost of doing business. Damn politicians are greedy bastards," Father replied.

"Doesn't sound very different from my home country, *mes amis*," mused Emil.

"It isn't. Just more middlemen and, therefore, more expensive," said Father. "So Robert, how are things going with my daughter?"

"Good," Robert said with a smile. "I've been playing the progressive just like you suggested. She's eating it up."

What the blazes?! Robert's words triggered a wave of anger within me.

"As expected," Father said. "Just stay consistent and humor her eccentricities for the time being. Once you are wed, she'll fall into line."

"Of that I have no doubt," Robert responded.

The note of superciliousness in his voice coaxed a guttural sound of rage from deep within me, along with a rising nausea. I shoved my gloved knuckles into my mouth and bit down to stop from letting either sound or sick out of my mouth.

Robert slowed his horse down, perhaps twenty-five yards away from where I hid. I held my breath and cast my gaze down at the ground, hoping to prevent the men from detecting my presence.

"To be honest, Theodore, I find her feistiness quite attractive. I've never been overly fond of passive women who simper and faint at the slightest provocation."

Father laughed. "There's no fear of that with my daughter. I'll be right back, just need to relieve myself." Father took Samson a little way farther up the hill for privacy.

Emil watched until my father had disappeared from view, then - "Robert, *mon ami*, it seems you've landed quite the honeypot. Miss Saskia is both intelligent and beautiful. And I would never describe her as weak," Emil said, as the men waited for my father's return.

"Definitely not," said Robert.

"Have you had the opportunity to...?" Emil's voice trailed off suggestively.

"Under her father's roof?! I'm bold, Emil, but not crazy," Robert replied.

Emil sighed. "Well, it will be a spectacular conquest."

"Indeed! I love the challenge, and look forward to the feeling of accomplishment when she finally submits," Robert said. "I prefer a strong willed broodmare any day. Plus imagine the young colts we will produce!"

That rat bastard! I fumed.

At that moment, Father trotted back down on Samson. "No more chitchat about horse breeding," Father said. "Let's get down to business."

Emil winked at Robert.

Whooping shouts were heard from the other side of the ravine. Father turned to Robert and Emil, "Seems like Hardwick and Whitaker have tracked the quarry. Let's split up and cover the creek from opposite ends. Let's have the good old boys flush our prey for us. What do you say?"

Emil gathered his reins and wheeled his horse around. "I'll go down now!" He clicked his tongue and the Arabian launched into a fast trot, then a canter as they rode away.

Robert said, "Bully! I'll head up yonder with you."

Father gave Samson a swift kick to the flanks, and took off with Robert in the opposite direction. Dust hung suspended over the trail from the horses' quick retreat.

I stood up slowly, then crept back to Devil and let him nuzzle me with his soft warm velvety nose. I scratched him behind his ears, just the way he liked. "Sad to say Devil, at this moment in time, you are the only male I trust," I said. Devil nickered a quiet response, and I pulled a green apple out of my pocket, and offered it to him. He crunched on it gratefully while I mounted up and guided him back to the trail.

Robert Logan was without doubt the single most condescending, pompous, arrogant man I had ever had the misfortune to meet - and in my circles, that was saying a lot. He was simply a well packaged typical male - a more handsome and more charming version than my own Father, but with the same rotten attitude. Well, Father was making a serious mistake in underestimating me. As for Robert, I simply rolled my eyes and muttered "Pittsburgh - ugh!"

The sounds grew louder, until I could see some of the hounds and a couple of riders cantering along the parallel trail across the ravine from me on the sister hill. The dogs began to bark with their specific 'we've found the prey' call.

All at once I saw a flash of white that my mind instantly recognized as fabric. *What animal could...?* My mouth gaped open as I realized - the men were *hunting a man?! Gosh-amighty?!* My mind reeled.

And who would they possibly choose to hunt? It couldn't be one of the regular help - that would make no sense. News would spread fast amongst the rest of the staff.

More likely, it would be one of the seasonal workers who came to help with spring planting? Or maybe even someone unemployed down by the docks in Poughkeepsie? I could imagine Maxwell offering some unfortunate man "a day job" with the promise of pay at the day's end.

Wait a minute! I remembered the year that one of the young stablehands had gone missing after the hunt. He'd been a handsome eye-catching lad...What was his name? Charlie?

How long had this been going on? Had my grandfather started this practice or was it Father's idea?

As I mulled this new bit of information over - I found myself surprised by just how unsurprised I was. Father and Teddy had always had a very cavalier attitude towards the help - except for Isaiah, Bette and Maxwell who were in Father's most intimate circle of trusted servants. Even Mrs. Doyle, whose chapped and capable hands wrangled the house staff into strict order was not here today, and now I finally understood the real reason for the "holiday" the staff received each year for my grandfather Ambrose's Hunt.

I now also understood why Father had prevented me from participating: no doubt he considered my feminine sensibilities were too delicate for such brutish matters.

But Father had also trained me to hunt warm-blooded creatures from a young age. And what prey could be more dangerous than a human male? A man could be calculating, smart, quick witted and able to fight back in ways that a deer or pheasant could never do. Maybe they'd recruited a former soldier who knew how to fight?

I wrinkled my nose as I remembered how Father had taught me not only how to kill a deer, but also how to field dress it. The first time had been dreadful. I was 13, and Father had given me his knife, but I had made the mistake of cutting open the animal's bowels - which made cleaning the beast a seriously unpleasant mess. Father had always frowned on any squeamishness, and I had been a Daddy's girl, determined to please.

I wheeled my darling Devil to follow in parallel. Whoever the unlucky bastard was, he disappeared back below the brush. A few moments later, some of our hounds raced up the trail, followed by that chubby Whitaker and his fellow Southerner, Hardwick, their horses straining under the weight.

As I followed the brush thinned out on the other side, and I caught a glimpse of the target. I gasped and sat upright in my saddle. It wasn't a man at all. I recognized the clothing as the same maid's uniform the female staff wore at Greythorne...

Oh my God! Could they be hunting Eve? Had my father lied? Is this what he meant when he said he'd 'sent her away?'

Oh, I'd never forgive myself if our affair had done this!

191

I held still until the woman reappeared between some trees. I recognized the frizzy hair and dress - it wasn't Eve after all. It was that young Fitzgerald brat who'd just barely started at the house. I pulled Devil to a stop and watched in dismay. What was her name again? Phoebe? No... that wasn't right. Frances? That sounded more like it.

"There! H'ya!" Hardwick cried, using a riding crop to urge his horse on. The dogs had flushed her out of the bush. I watched her race along the hillside opposite me in sheer terror, eyes wide, face pale, hair flying, arms and legs pumping as fast as possible.

Hardwick pulled his pistol out, and fool that he was, fired wildly. The bullet hit a tree trunk a few yards wide of the girl. She screamed and swerved away from the bullet's trajectory. But she miscalculated! She lost her balance as her left foot went off the side of the hill. Her momentum carried her over and down into the ravine.

The poor thing tumbled head over heel, hitting branches and rocks on the way down, crying out as she fell.

Hardwick and Whitaker rode to the edge of the hill and looked down into the ravine. "Damn, it's too steep for the horses," Whitaker said. Hardwick must have nodded. Before they could do anything, the hounds came tearing their way down the ravine and snapped at the poor girl. She wove about, disoriented, then started scrabbling along the ground to escape the dogs.

A masked hunter came galloping up the ravine behind the hounds and commanded the dogs to "leave it." The hounds stopped in front of the girl, and sat on their haunches like sentinels, tongues lolling, chests heaving. The girl tried to scurry away, but the dogs pawed the ground and growled at her. She stopped moving and simply sat on the ground, shivering.

"Hey! That's *our* catch!" Whitaker yelled down the hill at the masked hunter.

The fellow looked up at Hardwick and Whitaker, and removed his mask. It was Emil! He smiled at the men, his white teeth flashing a toothy grin. He called up to the men a taunt, *"Premier arrivé, premier servi."*

Despite the horrid circumstances, I had to chuckle at Monsieur Henry - he really was a most audacious fellow.

Whitaker yelled, "You son of a bitch!" He drew his pistol, but Hardwick reached over and put his hand on Whitaker's arm.

I couldn't hear what Hardwick said, but it made Whitaker's face turn red with rage. He hesitated then reluctantly holstered his weapon. Hardwick called to their hounds, "Hunt 'em up!" The hounds sniffed the air, then tails up, charged up the trail into the distance. The two men kicked their horses into action, and galloped away.

Meanwhile, on the other side of the ridge, I dismounted and crept to the edge of the trail. I felt compelled to watch the events unfold down below.

Emil dismounted and approached the girl, his revolver in his right hand aimed at her. With his free left hand, he started to unbutton the front of his riding britches.

I was taken aback and disgusted by the man's clear intention to ravish the poor girl. Was this also a normal part of the "Ambrose Hunt"? Men raping and killing. It beggared belief. These men had so much wealth and power, and at least some of them had a modicum of charm. Surely they didn't need to do this to prove anything to anyone.

"No, no, no, please, please," Frances cried, scrabbling backwards away from Emil.

Despite my strong distaste, I couldn't turn my gaze away.

"Now, *ma cheri,* where do you think you are going?" Emil asked almost kindly.

I was focused on Emil's face, when suddenly from under a bush, a man's right arm and hand reached and pulled Frances' head by her hair, extending and exposing her white neck. A second hand shot out with a knife that whipped across her bare throat. Blood spurted out onto Emil's breeches and boots. Then a second cut was made, this time, vertical from the jaw to the sternum. The right hand let go of the girl's hair and she collapsed in a heap.

Emil holstered his pistol. He sighed as he re-fastened his trousers. "I prefer my conquests alive."

The other man rose up from the shrubbery and removed his mask. I knew it was Teddy, even before he revealed his face. He was covered in mud and brambles and now the poor girl's lifeblood. In other words, he was a bloody mucky mess, and was in his element. This had always been his favorite way to hunt; to disguise himself with mud and plant matter so that the quarry wouldn't see him approach. He preferred the challenge of using a knife rather than a pistol or crossbow.

"Not me," said Teddy. He straddled Frances' lifeless body and cut open her gown from stem to stern. "I just want a little souvenir," my brother said, with that smarmy smugness I had heard all my life.

As he did so, I turned my head away. It was all too much for me... My brother and my father...Emil...all these men. Despite their wealth, pomp, fancy talk and social graces, they were cruel and beastly.

"You have peculiar taste, *mon ami*," said Emil.

I could tell that Emil was repulsed, but of course Emil was a guest of my father's and could not afford to be rude to my brother.

Teddy smirked, then rose up. "Ok, I'm done here. Let's go."

The men summoned their dogs, remounted their horses and wheeled away, as Teddy wiped his bloody knife clean on a rag. The hoof beats faded into the distance.

I approached the trail's edge, and looked down at the dead girl. She looked like a tiny broken doll. What a waste. How appallingly unsporting they were to hunt unarmed, untrained servant women who had no clue how to defend themselves. Wouldn't a soldier or sailor or dockworker with a knife in hand be a more honorable target?

Then it occurred to me - what if Father had lied to me about the Kelly women being dismissed and sent to Poughkeepsie? Maybe

Father and Teddy intended to hunt Eve, too? I untied my horse and we took off, as a hunting horn sounded in the distance.

Chapter 25

Hunters And Prey

Eve

I had never felt more alone in my life. Despite the tension between us, I had always been able to count on Ma to be my advocate and protector. Now she was badly hurt, and I was miles away at the other end of the estate, with a small army of murderous bastards in between us.

My left shoulder ached and burned. I was heartsick, tired, cold and thirsty. But I knew that I had no other option but to keep going. I pushed my way through the woods towards the creek, blazing my own trail between branches, over logs, and under thickets; anything to avoid the game trail. Glimpses of sparkling water flashed between the shrubs and tree trunks. The mist had lifted, but the clouds overhead had grown darker and heavier. The gloom suited my miserable mood. I was living in a nightmare. The blood I'd lost from my shoulder didn't help matters - I felt a bit lightheaded, and pangs of fear struck me hard, despite my efforts to stay focused on the present.

Blam! I jumped in fright, as a gunshot ricocheted in the distance. Men's voices shouted but they were too far away for me to make anything out. As I grew closer to the trickling water, the sounds of hoofbeats and barking dogs seemed to recede into the forest. Thank goodness.

A cottontail hare darted out from under some foliage as I pushed through to the creek, whiskers twitching and paws flying. I was already so jumpy, that the sudden movement made my heart leap up in my chest. Parched beyond measure, I knelt down on the ground, disregarding all niceties, and cupped my hands to scoop up the sweet refreshment. I gulped down several handfuls. Afterwards, I splashed the chilly water on my face, then gently poured some water over my left shoulder and arm.

I decided to risk another moment or two of being out in the open to unwrap the cloth and examine my left shoulder. The wound from the bolt had ragged puckered edges, and the skin around the puncture was red and hot to the touch - not good. I took a few moments to dip a corner of the rag in the brisk creek water and gently clean the wound. I stifled a groan at the pain. How on earth while I recover from this? Then I laughed bitterly - here I was assuming I'd make it through the rest of the day. Funny how one's mind can deny accepting what's real in the world. I wrapped the wound back up.

Once my personal ablutions were done, my mind and my sight cleared. I sat up and listened for a moment - the woods were quiet, except for the sounds of running water and the long repeated whistles of red cardinals that flitted above me. I whispered "Peggy, Nan, Franny - are you here?" No answer came.

I waited a few moments longer, chanced another few whispers for the sisters, but there were only the forest sounds and birdsong in response. I stood up slowly to survey my surroundings. Out of the corner of my eye, I spied something pale under a large hydrangea plant. What was that?

An ominous feeling rose up in my gut, as I drew close. It was a pair of pale bare feet... I ran the rest of the way, and to my dismay, I discovered that the feet belonged to...*oh, sweet mother of mercy! Not poor Franny!*

I yelped her name and moved to check her pulse, only to see that her throat had been cut in a strange criss-cross pattern. Out of this cross-shaped wound, her blood had flown thick and black. Franny's gown had been ripped open. The gorge rose up in my throat - I turned away so as not to vomit on the corpse.

Finally my stomach stopped heaving, and the wave of nausea subsided. A deep sadness rose up in its place. Even with my eyes closed, the image of Franny's brutal death was imprinted in my mind. The slashes of her throat reminded me of the first day I'd arrived at Greythorne when Teddy had ridden up with the near-dead buck slung over his horse's back. How could anyone be so savage and cruel? Damn these monsters to hell.

Tears rolled down my cheeks as I knelt by the sweet girl. I gently closed her eyelids with my right index and middle fingers. I pulled her gown together over her desecrated body to restore at least a modicum of dignity. I bowed my head in a moment of prayer: to the Morrigan to protect and keep Frances' soul.

I rose up with a solemn vow to Franny and myself, that I would do all I could to protect Peggy and Nan from the same fate. A narrow path led down the ravine, alongside the creek. Its trail meandered into a boggy marsh. The maples and ash trees gave way to wetlands of slimy moss-covered boulders, black, fallen tree trunks, spiders spinning webs, and even a pair of mallards, paddling and ducking underwater to snap up tidbits. Their quiet quacks were comforting. The little bog was hemmed in by boulders and heavy tree growth, so I had no option but to keep moving forward, the fetid smell of rotted leaves filling my nostrils.

Clammy mud and dead leaves started to accumulate on me, sticking to the lower skirts of my damp and soiled uniform. After several minutes, the long skirts of my uniform became so heavy with mud, it pulled me almost to a standstill. Amidst the shifting shadows and dark mossy tree trunks leaning crookedly over the marsh, I felt more and more like a trapped animal. In frustration, I lifted up the dress skirt, and used my teeth to start a rip at about the knee-line. Then with my good arm, I tore away the lowest several inches all the way around. I let the ragged pieces fall to the ground, and high stepped through the mud with my bare legs, squelching and squishing all the way.

To my left, a *flash of motion*; my heart skipped a beat and I held my breath. Was it one of the men, creeping up on me? I was a sitting duck - totally exposed and barely able to move in the mud. I squatted down to be less visible and watched.

It was a deer - thank goodness!- at the water's edge, pausing to take a drink. The doe looked up and caught my eyes, then flitted away to my right as fast as I could blink. Relief washed over me - if the deer could move that quickly it meant I had reached a dry edge of the swamp. I headed towards where the doe had stood, out of the mud and back onto dry land, taking a moment to wipe the mud and leaves off my legs.

"Help! Help me please!" A woman's voice cried out.

I rushed towards the voice, arriving back onto the hard-packed trail. As I raced around a bend in the path, I saw Nan. She was up ahead of me, sprinting at full speed, her filthy dress and slip billowing behind her. Behind me, I could hear hounds baying, and horses cantering. Damnation! Rage boiled up within me so strongly that all my fears were swept away.

I ran on a diagonal, planting myself directly in between Nan on my left and the dogs and hunters on my right. The men's silver masks obscured their faces with mocking empty smiles. As soon as I was in front of the animals and men, I stopped and screamed "Halt!" at the top of my lungs, my hair loose and swirling around my head, my arms raised in an unholy benediction.

The men guffawed, no doubt thinking my behavior was fool-hardy and ridiculous. Their scorn only served to intensify my fury. Behind my voice, my mind drove a strong *push* towards the dogs and horses. The prickling sensation erupted all along my hands and feet, as I did my best to speak directly into the creature's minds.

Stop, I commanded.

The horses locked their legs and skidded to a quick halt. The hunters almost flew over their mounts' necks, but managed to hold fast to the reins and stirrups. The hounds dropped from a fast run to rest on their haunches, panting heavily, sides heaving as they waited for my next command. Nan stood still, too - until I gave her a side glance and an order: "Nan! Go and hide!" She closed her open mouth, snapped out of it, and ran off the trail into a thicket of trees.

Even with their masks on, I could recognize Whitaker -- given away by his portly frame -- sitting astride a palomino. In a high-pitched tone, he cried out to his dried out string bean of a friend, Hardwick, "That fool Rennard brought us a witch to hunt!" At the same time, he raised his pistol and aimed it at me - but as with everything the man did, it was a mediocre shot that went wide.

Hardwick, who was apparently sporting his old Indian short bow and a quiver full of arrows, raised the bow and let loose an arrow towards me. The silvery tip of the arrowhead glinted in the light as it flew towards me - I stood my ground. I took a deep breath and concentrated - I whipped the air in front of me with my hands. The motion created a swirl of forceful wind which caught and reversed the direction of the arrow. Before Hardwick could react, the arrow struck him in the center of his chest with a satisfying *thunk*. He cried out and pitched sideways off his horse.

Hardwick groaned as he landed hard on the ground, then lay still, blood flowing from around the arrow's shaft lodged in the center of his chest.

"Oh my gawd, Winslow!" Whitaker exclaimed. He stood in his stirrups and urged his steed onward, toward his fallen fellow. The horse wouldn't move, just grunted in annoyance at his yanks on the reigns.

Whitaker threw off his mask, his face pale and eyes buggy with fear. "Hya, horse!" the exasperated man cried, whipping at his mount in futility. "Come on now, you sumbitch!!" Now terrified, he pulled on his reins and kicked the flanks of his horse, but it put its ears back, locked its legs and grimaced at him. The horse turned his head and snapped at Whitaker's booted leg. Realizing he could no longer control the animal, the man dismounted, but stumbled as he landed. The horses, now riderless, looked to me for a hint at what to do next.

"Go on, then," I said. They whinnied gratefully and bolted into the forest, disappearing past a thicket of oaks some distance away.

Whitaker fumbled to raise his pistol at me.

"Now, hounds!" I commanded. The foxhounds and retrievers rose up as one, eyes sharply focused upon me. "Go on and get that bad man."

I *pushed* the hounds and instructed them to corner Whitaker. The dogs pivoted to face their target, teeth bared, eyes staring. They growled and raised their hackles, slinking towards him, stalking low as though he were a juicy rabbit or fox.

Whitaker's eyes grew wide as he recognized the dogs' hunting behavior. He turned and began to trot as fast as he could into the bushes, firing his pistol blindly at me over his shoulder as he fled. I sidestepped as a bullet whizzed past me, then struck a maple tree trunk. With an explosive chitter of brown and fur, a terrified squirrel shot out of a hole in the same tree and scurried upwards to the safety of the higher branches.

I *pushed* into the mind of the lead hunting hound, which was gaining on Whitaker due to the man's slow, lumbering pace.

I feel the thrill of the hunt coursing through my limbs. My front and hind legs gracefully sink into the leaf matter and mud, my nose full of the awful sour stench of the man's body odor and stale tobacco breath. The target slips into the bushes, so I give a commanding bark, then leap into the chase. Barking in excited response, my fellow hounds fall in, right behind me. The landscape is a palette of gray shades, and my ears twitch as I hear the man huff and puff with great heaving breaths in front of me.

He picks up his pace and moves surprisingly fast now. He manages to reach and grab at the gray stone wall before I get to him. He scrabbles and tries to climb up the wall of stacked stones, using his hands and feet to find holds and pull himself up. Barely out of my

reach, he stops to catch his breath. He looks down, his jowls aquiver,
and eyes darting all over. I smell and sense his fear.

I rise up on my back legs, my front paws clawing at the stones as I
growl at him. The bastard reaches down with his pistol and swings at
me, striking my jaw with a hard blow. This is the final straw - I leap
up and sink my teeth into the ankle of his leather boot. His scream is so
loud I worry my ears might never recover. My hound friends catch up
to me, as the smelly man screams and falls off the wall. They'd seen
him try to hurt me.

"No pity," I growl to my pack.

"None," they howl back.

Whitaker shrieked and begged for someone to help him, as I
released myself from the mind of the hound. Right before the sucking
darkness pulled at me I heard a cry that resolved into a gurgle. One of
the dogs had ended him by a quick and thorough bite through the
man's neck. When the sensation stopped and I returned to my Eve
body, I swear I could taste his blood in my mouth still.

And all through that blood, the sour tang of fear. And
then...silence.

The dogs would be trained to sit and wait for their hunter to
come and claim the kill, then release them back to the kennel. I
hoped they'd wait all night. A cold drizzle started to fall as I sat on the
ground, my back against a tree trunk. I shivered and my left shoulder
responded with a throbbing ache. Branches rustled and I looked up,
afraid that another hunter was approaching, while I was exhausted
and defenseless.

To my relief, it was Nan. She emerged from the thicket and came
to squat before me.

"Eve, I can't thank you enough," Nan said.

I nodded as I looked her over. "Are you hurt?"

"No, but you are," she said, pointing to my shoulder.

I shrugged.

"Are you a witch?" Nan asked, apprehensive with a tremor in her
voice.

"In truth, I don't know, Nan." I knew there was no time for explanations, so I said, "I might be. But the important thing is that we are in this together. I'm going to get us out of here, any way I can."

Nan nodded.

"We need to get to Peggy," I said. "Give me a hand up?" That familiar exhaustion swept over me. I reached out and Nan helped get me to my feet. I was wobbly on my tired legs.

"What about Frances?" Nan asked me, clearly worried.

I shook my head, and looked at Nan with deep sorrow in my eyes.

Nan dropped down to her knees. "No, no, not Franny! Mary, Mother of God!" she cried. "She's gone?" She collapsed onto the ground, her hands clutching her head, knees to chest. Sad whimpers and moans rose up in the air.

Now it was my turn to squat down in front of my friend. I put my hand on her shoulder in comfort. "I'm so sorry Nan. I found her, but it was too late. One of the men..." Nan wailed, eyes wild with sadness and anger. I grabbed her and held her, tight as I could.

"I know, I know. It's so wrong. It's horrid, Nan, what is happening here. But if we don't get going, the men will get all of us," I said. "Then nobody hears about this. Nobody stops these bastards from doing this again and again and again. Frances, Ma, anyone else will have died in vain. We can't let that happen, can we?"

Nan shuddered and sniffled.

"They took yer Ma, too?" She asked, setting her hand atop mine.

"She's badly hurt - I don't know if she's still alive..." I said.

"Evie, I'm so sorry," she said.

A momentary sob shook me, but I managed to push the ache back down. "Thanks, Nan. We've got to go. Are you with me?"

In response, Nan stood and wiped her face on her sleeve, replacing her tears with a look of burning anger. "How will we ever find Peg?" She asked.

"Did you miss the part where I'm a witch?" I asked.

Reaching out and back with my feelings, I called out into the forest: "Black Queen, come forth and guide us!" Three black ravens soared downwards and croaked as they circled just above us.

Nan clutched my arm, terrified. "It's okay, Nan," I said. "They're here to help us...Birds lead the way."

The birds' wings flapped hard as they flew up. We followed them as they turned to the north. We jogged on for a bit, then tiring, slowed down to a steady walk. Nan's ankle was still tender, as was my shoulder, so we both helped one another as much as we could, winding our way across the estate for a while. We stopped every so often to look and listen for sounds of horses, men or dogs - but thankfully we didn't hear or see them.

Finally, our birds soared down, shrieking, and we heard Peggy's voice cry out, "Go 'way, you feckin' beasties!" We ran around a bend in the trail and found Peggy, terrified, dropped to the ground into a ball. We knelt down by her, as I sent the ravens to rise up and settle on a tree branch above us.

"Are ye hurt?" Nan asked.

"No, just scared out of me wits," Peggy said.

Nan took her sisters' hands in hers. "Peg, they got Franny." Peggy moaned in sorrow, and the sisters stood and held each other. "It's me fault," said Peggy. "I should've never brought her to work here in this bedeviled place."

"No," Nan shook her head. "We'll not be taking any of the blame for what those monstrous men are doing."

In the distance, I heard the horn blown and dogs bark and howl. I turned to the sisters, saying "You two need to clear out of here. Follow the birds: they'll take you out to the road. From there you can run to town and get help."

"What about you?" Peggy asked.

I shook my head, determined. "I'll divert the men, while you two get away."

Peggy and Nan gave each other a look - I knew they thought I was deluded. Nan piped up, "Eve, you need to come away with us. The Rennards are evil and, what's worse, they're richer than Croesus."

"Not Saskia," I said. "She's different."

"Perhaps," said Nan, though the doubt on her face was obvious. "But we're still out-numbered and out-armed. Miss Saskia isn't here, and the men wouldn't listen to her anyway. Even if by some miracle we are able to survive, they'll blame us for the dead hunters and Frances. Their word versus ours, we'll all be hanged for murder. That's how this world works."

I shrugged, then said, "You're probably right, but I guess I'm determined to fight. You two still need to go while you can. It's not just getting you out, I need to go back to the mansion and see if my Ma is still alive...Here, I'll summon a raven to show you the shortest way out of the estate."

"No," said Peggy firmly, as she grabbed my arm. "We'll not be leaving without ye, Eve," she insisted. Nan stood beside her, nodding in agreement.

I looked at the two sisters, and tears filled my eyes. It was more loyalty and kindness than I could have ever imagined.

"Okay, then, we stick together to protect each other and get out," I said. "I have but one plan in mind - we head back to mansion, hitch a horse or two to a wagon, bring my Ma if she is still alive, and then race out of here as fast as we can."

I cast my gaze upwards at a nearby raven preening in a tree branch and summoned it with a *push*. *Guide us back to the great house, and avoid all the men.* The bird croaked and soared down, then cast about hovering in the air, wings beating.

"Let's get going - the bird will lead us." More trouble was out there, and I wanted as much distance between us and it as possible.

Chapter 26

The Unmaking

Saskia

Devil galloped like an angel as we flew along the trail, with the start of a drizzle overhead. The air was a delicious elixir of foliage, soil and rain. Even though I was worried about the nature of this hunt, my body filled with inexplicable pleasure at the sensations of being astride my superb horse. I could tell Devil was enjoying himself, too, his ears pricked up high and tail streaming behind him, the cadence of his gallop as smooth as a boat gliding on still waters. A flock of geese flew overhead in their typical V; their silly sounding honks made me smile.

I had reached one of my favorite sections of our estate; the little beech grove. The trail led through a dense area of towering copper beeches and one massive, old oak. The base of the trunk had to be at least four feet across. I looked up at the majestic tree trunks which soared up at least sixty feet high. The silvery gray bark reminded me of an elephant's leathery skin. Aunt Winnie and I had visited the London Zoo while on our European tour and seen two elephants last year: they were magnificent creatures.

All of the sudden, Devil squealed and side stepped something on the trail, nearly losing his balance before regaining his step, if not his

206

speed. The high-stepping shifted me to the left of the saddle. Thank goodness the stirrups and saddle were tailored to fit me, or I would have gone flying. His behavior jolted me to stop day dreaming, and look at the ground below. To my utter horror, laying face down on the trail was another body...

This corpse, however, belonged to a man. A wealthy one! What would Father think when he found out? This would be an absolute disaster for our family. In my mind's eye, I could picture Father being apoplectic over the whole situation. Father had dedicated his entire life to build, protect and enhance the Rennard family's influence, status and power. All of it could come tumbling down in an instant if we were held responsible.

Oh God, it's Andrew Carnavoy! What happened? What happened to his head?!

The richest man in Dutchess County was recognizable only by his beautiful custom tailored hunting coat that I'd so admired earlier in the day. Now it was a sodden patchwork of mud and blood. The man's head was almost unrecognizable - it looked as though someone had dropped an anvil on the his skull. Gray matter had spilled out with the dark blood, looking like congealed eggs on top of the muddy ground.

A metallic taste rose up in my mouth, and I had to breathe hard through my nose to stop nausea from overtaking me. While I was not usually squeamish, this was one of the most appalling sights of my life.

Poor Gloria. As much as she loved to complain about her dear papa, she was daddy's little girl, and his sudden death would be a devastating blow to her and to the entire Carnavoy clan. There would be an uproar, and our family would be cast under a shadow for the death on our property. Even though Gloria was a gossipy bore, she carried a lot of power in our circle of friends, just by virtue of being a Carnavoy. This was not going to be a simple problem to erase.

Devil slowed down and tossed his head to and fro, looking around as much as I did, to see if any other unpleasant threats were about.

My pulse was racing, and I still felt queasy after that horrid sight. I pivoted Devil to the right and urged him on with a gentle verbal cue. The rain began to patter down more heavily, and I shivered as we rode a short distance away from the corpse.

The man's gruesome death was shocking. It was also bewildering - he must have been thrown from his horse, which was hard to fathom considering he was such an accomplished horseman. He'd won many a blue ribbon at equestrian jumping competitions from Massachusetts to Virginia. Gloria had complained more than once that her father spent more time breeding racehorses, than to his wife Margaret or children.

When I could no longer see the body, I pulled Devil over and tied him to a branch that spread over some tall grasses. Poor Devil had been badly spooked, so a nice patch of sweet green foliage would be ideal for him. Meanwhile, I needed to understand what I had just seen, so I walked carefully back over the trail, looking for any clues that might help to explain Carnavoy's death.

Block it out. Just focus on the other details here. I took a deep breath.

I had just begun to settle my heart rate down again, when something strange did catch my eye up ahead. A flock of ravens circled two hundred feet away overhead, cawing and swooping down, as though there was carrion below. I jogged over and saw a pair of shiny black riding boots, toes pointed up to the sky, by the side of the trail. Oh my God! Not another!

My stomach plummeted as I got close enough to identify the rider. It was that sourpuss Southerner, Winslow Hardwick, lying on his back, eyes open. An arrow from his own Cherokee bow was embedded deep in his chest. Well, that was a nice bit of irony.

I knelt down and slid off one of my lambskin gloves to touch his pasty gray skin - it was barely warm. I scanned his body and noticed he'd lost bladder control, too. The man was lying dead in his own piss, and been in that position for a while, then. And the arrow. His own; but how? It was all quite perplexing. I walked slowly around him, studying the area for any hints of an explanation.

Perhaps Carnavoy hadn't just fallen? It was hard to believe the noted horseman would meet his end by mare, doubly so in the evidence of Hardwick being slain by means of his own weapon.

Why would Hardwick and Carnavoy be killed by the hand of another hunter?

Why would the men turn on each other, when they had seemed so jolly and filled with the spirit of brotherly love just the night before, and even this morning? It made no sense. My father had always been devious, but this seemed entirely unlike him. And my brother? While he could certainly be an *enfant terrible,* he was tightly reined in by my father.... But maybe things had changed during my absence? Something dreadful was afoot -

"ROooooooo..."

The baying howls of one of our foxhounds came to me then, loudly and clearly to my right, from the periphery of the property. I ran back and untied Devil, mounting speedily, then coaxing to speed up. I urged him on with my heels, and we arrived at the eastern wall of Greythorne. A thicket of thorny plants stood before a ten-foot tall stacked limestone wall. Several of my father's scent hounds were keeping guard in position around some sort of quarry, but there was no hunter anywhere nearby to be seen. So strange. The dogs smelled my scent and when I gave them the command, they obediently sat still on their haunches, tongues hanging out and chests heaving.

Cold, unrelenting fear struck as I saw splashes of red and scarlet on the hounds' snouts and bodies. I realized it was blood, spattered on their faces and chests. I pushed past the dogs on foot, and came upon a badly mauled boot and leg, riding breeches torn and ripped asunder. My eyes followed from the foot and leg upwards -

It was another of my father's guests who lay dead before me. This time it was that odious fellow, James Whitaker, his legs and his neck torn open with severe puncture wounds. A pool of coagulating blood lay underneath his body. His eyes were open, fixed in terror, and his hands showed defensive wounds. He must have bled out. It was beyond strange...

Our dogs were trained to flush out prey, but never to bite a human so aggressively. And yet, I could see traces of blood in the dogs' coats, especially around their mouths. I decided it would be best for me to stay on Devil and not get too close just in case. I talked slow and low to the dogs, as Maxwell had taught me to do. "Good job, dogs. Good job." The hounds came over, wagging their tails, tongues lolling, looking as if nothing untoward had just happened.

Now there were *three* dead men on property! I struggled to make sense of what was unfolding. A new fear arose - what about my father and my brother? Were they okay? Had they been hurt, too? Or were they responsible for this catastrophic mess?

An idea rose up in my mind. I reached into my pocket and pulled out the blue silk pocket square that Robert had given me in the morning when I'd hid behind the pillar. I bent down from my saddle, and dangled the fabric to the hounds' noses.

"Do you smell this man?" I asked the hounds. Their eyes sparkled with excitement. They rose up off their haunches, beginning to paw at the ground, bark and bay. Their eyes focused on me, awaiting my command. "Alright then, go hunt him up!" The hounds barked and raced away in a hurry. Scent dogs were remarkable beasts with incredible stamina. Even though they'd been on the go since morning, they showed no signs of slowing down.

"Good dogs!" I shouted, as I jumped back on Devil and followed after them. Their steady barks helped Devil and I keep on track, as they disappeared into the countryside.

I was fairly certain that Robert would be riding with my father. I needed to understand what was happening and what they were up to. Whoever it was that had hunted the men, had outsmarted them and used their own weapons against them. If it weren't so horrific, it would be really quite poetic. An example of hubris crushed by a remarkably clever opposition.

We tore across the landscape, the rainfall growing so heavy it became difficult to see more than a few yards ahead. Crack! Lightning forked across the landscape, followed by the deep bass of thunder in the distance vibrating through my chest. Devil whinnied loudly in protest, his ears laid back and nostrils flared. The fear that had clamped onto my gut, kept getting stronger and stronger. Ominous dread filled my chest. Time was running out, but it was not at all clear for whom.

Chapter 27

Daughter Of The Morrigan
Eve

Peggy, Nan and I followed my raven as it soared up ahead, guiding us towards Greythorne. The rain turned from drizzle into fat, heavy drops. The only bright spot with the rain was that maybe it would make it harder for the hunters and their hounds to smell and see us.

Nan's ankle was swollen but she was able to bear some weight on it. Peggy was right there with her sister, lending her some support to keep the pace. Forging ahead, I pushed branches aside with my uninjured arm and tried to pick the smoothest path forward for us. From the bird's eye view, it looked like it would take us about half an hour to cut across the grounds.

With a crash of thunder, the gray skies finally unleashed their threat of rain in earnest - the water came down in dense sheets, muffling sound and quickly saturating the soil. The storm dumped on us, forming rivulets of water that flowed down my back between my shoulder blades. Our clothes hung heavy. I was chilled to the bone. The ravens kept going, undeterred by the steady drumbeat of rain.

Was I doing the right thing? Maybe I should have insisted that the sisters leave without me? Or maybe I needed to accept that Ma was likely gone, and that returning to Greythorne was a dangerous fool's errand.

No. She'd come back for you. That little voice inside my head whispered that I *needed to know for sure,* before I would be able to let go and grieve my mother. What if she were still alive? Perhaps the wound wasn't mortal and she could be nursed back to health? On the other hand, what if we were making a fatal error by returning to the mansion? I knew at some point the men who were still alive would head back there, and overcoming them was not going to be easy. I was exhausted, hungry, beyond tired, achy and sore. My mind swirled with a torrent of thoughts, as heavy and thick as the rain pounding us and the surrounding landscape.

We followed the ravens as fast as we could, Nan and Peggy doing their best to keep up. A tiny sliver of hope bubbled up inside me - if there were any chance that Ma was still hanging on, we could load her onto the back of a wagon. After that, maybe race to the nearest town and find the local doc to fix her up, and then disappear. To where? That was something I wasn't sure of quite yet, but we'd leave this hell far behind.

That tiny voice within me whispered that perhaps Saskia would be at the mansion, and assist us. I tried to shrug it away; you're nought but a naive fool! But the whisper continued, and hope bubbled up inside me.

The rain made it hard to see more than a few paces ahead and my hair was soon sodden, dripping water into my eyes, no matter how much I tried to push the curls away from my face. Peg and Nan were in a similar state of misery. We hiked down the hill along the creek. My heart filled with sadness over poor Frances, and when I let myself check in with my own feelings, I was frightened and sorry for all of us as well. Just a few weeks ago, I believed I was on the cusp of the best opportunity of my life. In reality, working at Greythorne was likely going to end my hard-scrabble life in the most miserable fashion.

After what felt like forever, the trees grew more sparse and we could spy the open lawn of the mansion up ahead. Greythorne loomed tall in the distance across an open grassy field. We paused to take a breath and study the grounds, in case anyone was lurking about. Maxwell or Isaiah would never let us escape off the property, and who knew whether others had been instructed to do the same.

"I don't see anyone, do you?" Nan asked. I shook my head.

"Okay so what's the plan now?" Peggy whispered.

"First, I need to see if my mother is still alive," I said.

Nan grabbed my good arm and turned me to face her.

"You're mad if you think it's a good idea to go inside the mansion," she said, a desperate note in her voice. "What if we grab some horses, and make a run for it while the place is deserted?"

"I just have to know for sure," I said. "I won't be able to live with myself if I abandon her now."

"Right, well I do agree with ye there on principle, but how in hell will we manage to get away? The police and local folks will think us a fine trio of Lizzie Bordens, killing upstanding men," Peggy said.

"You're not wrong, but I don't want to give up yet... I've thought it over - the staff are mostly gone on their 'holiday' and I know that three of the hunters are now dead, which leaves just four men out there," I said. "They're still racing around the woods looking to find us, and the last thing they'll expect is that we would head back to the mansion."

Peggy sighed and nodded. "I don't think we have much choice."

"And you think we can take on the Rennards?" Nan asked with her usual pessimism. "Neither Peg nor I are fighters," she said. "We grew up with sisters only, and no idea how to handle a knife or a pistol..."

"Nan, we need to at least try," said Peggy.

"I don't want to fight the men, unless I am forced to," I say. "Look, I know, there's a lot to deal with, but I think that if we work together we just might be able to get away...and I'll not be afraid to use whatever I have at hand," I said grimly.

"Here's what I propose: we skirt around the mansion, then you two run to the stables and grab a horse or two and hitch them up to a buggy or wagon. Nothing fancy, preferably something the workers would use to haul lumber or coal. Meanwhile, I'll run inside and check on my mother," I said. A lump rose in my throat as I realized how scared I was by the thought that she might be gone.

The rainfall started to ease up, and the clouds lightened. A drizzle continued to keep the air damp, but it was a relief to be done with the torrential downpour. Peggy's face was sad but thoughtful, her head cocked to one side as she glanced around the terrain.

"Even though it scares me to the bone, your Ma could very well still be alive. It's right to want to see if she can be gotten out of there..." Peggy said. Nan sighed with reluctant acceptance as I realized we were all on the same page. "I'd do the same for Frances, if..." my voice broke a little in sadness over the losses of the day.

"I know you would," Peggy replied, and gave my right shoulder a gentle squeeze.

"We'll need money," I said. "For a train or a ferry. For accommodations and food."

"That old crone Doyle keeps the pay in a desk drawer in her office," Nan said. "It's under lock and key no doubt, but you can probably manage, hey? Mr. Rennard also keeps some cash in his study. Mostly he's careful, but sometimes he does leave some notes loose in a desk drawer. At any rate, whatever you find won't be a drop compared to what they've taken from all of us."

"Agreed and understood," I said. I hesitated, then blurted out, "I'm hoping Saskia will be home - I need to talk to her. She could be willing to help us - she might even want to leave with us."

Nan snorted and Peggy shook her head in response. Not the answer I'd hoped to hear. By now, we had gotten almost to the edge of the woods.

Peggy looked me in the eye. "Eve, you're tenderhearted, but folks like Miss Rennard are nought but interested in themselves...Sorry to say, even if she's shown you some *special* - um - *attention*," my face

215

turned bright red as Peggy continued with determination, "Well, it don't mean she gives a shite about ye. What if she just turns ye over to the men?"

I sighed. I didn't have the energy to argue, and I definitely didn't want to discuss any of this with them. I was more than a bit relieved that Peggy hadn't seemed to judge me, but I had no desire to discuss Saskia and my relationship with either of the Fitzgeralds. In my heart, I hoped Saskia would be horrified by her family's behavior, and would at the very least want to help us to get away.

"My first priority is my mother. It shouldn't take long for me to get inside and find Ma and some money for us. Whether or not she's alive," I said.

"Eve," Peggy put her hand on my shoulder, "Thank you for coming back for us. Alright, let's give your plan a go. We'll sneak into the barn and hook up a buggy to the horse. But how will you let us know you've found what you're after in there?"

I was about to respond, when--

Crack! The sound of a rifle shot echoed across the forest.

My ears reverberated. I winced.

A bullet whizzed by. Terror whipped through me, and time seemed to slow down to a crawl. I watched as the bullet flew past me. A fraction of a second later the bullet struck! Nan's eyes widened and her mouth opened in a silent scream as the bullet penetrated the front of her throat and flew out the other side. Blood began to spray out in a rhythmic pumping motion from the wound. Nan crumpled down to the ground, pulling Peggy down with her. I threw myself down as well.

I scanned the environment around us, looking for any clues as to where the gun had been fired from. I could see a whiff of gun smoke from under some bushes a hundred feet or so away from us. Should I charged towards the hunter? Or try to help Nan and Peggy? I decided that a chance to save Nan was more important than anything else I could do.

"Noooo," Peggy wailed as she held her sister in her arms. I

crawled over and drew close. Nan choked, her brilliant green eyes filled with pain and shock. She convulsed, her back arching and limbs splayed. The enormous blood loss was dreadful enough, but the bullet's damage to her trachea meant that she was also suffocating. She grasped our hands, writhing on the ground, her eyes growing more and more filled with terror...and then suddenly she stopped struggling. Her hands released us, and her head lolled back, eyes open, but sightless. Her suffering was mercifully short, but that was no comfort to me or to her sister, Peggy.

Peggy looked up at me stunned, mouth agape, eyes filled with tears. "Can you not do anything to help?!"

"I only wish I could," I replied. I'd never felt more impotent. "Are you hurt? Can you get up? We need to keep moving so we don't get killed, too."

Peggy looked at me with a mix of despair and rage. "Christ on a shingle Eve, what's the feckin' point?! We're both gonna be dead in no time, and then at least I'll get to see my sisters again." Peggy wept quietly, her eyes filled with grief. Truthfully, she was likely right. But I was stubborn and unwilling to yield.

"Peggy, please, don't give up," I said. I grabbed her and forced her to let go of her sister. "Three of the men are gone; maybe we can outsmart the others and escape? I need you to run and go hide over there, amidst the trees. Keep low to the ground."

I pointed to a stand of large oak trees, and after a moment, Peggy got up and quickly darted towards them, disappearing beneath the thick foliage.

I focused on where the gun smoke had lingered a few moments earlier, but I couldn't hear or see anyone. Surely they were still out there. Then a flash of movement caught my eye. It was that smarmy mealymouthed Robert Logan!

He rose up from under the bushes, raising up on one knee, then coming to a stand. He must have been lying on his belly, for his coat and pants were covered with leaves and dirt. He smirked as he worked to reload his rifle.

My sadness was swept away by a mighty wave of fury, swelling up within me. I raised my arms up in the air and pulled my soul towards that higher energy that was quietly guiding me, from beyond my awareness. Without knowing how or why, I realized that I had summoned the power of the Morrigan to my aid. An almost explosive barrage of fiery hot prickles ran up and down my skin, as I dug deep and pushed my arms to force a blast of wind energy up towards the bastard.

The wind blew across the space between us, collecting dust and leaves, small stones and twigs, before finally reaching and slamming into Logan. He had just brought the rifle butt to his shoulder to sight and aim, but found himself being thrust back and up into the air. His arms and legs windmilled, until he clipped a large oak tree trunk, which caused his right leg to snap. His head smacked the trunk of an adjacent tree, and he let out a weak, "Oh," upon impact. He slid down to the forest floor, unconscious, leg bent at an unnatural angle, rifle discarded a few feet away.

My legs buckled and my vision turned gray for a few moments from the intense burst of magic. I fell to my knees, my hands sinking into the mud.

When I was able to focus again, out of the corner of my eye I spied the beautiful Palomino horse Whitaker had ridden, still saddled, chomping on tall grasses and watching us with a disinterested stare. I roused myself and *pushed* to the horse. *I need your help,* I told her from my mind to hers, summoning her to come to me. I felt her hesitate, then give in. As she came over, I felt that familiar swoosh of darkness come over for me, and my sight went black for a moment as I sat onto the ground, exhausted.

"Eve!" Peggy whispered. "How did you do that? Are you okay?" I opened my eyes to see Peggy kneeling beside me, shaking my shoulder a bit, and I recovered a little, my eyesight still a bit blurry.

"The bastard deserved it," I said, my voice hoarse from fatigue. "I wasn't going to let him take anyone else down."

I sat up, and wiped my muddy hands on my tattered skirt. I

looked over at Logan, but he was still out cold. Meanwhile the pretty mare came trotting over. Peggy helped me stand up.

"This is Whitaker's horse; I asked her to come and help us," I replied. I let the mare smell me for a moment. She nickered quietly, her deep brown eyes staring at me.

"Come and help us?!" Peggy repeated, her eyes wide with astonishment.

"I know it sounds mad... but Peggy, can you manage to keep on? We need to stick with the plan from before..."

Peggy nodded sadly. The poor thing was trembling all over - maybe from being cold, or in shock, or likely both. I offered my hands as a cradle and she stepped up and swung her right leg over the horse. She settled herself on the saddle and gathered up the reins. "Thank you for not giving up on me. I'd be dead by now, if not for you."

"Nonsense," I said. "We need to see this through and stick together." I reached out and took her hands in mine. "Please forgive me - I am so sorry, I was unable to protect your sisters."

"Not your fault," Peggy said, through chattering teeth. "Nan had the right of it: we shan't feel guilty for the wrongdoings of these evil men."

I stood still beside Peggy and the Palomino. Above us, three ravens hovered, keeping watch over both of us. We eyed our destination for several moments from behind the screen of trees and shrubs. The barn door was open, but we saw no sign of any stable hands or groundsmen. Meanwhile, the mansion's windows reflected the cold silver gray of the clouds. There was no light on inside that I could detect.

"I don't see anyone. The place is dark and quiet as a tomb," I said.

"Neither do I," said Peggy "but I wouldn't put it past that worm Maxwell to come crawling out from some hole in the ground."

"Ha! Well, if he shows his face, he'll regret it," I said darkly.

Peggy nodded. "I'll stay out of sight as much as I can in the barn. When you're ready for me, I'll meet you at the front door and help get you and your Ma up into the wagon."

"Let's get going," I said.

Peggy gave the mare a gentle squeeze and began to trot across the open grass to the stables, while I took off towards the mansion. My heart pounded in my throat as I raced across the wet grass. Every moment in the open felt like an eternity.

Chapter 28

Blood And Bone

Eve

I scrambled across the grass, fear racing through my chest, as swift as I could. Not an easy task, considering how exhausted and drained I felt.

The mansion soared up high against the lead-gray sky, malevolent and brooding. When I reached the servants' entrance, to my extreme relief, there was no sign of anyone. I held my breath while I turned the bronze handle of the servants' entry door. It swung open without a sound, thank goodness; the hallway before me dimly lit and silent as a mausoleum.

I glanced behind me, but I lost the sight of Peggy and the horse as they moved behind the barn. Shaking with fear, I tiptoed my way down the hallway. The silence was eery and oppressive. Normally, the manse was a bustle with activity - it took many hardworking folks to make a place this enormous run well. While I was grateful that none of the other servants were here to be tortured with us, I also felt a profound sense of sadness that we Irish lasses were considered both attractive targets and entirely disposable. I wondered whether Mrs. Doyle knew or suspected anything; the woman was sharp as a tack, so it was hard for me to believe that she had worked there for years with no inkling.

I crept down the last turn of the hallway, and peered around the corner into the kitchen. The hearth fire glowed orange and yellow, giving off a delicious warmth and casting shadows against the walls. Steam billowed out and up into the air from the black iron water kettle suspended over the fire. The bubbling water and crackle of the fire were the only sounds. Pale gold-skinned apples and more of Bette's baked berry scones sat waiting in silver serving baskets on the counter. My stomach rumbled so loud I was sure if anyone were nearby they'd have heard it. I ran across the kitchen, grabbed a couple of apples and scones and threw them in my dress pocket, and then took the cellar key to unlock the door.

Just as the lock clicked open, a hunting horn wailed outside - it sounded close. *Damnation!* The men must be heading back to the mansion. It meant that Peggy and I were on borrowed time. I grabbed the lantern and raced down the stairs.

At the bottom, I stepped into something dark and sticky and an unpleasant odor filled my nose. *Ugh!*

I raised up my lantern and realized I'd stepped into a puddle - of Bette's blood. Her body was splayed across the lowest steps, her neck gashed open, blood having pooled and congealed beneath her. I took one of the scones out of my pocket and pressed it to my nostrils as I passed over her; the pastry helped a little to block the smell of death.

Judging from the fact that Bette hadn't moved from where she'd fallen, I hoped that Isaiah hadn't yet found his wife. I knew he would be devastated, too - the man had worshipped her, despite her prickly personality. My friend Dina would grieve her sister's loss bitterly.

Now that I understood the vile arrangement the Rennards had made with the Franklins, I realized Isaiah had just been protective of his sister by not letting her come work at Greythorne. Probably that was also why Bette had been so unfriendly towards me: why bother to get to know folks who wouldn't stick around for long, or might end up at the wrong end of a bullet or arrow?

I held the lantern high, bracing for the sight of my mother's corpse. Bloodstains and bloody handprints marred the floor and walls, but there was no sign of her. Where on earth was she?! I made my way along the shelves, and whispered "Ma, it's me".

Fire popped, water boiled, but no response came.

I peered around the nooks and crannies of the stores. On the opposite wall, the doors of one of the great furnaces were swung open, and as I approached, soft eery whispers filled the air. I could not make out any words. It was mysterious but I was soon distracted as -

Out of the darkness, a pair of empty eye sockets emerged first in my candle's light, followed by the outlines of three partial skeletons laid on the stones before the silent furnace. Two of the three had no skulls.

On any other day, the sight would have scared the daylight right out of me. But after what I had seen in the forest, I was almost too exhausted to react.

Someone had laid them out on the ground. But why? I drew close enough to examine the bones, especially noting the obtuse width of the pelvic angles - which confirmed that these skeletons had belonged to women.

"What did the bastards do to you?" I whispered. I lifted the lantern to illuminate the inside the furnace. Nothing but ashes. My mind and gut roiled with disgust and horror.

The second furnace, lit and generating heat, stood beside its frigid twin. I considered opening the furnace door and looking inside, but my courage failed me. Even if my mother or another body lay in there, there was nothing I would be able to do, and the sight would haunt my nightmares forever more.

The rest of the cellar looked to be in order, except for a smattering of blood drops leading to the farthest wall, cloaked in utter darkness. A draft of cold air blew towards me, making the flame in my lantern gutter and sway. Stepping into the darkness, I headed into the draft. After a few moments, I began to see a vertical line of soft light emerging from a crack in the wall. No, not a crack: a doorframe. My right hand reached across the wall and found purchase on the ledge of a hidden door. Gripping tight with my fingers, I carefully pulled it open.

Inky blackness stared back at me. I stepped inside a small, cool space.

Despite all I had seen so far, the horrors that awaited me within stole my breath once again.

The stone walled rectangular room was the size of a smallish bedroom, but everywhere were the hides and bones and innards of every conceivable creature. On the walls were iron sconces holding oil lanterns whose yellowish light flickered with the air movement from the door opening, and my entry. In the center was a wood trestle table, marked with blood and grime, and replete with menacing metal tools. Most were foreign to me, but I noticed a shiny saw, several scalpels, and a large hypodermic needle. On top a taxidermy project looked to be under way. A deer head rested on the table, with a wooden plaque next to it, materials for filling the head, and elixirs to treat the skin and bone neatly arrayed next to it. The stench of chemicals, alcohol, animal entrails and blood made breathing almost intolerable.

Wood shelves were mounted against the walls between each wall sconce. One shelf held an array of animal skulls - bird, deer, rabbit, fox and more. Three more shelves held assortments of bones arranged by type and shape - vertebrae in one pile, long bones like femurs in another, a third with scapulas and pelvic bones and other irregular shapes. On the center wall opposite the entry, was a collection of human skulls all precisely positioned. And again beneath that shelf, were other human skeletal bones arranged by type and neatly piled up. A third set of shelves held tools, wax, molds and a variety of strange shapes. A closer look at the glass jars filled with murky liquid revealed various organs floating within - one was filled with eyeballs, the optic nerves still attached at the back like wrinkled pinkish strings. A second jar was filled with dark maroon kidneys. A third contained tongues -they arched and curled around each other, the tastebuds raised like tiny bumps on the tongues' surfaces.

I slid down to the floor in despair. My mother was nowhere to be seen, and I could not sense her presence. I was too late - her body must have been moved to prepare her for the same grim appalling nightmare that these other human beings had endured. The nausea and terror coalesced within me into a hard ball of rage and hatred that stuck in my gullet.

Dozens. There were dozens of victims. These monsters...

I realized my plans had to change. Knowing now what these men did, there was no way I could just flee this place. Even if I survived, they would continue to terrorize women next year and then again every year after that. I couldn't live with myself if I allowed that to happen. Going to the local authorities would be futile - men like the Rennards were above the law, simply by their wealth and power. They could and would pay people off with minimal difficulty. And migrant folks like us, whether Irish, Italian, African or Jamaican - we were all just grist for the entertainment of these obscenely wealthy white men. The injustice raked at me.

I knelt down before the shelves of the dead and prayed.

"Morrigan, oh Morrigan, hear my prayers.

Grant me vision and power to fight evil in this dark place.

Guide me in seeking revenge against those who desecrate the bodies of women -

I place my heart, my mind, my soul and my body in your capable hands

as I wage this battle against evil, in your name."

As I rose up, a shimmer of light and power surged through me. I raised the lantern high and exited the ossuary and the cellar, climbing up the stairs to the kitchen. There was no sign of life as I hung the lantern back on its hook, and crossed the white-tiled room. I paused and strained to listen for any sound. To my dismay, I heard footsteps coming down the hall, and someone whistling outside the kitchen.

Heart racing in my chest, I duck-walked my way out the kitchen's back door towards Mrs. Doyle's office to avoid being seen.

Aside from the slightest creak of the office door, I made no noise as I slipped into the nearly-dark room, which was a well-organized and immaculate space off the kitchen hallway. The room had little decoration, save a white ceramic vase holding a few pink peonies. A photo of a younger version of herself and her family from ages ago stood faded and yellowing in a pewter frame on the desk. My steps took me over to the wooden desk and I quietly pulled the drawers open two at a time. Ledgers, note pads, writing implements and ink, a bronze letter opener, corkscrews, pocket chains, all neatly organized. No money. *Damnation.*

The lower drawer on the left was locked...she had some keys hanging on a hook under the desk, so I tried each one. No luck! I was not surprised, considering how my day had gone so far. Frustrated, I grabbed a bronze letter opener from the top of the desk, and slid the tip inside the lock. I jiggled it carefully from side to side, my hands sweating and my ears on high alert for anyone nearby...

At last, the lock gave in!

Inside the drawer was a decent stack of paper money and coins. A brown leather drawstring pouch in the same drawer would do nicely as a purse. After gathering up the cash, I closed the drawers and made everything look as I'd found it, then headed back into the kitchen.

With no sign of my mother's body, and the money secured, there was only one thing left to do: but the thought filled me with anxiety.

Would Saskia believe me? Would she come with me, away from her family? Away from wealth and power?

I was weighing the risk of searching for her, when I heard a scream outside.

Peggy!!

Looking around for a weapon, I spied one and grabbed the first thing that came to hand: Bette's beloved machete. I tore out of the house at full speed, determined to protect Peggy and take revenge.

Saskia would have to wait.

Chapter 29

A Twist Of The Knife

Saskia

Devil and I had kept up pretty well with the foxhounds as they worked to find Robert. Even when we couldn't see them snuffling under bushes, their barks and yips guided us to follow. Finally, they emerged onto a trail, and we were able to quickly catch up with them. We followed at a trot behind the dogs, as they sniffed their way across the terrain. Finally the lead hound barked twice, raised his tail high, and took off at a rapid clip. It was their signal that the leader had found its quarry. The rest of the hounds followed, and Devil and I picked up our pace. The dogs followed the scent trail with intense focus until we entered a more open area.

The dogs led us to a man, whose right leg was bent an unnatural angle beneath a tree. I pulled Devil to a stop. It was Robert, lying unconscious in the mud and moss under a wide-branched oak. The dogs were snuffling and stalking around him, but a quick command from me hushed them into sitting still on their haunches.

I hopped down and grabbed the Winchester. Slung across my back the rifle was a heavy nuisance, but better safe than sorry.

I knelt down beside Robert. The dogs' yapping hadn't roused

him. His eyes were closed, and he hadn't sensed my approach at all. Although my feelings had been deeply hurt by his duplicitous attempts to manipulate me, there were more pressing issues to deal with. He was a guest of my father's, and it would be far better for me to not burn bridges, so I mustered up my most caring facial expression and gently placed my hand upon his shoulder. I shook him gently and uttered his name.

No response - until suddenly, "Don't touch me, you bitch!" he screamed. He slapped my hand away with a feisty defensiveness, before his eyes were fully open.

What on earth?! Shocked, I rocked back on my heels and paused. *"Bitch?"* Who the heck did he think he was speaking to? Despite my best intentions, hot boiling anger bristled up within me. It was clear to me that Robert's true nature was horrid. I mean, what sort of cad would dare to talk to any woman in such an appalling manner? Not to mention take part in hunting, raping and murdering....

I took a breath to calm myself, and then forced myself to speak soft and low to him.

"Robert, it's okay. It's me, Saskia."

He focused and recognized me, smiling with relief. "Oh, thank goodness!" Robert said. A moment later, he tried to sit up, but cried out as he accidentally moved his broken leg. I put a hand on his shoulder to stop him from moving in a way that could increase his pain or injuries.

"You need to keep still. You're hurt," I said.

"My leg is killing me," he replied.

"Hold on," I said, "Try not to move, but I will help you get more comfortable." I lifted his head and shoulders so that he could better see and tucked some fallen leaves under his head as a makeshift pillow.

He reached out his gloved hand and I gave him mine. He kissed it and brought it to his chest, but he clutched my hand far too tight within his giant paw. I did not appreciate my hand being crushed, and had to bite my tongue to stop from snapping at him.

"Robert, you're hurting me," I said with as much faux kindness as I could muster.

"Oh, I'm sorry! Sometimes, I don't realize how strong my grip is." He let go in a jiffy. I gently wiggled my fingers to restore blood flow.

"I don't feel well at all," he said. "I have a horrible headache and when I look at you, I find that I'm seeing double."

"What on earth happened?" I asked.

"It was that she-devil servant of yours, Eve! She's a witch!" he said.

Aha! So Eve *was here* on the property! Father had indeed lied to me.

"A witch?" I repeated. "Why do you call her such a thing?" I asked.

"I know, it's difficult to fathom," he said. "But Saskia, you must believe me! She's killed both Whitaker and Carnavoy. Don't ask me how, I know not, but I've seen their corpses. When I came upon her, she waved her hands in some sort of incantation, and the next thing I knew, I was flying backwards in the air and hit a tree."

Carnavoy was definitely dead. Could Eve have somehow caused the horse to throw the man off? And what about his head being trampled? Perhaps that wasn't intentional, but just a result of Eve redirecting the horse?

I had seen Eve interact with birds and even with that rattlesnake when we first met...Perhaps her abilities extended to connecting with all sorts of animals? My mind spun in circles... Whitaker being torn up by our dogs? It had made no sense that our hunting hounds would maul; they were trained to sight, scent, flush or retrieve, but *not* to *kill* unless commanded.

What if she had...?

While Robert was portraying himself to me as an innocent victim, I knew what the men had been up to. If Eve were hunted and her life threatened, would she not use whatever powers she had at hand to protect herself and eliminate her attackers?

When we were in my bath the first night, Eve's emotions had

caused the lights in my room to flicker and the water in the tub to rise and fall. The lights had flickered again when she was pinched while serving our guests. What if her magical powers included the ability to alter aspects of the weather, like the wind or light?

My mind swirled as I began to realize just how magical and powerful Eve might be. I cast my mind on all of the little moments I had witnessed. Eve was no ordinary woman. She possessed extraordinary powers, and it seemed as though she'd just begun to harness them and take her power.

Eve really was amazing. With Eve by my side, we would be invincible.

I had to admit, I was sorry I'd missed seeing her fling Robert. Lying here, weak and pathetic, with his broken leg, he seemed like a badly behaved cur, who'd gotten what he deserved.

"Don't worry, Saskia my dear," he said in a most patronizing tone. "I will protect you from this evil peril. And later when I am healed, we can hunt this witch together!"

I had to stifle a laugh. This was the dreamboat my father wanted me to marry?! Was Robert really serious? How on earth would the man protect me, when he couldn't even defend himself, and was now incapacitated? His right leg was dreadfully broken. He'd be lucky if he didn't have to walk with a cane for the rest of his life.

I was no pitiful damsel in distress. And he was certainly no prince in shining armor, who'd arrived to rescue me. In fact, I could see now that life with him would be utterly intolerable. I was tired of men who believed that without a man at my side, my life would be empty and devoid of meaning. I was even more exhausted by men controlling how I should live.

"You must watch out - she is dangerous," he said.

And with that statement, I suddenly realized the truth of the situation, and the opportunity that lay before me.

"As am I," I said.

A flash of silver winked in the air as I drew my blade, then thrust it beneath the ribcage, angling upwards to sever the aorta and then strike the heart. His eyes widened in surprise. Blood sprayed up into the air as Robert gurgled and gasped.

I leaned in and spoke clearly, so that he would hear and register each and every one of my words. "I heard you jape with my father about pretending to be a progressive, so that I would be fooled into marriage, only to submit to your will afterwards. I heard you tell Emil that I was a mere a broodmare waiting for you to dominate me."

I paused, as Robert's eyes reflected that he'd understood every word I'd said.

"Let me be clear - I am in charge of my own life and my own destiny. I will not allow any man to dictate how I may live my life."

He stared at me in shock, then began to cough up blood. My aim was true. Within a few moments, his heart stopped beating, and he was gone.

Unlike my brother, I didn't believe in unnecessary suffering or in taking appalling trophies. A quick end was most compassionate. I wiped my blade clean on Robert's jacket, then stood up and glanced down at my outfit. Unfortunately, some of the man's blood had sprayed across my shirt and jodhpurs. I shrugged and was surprised to realize that I no longer cared whether my clothes were stained or pristine. What mattered was my life, and how I would live it.

I went back to Devil and untied him. I climbed back up, and gently nudged him to a trot. A huge sigh of relief passed through me as I realized I had eliminated a weighty worry, thanks to my seizing a fortuitous opportunity before any hesitation could stop me. The man had been even more dreadful than I could have predicted, and if this was the best of the lot, according to my father, then I was clear about what I must do.

What was it with these men? That they are so certain they know best and should own and control our lives? I was tired of the manipulation, and determined to show Father and Teddy that I was just as capable of being ruthless and efficient. As for Robert, I could easily blame his death on the now-dead Fitzgerald girl.

I climbed back onto Devil, and whistled the dogs to come with me. I had a fresh goal for this day - find Eve and convince her to leave the estate with me.

Hiring Eve had been most fortuitous. Not only was she an excellent personal maid, she possessed beauty and unique power. She would be the perfect solution to my problems. And obviously, my rescuing her from being hunted, would lead her to be even more devoted to me than she already was. With her, I would be unstoppable. No man could tell me how to live my life. It was the most tantalizing realization...

We would be able to travel wherever we wished. Paris, Rome, Florence, Madrid, Tokyo, Hong Kong - the world would be our oyster. A new vista of possibility stretched before me. I would no longer need my father or my brother for protection. Eve would live a life of leisure and be elevated to the status her talents and beauty deserved. And if danger arose, she would be my shield and protectress.

And after seeing the hunt, I had plenty of leverage. I certainly did not want or need to ruin their lives, but I finally could prevent my family from ruining mine. And if push came to shove...

"Ahhhh!" A woman's voice screamed in the distance and interrupted my thoughts. I turned Devil in the direction of her voice, and urged him to fly down the trail. I prayed that it was not Eve who was crying out for help....

Chapter 30

A Conspiracy Of Ravens

Saskia

Devil and I flew all the back to my home; my heart pounding with with anger and fear. What if that was Eve I'd heard screaming? What if Father and Teddy had tried to corner her? Maybe they still didn't realize how dangerous she could be? It was strange to realize that my loyalties were split between my family, and a young woman I had known for less than a month... I wasn't sure what I was going to find once I got there, and even less sure of how to best proceed.

I got to the tree line and pulled Devil to a wall of cypress trees that acted as a wind break protecting Greythorne. The dense green branches would hide his presence. I didn't really think that Devil was in any danger, but I wouldn't want to take any risks as far as he was concerned. A horse of his breeding and pedigree was priceless. It was really the one and only good thing that had come from Father's acquaintance with Robert.

Once I was on the ground, I rushed forward under the shrubbery until I laid eyes on the source of the screams. It wasn't Eve - thank goodness! It was the buxom Fitzgerald girl. Peggy, I think? Though not my usual type, I'd always enjoyed eyeing her voluptuous curves as she bustled about the mansion. Now Peggy found herself being thrown about by Father's manservant, Maxwell.

I lay flat on the ground, rifle at the ready. I slowed my breath and held as still as I could manage.

The man had always been an undeniable creep, but Father had always insisted on turning a blind eye to Maxwell's off-putting behavior. I knew that it was no mere coincidence, when Maxwell would just "happen" to come upon me at the lake while I swam. I'd also seen him linger in the bushes outside the servants' bathhouse. He could be slimy and obsequious when needed, and my father valued loyalty above all other virtues or vices.

On more than one occasion I had thought about complaining to Father about the man. The only reason I hadn't done so, was due to Maxwell being quite discreet regarding my personal peccadillos. And likely also for my brother's. It occurred to me that Father probably knew at least some of Teddy's quirks, and Maxwell's trustworthiness would be worth a great deal to Father. And clearly Maxwell was all too happy to assist Father and Teddy with their foul hunts and other detestable behavior. Such loyalty from a servant would be of the utmost value to my family.

But here, out of my father's view, Maxwell had apparently decided that he was entitled to partake in some of the 'female delicacies' of the day. His face was utterly gleeful as he wrestled Peggy. His arms were wrapped around her, as he tried to force her onto the ground, but the woman was not having it.

"Oh no ye don't, ye bastard!" she yelled, and pummeled the man's bald head with her fists. Rather than being meek and timid, she was doing her best to fight the man off. When he did finally tip her to the ground, Peggy flailed her legs in the air, and pushed hard against him. Quite impressive really. I had to give her some credit for being tougher than most in her position. I lifted up the rifle and sighted along the barrel.

"Behave, you little bitch!" Maxwell snarled as he struggled to get her to submit. Old Maxwell had bitten off more than he can chew.

An amusing thought. In truth, the bonny lass was giving the man a fair fight. He clapped one of his hands over her face to stop the screaming. Big mistake: Peggy quite rightly opened her mouth and bit down hard on the man's hand. Well done!

Maxwell screamed, and let go of Peggy as though he had accidentally grabbed a hot poker. Peggy rolled away from him, and spat something out of her mouth. She scrambled away from his reach, then rose up. She spun her eyes and head all around the grounds in terror, then startled to stumble away.

Meanwhile, Maxwell hopped around, mad as a hatter, clutching his injured hand with his other and wailing obscenities.

"Faaaack! Ye fecking whore! I'll skin ye alive, ye miserable bitch!"

He paused his invectives and held his hand up to examine an index finger that was one knuckle shorter than it should have been. Blood streamed down his arm, dripping into the mud. With his good hand, he reached into his trouser pocket, produced a kerchief and wrapped up his injured digit.

While he'd been fussing, Peggy rose up from the ground, turned and started to run towards the barn.

Maxwell, business with his hand put aside for the moment, looked up and realized Peggy had almost gotten away. He raced after her, pulling his gun out.

She'd almost made it all the way to the stable door when he fired.

Peggy jerked, took two wobbly steps, then toppled to the ground. I couldn't tell where the bullet had struck. Her hands and feet scrambled and scraped at the ground in desperation.

Maxwell jogged over to her, flipped her over, and pinned her down with one arm across her chest. With his uninjured hand, he flipped up her tatty skirts, and unbuttoned his fly. Enough was enough for me - I cocked my rifle and aimed at Maxwell's rump.

Crack! I fired and felt the rifle butt slam its recoil into my right shoulder. Beyond the smoke from the rifle I looked ahead. Darn! I had missed the scoundrel! At least the shot had convinced him to hop off the woman and lay low on his belly, looking over his shoulder, trying to figure out where the shot had come from. I prepared to reload, when all of the sudden, an enormous shadow crossed the sky above us.

Gosh almighty! I looked up and was gobsmacked. The largest cluster of ravens I'd ever witnessed swarmed and circled overhead, cawing as they drew lower and lower. My mind flashed back in time to the day I arrived at the Tarrytown Inn with Aunt Winnie, and ravens flew down and accosted us. In a flash, I realized I knew what that meant - *she* must be nearby. Maxwell's luck was about to turn direly against him.

Maxwell glanced up at the sudden darkness overhead, then shook his head. The man, clearly driven by his most base animal instincts, had decided that regardless, he was determined to finish raping the poor injured woman. He clambered back upon poor Peggy.

The front door of the mansion flew open with a bang! Out came Eve! She ran down the steps, her long copper hair unbound, a machete in her right hand. She was a glorious sight to see as she moved at lightning speed towards Maxwell and Peggy.

I held my breath as Eve reached them and swept the machete down, slashing both of the man's Achilles tendons. He screamed to high heavens, and spun around to see the source of his attack.

What a woman! I was thrilled by her courage and strength.

"Let go of her, you foul beast!" Eve cried.

Peggy took the opportunity to push him off and claw herself away from him.

"Peggy - come with me! You need to get out of here!" Eve commanded. Eve kicked Maxwell in the side and he balled up his body in pain.

Eve leaned down and offered a hand to Peggy. She helped her friend stand up, then turned Peggy and pushed her into the barn. She limped inside.

I watched Eve's kindness towards her friend, and it warmed my heart. If she could be so kind and caring to someone so unimportant, I would likely be treated with all the adoration and warmth I had ever dreamt of. Unlike the social snobbery of the women in my circle, someone like Eve would put me first and would not care for petty selfish things like the latest dress or chapeau.

While Eve was helping Peggy to escape, Maxwell pulled his wits together. I did not see him draw his pistol out from a leather holster on his right hip. I lay on the ground so gripped by what I was watching, that I forgot my rifle, and that I had the ability to intervene.

CRACK! Maxwell fired his pistol at Eve. The bastard!

Eve leapt and swerved to the right to avoid injury, but not quickly enough. The bullet grazed her left hip. Instead of a girl's cry of dismay, Eve let forth a roar of fury. Far from stopping her, Maxwell had sealed his fate.

Peggy, now on horseback, rode over to Eve, saying, "Oy Eve, come with me!" she cried, reaching her hand down to pull Eve up. Blood flowed down Peggy's right thigh and leg, and the woman looked white as a sheet. The mare sensed the tension. She pawed the ground with her forelegs and shook her head, impatient to get going.

Eve looked at Peggy and shook her head. "I need to stay and finish this," she said. "But you've got to get away - now! Ride as far and fast as possible and do not stop. Find someone who will believe you." Eve slapped the horse's rump.

I watched Peggy and the mare tear down the path towards the main road, away from Greythorne.

Eve limped towards Maxwell, her wounds dripping blood. The man was rolling on the ground crying in pain. Between his moans and groans, he threw an assortment of vile curses towards her.

Eve leaned over him and the ravens rose up above them. "Who's crying now?" she asked him, anger quivering in her voice.

Suddenly he sat up and lunged at her. Somehow he managed to get his hands around Eve's neck and he began to choke her. Enough! I cocked my rifle and fired at Maxwell.

CRACK!

Damn! I missed the man again, but he and Eve both heard the shot and paused. It was just the interruption she needed. Eve raised her arms and her hair began to float upwards, as a strong wind began to blow. Her eyes sparked with flashes of electricity.

"Damn you to hell!" Eve screamed. She commanded the black-feathered beasties to descend upon at Maxwell. He looked up and squealed in fear.

There were truly more ravens in the sky than I had ever seen in one place. It seemed as though every black bird in the Hudson Valley had been summoned. They grew close and formed an ebony morass. A shifting and foreboding shape of a woman in the air - with flowing hair and gown. I rubbed my eyes to make sure I wasn't imagining things. The feminine image hovered over Maxwell for a moment. His jaw went slack and eyes were wide with fear as he stared up at the birds in their formation. With a sudden cry from Eve, the birds launched a terrifying attack on the man, with beaks open and claws at the ready.

"Argh! Gedoff me!" He screamed as he tried to bat them off. But the ravens were unstoppable - they tore and picked at him with ferocious intensity, pulling strips of skin away with their orange beaks, and ripping his clothes and body with their talons. For the next moments, I had to avert my eyes.

When his screams died down, I looked again. He lay collapsed on the ground, his clothes ripped and ragged, his face a bloody ruin, his eyes empty black sockets. The birds had pulled back, then soared down together.

The birds were so thick and countless, I could scarcely see Maxwell at all. They began to lift him with their beaks and claws. The birds carried him into the barn, and Eve followed, guiding them ahead.

I ran up towards the barn door in time to see Eve direct the birds to bring Maxwell over the opening in the barn floor. They lined his body up directly over the open trap door and then let go. He fell, screaming down into the cellar, the sounds of his bones cracking and a heavy thud as he crashed down to the floor. I shivered at the sound.

The ravens rose up in unison and screeched as they soared past me out the barn door and back up to the sky.

Eve staggered over and leaned in and said, "Enjoy a taste of your own medicine." She closed the trap door and locked the latch. His cries were silenced by the door's closure.

I was utterly enthralled by everything I had just witnessed. It was beyond anything I had even imagined possible.

"Eve!" I called out as I ran to her. She turned to me, startled. I was a bit disappointed that I couldn't tell if she was happy to see me or not.

"Did Peggy get away?" she asked me, her voice gravelly and weak, just before I reached her.

"Yes, yes, I think so," I said.

"Good." Eve nodded, then collapsed onto the ground. I leant over her and touched her face, but she did not respond.

"Eve are you there?" I asked. "Can you hear me?"

There was no answer. Eve's eyes were shut, and her breath was steady. She must have completely exhausted herself. She'd been hunted and wounded, and had ended up utterly drained and passed out. I sat down beside her, legs crisscrossed in front of me, and took a moment. Even in her bedraggled state, she was beautiful. Her face, peaceful at the moment, beckoned towards me - calling me into a new and entirely unpredictable future.

As I sat there debating our next steps, I heard the sounds of horse hooves galloping towards us. My time to take a stand and make my choice was fast approaching. For the first time in my life, I was afraid.

Part Four

Chapter 31

The Phantom Queen Rises

Eve

"Eve. Eve, lass." I was tranquil and at peace, deep in my sleep...when I heard a familiar voice call my name. I tried to open my eyes, but I was so very, very tired. My mind felt as though I were floating adrift upon a cotton sea. Trying to wake up seemed at the very least undesirable, if not impossible. Still... someone was tugging on my consciousness.

"Eve, can you hear me?"

Finally, with a groan and a stretch from my head to my toes, I pulled my mind together and opened my eyes. Someone was holding my hands and calling my name over and over. As I raised my eyelids, a familiar shape grew sharp.

"Ma?!"

I tried to sit up, but pain shot through my shoulder and my hip. My whole body ached with pain and fatigue. Ow!

"Don't try to sit up," Ma said. "You've been through the wringer and used so much power, it's wiped you out."

"Am I...? Are you...?" I asked.

"No, you're still very much alive," she said.

She didn't answer my second question. A wave of sadness swept over me as I recalled the day's events. My eyes brimmed with scalding hot tears that spilled down my cheeks. My shoulder throbbed, and the pain in my side was sharp and burning.

"I failed," I whispered. "I failed you, I failed Nan, I failed Frances, I failed myself."

Ma reached and took my hands in hers. Her rough and calloused hands felt so comforting and familiar. "You didn't fail me," she said. "I failed you. I protected you too much. I believed it was the right thing to do. Instead it made you naïve and vulnerable."

"I don't blame you," I said. "It was my fault that Da died."

Ma shook her head. "No Eve, 'twas just an accident and you were just a child. No use in looking back with regret. You cannot stay here. The men will kill you. You need to fight. You need to live. You need to wake up..."

Ma tried to pull her hands away from me, but I gripped on tight.

"If I wake, will you still be here?"

"I'll always be part of you, my *Aoife*. My blood, your Nan's - we are all connected. All the way back home..."

I opened my eyes and took in where I was. I was under a large weeping willow by the bank of a river, emerald green grass all around me. The soft rolling hills of the Irish countryside surrounded me, and the fresh scent of recent rainfall filled my nostrils.

Ma rose to go. As my eyes focused, I watched her grow taller than she'd ever been in real life. Her face and clothes dropped away like a watercolor-painted façade washed away in the rain...

From within a streaming light, a woman emerged. She was hooded in blood-red robes, with fiery long curls and deep green eyes. When she spoke, her voice's timbre was like aural honey – a harmonious lilt with a bottom note of iron-hard strength.

"Who are you?" I asked.

" I am known by many names, but you know me as *Mor-Rioghain*," she replied.

The Phantom Queen...

"I didn't ask for any of this," I said. The sound of my own voice surprised me – it was sharper and stronger than I had ever heard it before.

"No one ever does," the spirit woman replied. "But that doesn't change the reality. You were given a gift, a power that no man can ever wield. But what use does power have, if not used in the service of the powerless? If you don't protect those who are ill treated by ravenous evil folk, then who will?"

"How can I possibly make a difference? My parents are gone, my friends are gone. I'm all alone. Life has been hard and painful. What's the point of continuing to struggle?"

"The mantle is heavy, but you have the shoulders and tempera-ment to bear the weight, *Aoife*. You are no coward, and your life has value. You have the power to heal the sick, and protect the weak..."

"But where do I go from here? Even if I survive, I'll be a hunted, wanted woman..."

"There are others who would wish for you to succeed and who would long for the help and healing you could offer them. They are out there, waiting for you, though they do not yet realize it. Fight like hell and come back, come back to the land that birthed you. If you can find your way, I will be waiting for you here..."

A bright light behind the *Morrigan* grew in intensity, until I had to squint and close my eyes against the light of a blazing hot sun.

And then, just like that she was gone. I shivered, alone in the darkness once again.

Chapter 32

All Her Pretty Tricks

Saskia

I sat calmly next to Eve, who was out cold on the ground. I'd bound her hands with a piece of fabric--Robert's hanky, actually--that I had ripped into strips and tied around her wrists. The measure had been mostly for appearances, as the girl was unconscious. But I also knew the men would consider Eve dangerous, and may even want to shoot her on the spot. So, my efforts were more to protect her from them, as to protect me.

Father cantered up astride the mighty Samson, crossbow raised and a wild look in his eyes. Teddy and Emil circled their horses around Eve, pistols pointed at the unconscious lass.

"Oh thank heavens! Saskia, my dear! Are you alright?" Father asked as he stopped his horse, his gaze snapping directly to the blood on my clothing. He leapt down and ran to me, his hair and clothes tousled and unkempt, and a look of fear in his eyes. It was the latter that chilled me to the bone... I'd never seen Father afraid of anything.

"I'm okay Father, I'm not hurt," I said. Father held me by my shoulders, and looked me over from head to toe, then gave me a big bear hug. "If anything had happened to you..." He paused and shuddered.

Now that he knew I was okay, Father pivoted from worry to fury.

"What the hell do you think you're doing being here today, of all days?!" Father roared at me. "You deliberately disobeyed my instructions that you should be gone from the property. This hunt is no suitable place for my daughter."

"But Father, I have no idea ...what's going on? It's just a hunt, no?" I asked, my voice ringing with innocence.

"The day has been utterly catastrophic!" Father proclaimed.

"What on Earth?" I asked, wondering how much the men already knew.

Teddy looked at me. "We found Robert dead in the woods; he'd been stabbed in the chest," he said.

"What?! No! You mustn't joke about such things, Teddy!" I said, my voice wavering and trembling with would-be shock.

Father came over and placed his hand on my shoulder to comfort me. "Unfortunately, your brother is not joking," he said.

"What could possibly have happened to him?" I asked Father, sniffing and widening my eyes for effect.

"Must have been the witch," Teddy added, although he gave me a most peculiar look.

I fell to my knees and clapped my hands over my eyes. "Oh, Robert," I said, as I sniffed back tears. Though Father no doubt thought I was crying for Robert's loss, it was actually relief from an unwanted and undesirable marriage to a vile and pompous boor.

Father offered me a hug. "I'm so sorry my dear," he said. "He was a fine young man."

As he looked past me, Father's eyes turned to slits, brows contracted and jaw clenched, as he gazed at Eve, passed out on the ground. He drew his pistol, then kicked Eve in the leg with the toe of his riding boot. She didn't rouse, thank goodness. "Is she dead?" he asked.

"No, just passed out. It seems likely she's lost a lot of blood," I pointed to Eve's bloody shoulder and thigh wounds.

"We should finish her," said Teddy. *Click!* My brother cocked his pistol and aim it directly at Eve's head.

I rose up and flung myself across Eve's body. "Teddy, no!" I shouted, hoping to strike a mixture of dismay and authority over my younger brother.

"Get out of the way!" Teddy snapped at me. But I refused, determined to protect Eve.

"Mademoiselle Saskia, perhaps you do not realize..." Emil chimed in. "I am afraid that your maidservant is a most fearful and dangerous creature. You are wise to have tied her up." He leaned over from his horse to Teddy and put his hand on Teddy's to encourage him to lower the pistol.

Father reached down to pull me away from Eve. He was flabbergasted with dismay at my desire to protect her. "Did you not hear your brother? That witch or demon, or whatever the hell she is, somehow has managed to murder Robert, and my dear friends, Andy, James and Thomas, four of the wealthiest men in the country."

"But how on Earth could she do such terrible things?" I asked. "She's just a maid."

I ignored Father's outstretched hand.

"Saskia, have you gone mad?" Father asked, his voice rising in anger.

"No Father, please stop and listen to me. As you can see, she is unconscious and not a danger to any of us at the moment. If all you say is true, it seems a pitiful waste to just kill her, when if she is truly as powerful as you say, there could be great value in keeping her alive and using her powers for our benefit," I said.

Emil came up next to Father and looked down at me. "Your daughter is quite wise, Theodore," he said. "Where I come from, this woman would be revered for her tremendous power. What you call a witch, I would call a *caplata*, a priestess who can speak to the spirit world. No reason we could not take her power for ourselves...A woman with such strong gifts is unique, and her life blood should not be wasted. I know a ritual from the islands, that would allow us to take her abilities for our own use," he added.

Father looked at Emil. "What kind of ritual?" he asked.

"It is simple but powerful," Emil replied. "It is not commonly known or shared, but in my family the knowledge has been passed down from generation to generation. It is why I have been able to achieve such success."

He looked up at the sky which was beginning to turn towards sunset. The pale shadow of the moon was slowly rising from the horizon. "We must wait for the moon to be fully risen before we can start," Emil added. "After we drain her of her powers, we can turn her over to the local authorities - she can face justice for the crimes she has committed. When people learn of her crimes and witness her execution, your family will be considered fortunate survivors of a terrible spree."

"In the meantime, how do we keep ourselves safe and the girl subdued?" Father asked.

Emil knelt down and felt Eve's pulse, then lifted her eyelids. Eve did not respond. "Her pulse is weak and quite fast," he said. "She is not any danger to us at the moment, when she is so exhausted. But we will need to feed her some special foods and give her water and wine, to raise up her powers for our benefit."

Emil rose up and added, "We can take turns keeping watch on her, until the time of the ceremony tonight." Emil offered his hand to me, and this time I accepted.

"Very well, Emil," Father said. "I trust you to help us salvage a desperately dreadful day from completely ruining our lives."

Emil nodded. "Let us move her to the house," he said. He and Teddy bent over and each lifted her up - Teddy by her legs and Emil by grasping under her shoulders.

A small wave of relief flooded through me, as I realized I had managed to wrangle a few more hours to figure out a way to get Eve and myself out of here.

Chapter 33

Nobody's Plaything

Eve

I woke to the soft stroke of fingertips caressing my cheek. The warm and gentle touch felt comforting and kind. My heart thrummed in response, only for my awareness to suddenly be flooded with sensations of pain from all over my body. In particular, my left shoulder throbbed and my right hip burned as though it had been stuck by a hot poker. Every inch of me felt as heavy as a lead weight, and mentally I was exhausted. Where was I? What was going on...? My brain felt as slippery as a rainbow trout, sliding out of my grasp.

But then a brisk breeze blew over me and I shivered involuntarily as the memory of the last twenty-four hours of terror rushed in. I groaned and slowly opened my eyes.

Close up, a woman's face leaned in. It was Saskia; relief flooded through my body as I saw her and my heart lunged into an excited rhythm. No matter that I was exhausted, her presence beside me filled me with heat and longing, despite all I'd endured today.

"Eve, I'm so glad you're awake," she said, holding a cut crystal glass in her hand. "Here let me give you some water, you must be parched!"

As soon as she suggested water, I realized I was desperately thirsty. I nodded, and she gently raise my head up with one hand, while offering me a glass filled with fresh water. I drained the glass, and felt the cool water flow down my throat and revive me.

"I've been so worried about you," Saskia said. Her eyes sparkled as she leant down and gave me a gentle kiss on my lips. Her velvet soft mouth and sweet breath filled my senses with her deliciousness. Wanting to savor it, I took a deep breath in, and was startled when a sharp whiff of men's cologne, tobacco and leather rose up in my nostrils.

Fear swept through me as I focused and recognized the massive stag head on the wall across from me. Somehow, I was in Mr. Rennard's study, though I could not fathom how I'd ended up here.

My eyes flashed with worry and I opened my mouth to speak, only for Saskia to place a fingertip to my lips. "It's okay. We're alone," she said.

I struggled to move and sit up but my arms and legs would not respond. Looking down, I could see ropes criss-crossing my body. I had been lain on Mr. Rennard's large oak desk, with lengths of rope binding my body to the table. Even moving my feet or hands was impossible as both ankles and wrists were bound by leather straps which chafed against my skin as I struggled. I tried reaching for my magic within me, but I was too weak. I couldn't feel any prickles or tingles.

It seemed as though Saskia read my mind, "Just rest for the moment, my darling," she said. "I need to speak with you so that we can make our plans..."

My darling! This new-found effusive tenderness from Saskia somehow did not ring true to me. "What's happening? Why am I tied up?" I asked, a note of suspicion creeping into my voice.

"Funnily enough, the men are afraid of you," she said. "I, however, am not. I see for you the magnificent person you are," she added. "Here, take a few bites of this - it should help you to recover some of your strength."

She offered me a spoonful of something utterly foul tasting. It was bloody and metallic and gummy in the worst possible way. I gagged on it as I swallowed. "What on earth was that?!" I said.

"Raw deer liver. You've lost a lot of blood," she said. "I know it looks and smells awful, but according to Emil, it is the ideal food for you."

"Emil?! You must be joking! Saskia, cut me loose," I said.

In reply, Saskia got down on her knees so that we would be eye-to-eye. Her eyes were luminous, her cheeks flush, her lips a soft full pink. As she leaned in close to my face, I could smell her delicate lavender scent.

For the first time I found the smell cloying. My throat closed up of its own volition.

"That's why I'm here, silly," Saskia said, patting my head. "To set you free. We could be *amazing* together. With my family's name and wealth, and your powers, we could go to Paris and have the most extraordinary life," she said.

"What about all of your father's plans?" I asked.

Saskia shrugged as if she had not a care in the world. "Darling, with you by my side, I can face the whole world, including my father!"

Sweet mother of mercy! Her calm demeanor revealed a profound lack of human kindness. Rage and despair begin to fill me, until it spilled over in an angry outburst. "You brought me here, knowing what your family is like?!"

Saskia sighed. "Eve, darling, don't be naive! This is what the world is like."

"Oh stuff that," I spat back. "My Ma is dead thanks to your family. So are two of the Fitzgerald sisters," I said. My thoughts drifted to Peggy for a moment. Last I saw her, she was riding hard down the road. I hoped she had gotten free of the men.

Saskia looked at me with a wry expression. "Well, yes, what the men have done today was horrid, but frankly Eve darling, you've personally killed three men in less than 24 hours, so perhaps you're not really in the best position to judge anyone."

I was gobsmacked - how could she possibly equate men hunting and torturing women, with my defending myself? And then I realized that she saw no distinction at all.

Saskia continued, without awareness of the impact of her words on me. "So what shall it be? We can have the life you dreamed of when we first met. The two of us together need not be obedient to any man. I can take us anywhere in the world we wish to go, and you can keep us safe," she said.

"What about *your* family? Thanks to your father and brother, my family and friends are dead."

"You cannot possible think I'm responsible for their behavior. I have been on track to forge my own path; separate from my father and brother," she said. Her eyes flicked away from me.

I sensed that she was not being entirely truthful. Something about the way Saskia uttered those sentences struck me. She had a gleam in her eye, and as I looked her up and down, I spied a splatter of blood across Saskia's blouse which made me gasp. *She couldn't possibly.* Before I could stop myself, the question blurted out of my mouth.

"Saskia, did you kill Robert Logan?"

Saskia didn't respond immediately. She smiled, ruefully, and closed her eyes for a beat. When she opened them again, she stared me down with a furrowed brow.

"Just finishing what you started, love." She was frighteningly matter-of-fact in discussing killing a man. It was as though she were discussing something as mundane as getting her bath ready.

"And you really think your father will let you go to Europe, *and* take me with you? Now who's being naive?!" I said.

"Well, there is one idea that could solve everything," she said, a strange expression on her face.

"And what would that be?" I asked, afraid to hear the answer.

"If my father and brother were to die, there would be no obstacles, and you, dearest one, would be by my side as my queen for the rest of our lives," she said.

"You've gone mad!" I replied, not knowing what else to even think.

At that, Saskia grimaced, and who she had been to me, was shattered. The spell she had cast on me was broken. I saw her now for who she really was: a shallow, narcissistic social climber who cared only for her own needs and pleasures. She and her kind were takers in life; remarkably greedy ones at that.

Outside the study door, I could hear the voices of men speaking as they approached. My heart began to pound in my chest. "Untie me for heaven's sake!" I urged.

Saskia leaned in and whispered, "It's up to you, now to choose, but we are running out of time." This time when she grew close to me, her entire being felt repulsive. As I made a face, Saskia hissed at me. "Don't be a stupid *bridget*! You could have the world at your feet."

That insult was the final straw. I spat in Saskia's face. "You're no better than the rest of your family."

Saskia was shocked and furious. I'm sure no one had ever spat on her or disparaged her in her entire sheltered life. She'd been raised as an American princess and expected the world to heed her every wish and whim. For a lowly servant to challenge her, was clearly more than she could tolerate or accept.

I didn't care, though. I took a deep breath in and said, "You would make me your slave forever, in *your* gilded cage, ready to perform for you at your bidding."

Her face grew red with rage and she whipped out her hunting knife. "How dare you! After all I have offered to you. If you won't cooperate, then you force my hand." She glared at me, as she pressed the blade into the skin of my throat, directly below my jaw. I could feel the blade slice into the skin, but I would not give her the satisfaction of having me beg for mercy. I looked at her with a fierce loathing. If these were to be my last moments on earth, I would go without fear or weakness.

Chapter 34

The Phantom Queen's Justice

Saskia

What nerve the little bitch had! Outwardly I held still, watching in fascination as beads of bright red blood appeared on the edge of my dagger. Eve's ivory skin was almost translucent under the pressure of my knife. But inside my mind was seething. How could she turn down my offer? I was everything the wench had ever wanted and more. Clearly, I was wrong in thinking that the girl had much intelligence. Eve was a naive little do-gooder, who played small in a tiny pathetic life with no great dreams and nothing of substance to accomplish. I found myself beginning to despise her.

But, damn it, didn't I need her magical protection?

The study door flew open. Emil, Teddy and Father entered and headed towards me.

"Stop that, Saskia!" Father commanded. "You were supposed to guard her, not kill her!"

My heart sank as I knew my opportunity to take Eve away had slipped away. Gone was my chance for true, unfettered independence. Gone was my future of travel and leisure and liberty. I reluctantly lowered my blade and sheathed it. Not only could I not compel

Eve to listen and come along with me, I also had to face the harsh truth that breaking away from my father would be almost impossible now.

Although Eve was acting tough, I saw her breathe a sigh of relief as the blade left her throat. What a fool she was! I could have given her the sun, the moon and the stars, but instead she'd likely face the death penalty. The good people of New York would be horrified by the murders here at Greythorne.

Eve's phony moralizing was nauseating. I had loathed similar sentiments in school, and at church. Eve was the last person I would have expected to subscribe to a moral code, especially since she had been a very willing and delightful participant in our dalliance, not to mention the murder of three of the world's richest men.

I tried to reel in my anger, as the men gathered around the desk and looked down at Eve. I needed to keep a calm and level head, while I tried to find any way to salvage my plans. Maybe, despite her bitter words, Eve would come to her senses and realize that the offer I was making to her was once in a lifetime. Only a fool would snub such an opportunity, and I prayed that Eve was not a complete imbecile.

To my surprise, it was Emil who spoke next. He gazed at Eve with respect in his voice, and even lowered his head as a sign of respect towards her. I was shocked by the gesture.

"Mademoiselle Eve, it appears you are quite powerful. Your name suits you - like the first woman in the garden of Eden."

"I'm not interested in your sweet talk," Eve replied. "Set me loose, and I will let you leave with your lives."

"Ha!" said Teddy as he grabbed Eve's jaw with his hand and turned her head with force to look at him. In his other hand, he held his hunting bowie knife, identical to mine. Father had given us the matching blades when Teddy turned twelve and I was thirteen.

"Naw, Father. Saskia had the right of it: let's slit her throat and be done with it," snarled Teddy. Eve shuddered in response to his touch, which only made Teddy smirk in amusement and pleasure at feeling her tremble under his touch.

Father raised his hand with a look at his son that would have frozen water. Teddy released his grip. Meanwhile, Eve kept silent. Perhaps she was being smart for a moment, and realized it would not benefit her to trigger a sudden rage reaction by my brother or father.

"In Haiti, we have a long tradition of *sèvis lwa* - what English speakers call *voodoo*," Emil said. He leaned over Eve and spoke. His lilting baritone voice sounded quite melodic. "Like me, you come from an island country with a deep belief in the spirit world, yes?" he asked.

Eve glared at the man, but said nothing in response.

Truthfully, I wasn't sure what the man was babbling about either. He looked at me and saw an expression of disdain in my eyes before I could conceal it.

But Emil merely smiled, his white teeth flashing. No doubt, he had been treated this way many times before. He turned and brought over a decanter filled with red wine, and a special blade that he pulled out of a leather sheath. It was silver, long and narrow, and came to a sharp point with a smooth handle made from deer antler. It looked wicked sharp as it glinted in the evening light.

"Shall I fetch the goblet?" asked Teddy.

Father shook his head. "Absolutely not, Teddy." My brother's face turned red with embarrassment.

Father ignored Teddy's reaction and turned towards me. "That honor belongs to Saskia, the *jewel* in our family's crown!"

"But she's a woman!" Teddy protested. "It's unheard of!"

"She survived the witch. She brought the witch down. And she chose her family over heresy. I can think of no greater honor than to have her join the culmination of this year's Ambrose Hunt."

For the first time in my adult life, Father regarded me as an equal. I stood erect, shoulders back, embracing the pride he had bestowed upon me. Perhaps I still would have a voice for my future, after all. If that were the case, then Eve would have served her purpose well. *Désolé, ma chérie.*

"Preposterous!" Teddy was shouting now, his face reddening with rage. "I took down two of the targets myself. I managed to track and avoid death at the hands of a witch. Something not even your esteemed friends were capable of accomplishing!"

But Father simply replied, "And when you *capture* a witch, then you can speak about this." Father had the gift of knowing exactly where to cut and wound each one of us.

Teddy's eyes flared with anger and he tightened his fists, but he knew better than to confront Father.

Father looked at me, and pulled a heavy key from his pocket, then nodded his head toward a section of wood panelling. I nodded back as I took the key from him, then walked over. In a groove between plants was a hidden switch. I pressed it and the panel swung open to reveal a large mahogany cupboard which had two large brass handle pulls on each side of the cabinet doors.

I slid the brass key into the lock, and it turned smooth as butter, clicking open. After that, I grasped the pulls and the doors swung open towards me. The cabinet had been finely crafted, so that the doors opened with not even a whisper.

Inside the cabinet, were multiple highly polished mahogany shelves. Upon each one stood items from my father's rarest collectibles. On the middle shelf, resting on a square of burgundy velvet cloth, stood the skull goblet. Its obsidian eyes glittered in the light. I reached in and pulled it out, feeling the coolness of the bone against the skin of my palms. It was heavier than I had expected, and I used both hands to bring it to my father.

Eve's eyes widened in horror as she watched me bring the goblet forward. "Did you know all of this, all along?!" she asked.

I was about to respond, but Father cut me off. "Saskia, Teddy, and I - we each have our role to play in this family. The Ambrose Hunt, started by my dear departed father twenty years ago, was designed to unite the most powerful of men in a sacred ritual to draw and share our power with one another. The taking of life and sharing of our blood, brought us to a state closer than anything other than birth could achieve." Father paused in contemplation for a moment, then continued, "And in some ways, truly it is closer, for we choose one another, while how we are born and our circumstances at birth, are not in our control."

Father paused, then looked at me, his eyes shining with pride. "This year although we have lost a few of our blood brothers to this witch, we now have the opportunity to achieve a level of personal power beyond anything even my father Ambrose could have imagined. I thank you Emil for your guidance in this ritual."

"*Mon plaisir, mon ami,*" Emil replied. He reached down to pull up the sleeve on Eve's right arm. She flinched at his touch, and I saw her jaw working. Yet she remained silent as he exposed her cream-pale wrist and forearm. "We wish to tap into your powers so that we can grow in strength," Emil said. He looked outside through the windows at the moon now risen above the tree tops in the darkening night sky. "Come Rennard family, it is time."

Eve closed her eyes. Perhaps she was too exhausted to have much fight left in her.

Father came to my side and held down Eve's right arm. Teddy went across the table, and held down the other limb. Even though the girl was bound, they were taking no chances.

I stood waiting beside Emil, goblet in hand.

Eve took a deep breath and squinted in concentration. Suddenly, a prickle of electricity raced across my skin, but it quickly faded away. The effort seemed to only weaken Eve. She had stopped pulling against her bonds, and instead lay quietly, breathing slowly in and out.

Emil took my hands and guided me to hold the goblet directly under Eve's forearm. He placed the tip of his dagger at Eve's wrist when all of the sudden, Eve's eyes flew open, as did her mouth - and she spoke in a blood-curdling tone, as though she were possessed by a demon. "*Badb, Macha and Nemain - come!*"

259

I think all of us fairly jumped out of our skins at that. I'd never heard anything so terrifying, and prayed I never would again. All of us looked around, craning our necks in every direction. Emil frowned, clearly upset that the moment of his ritual knife work had been interrupted. My heart raced with panic, worried about the strange incantation Eve had just cast.

But the moments stretched on, until my brother Teddy began to chuckle. We all sighed with relief and the laughter became contagious. For her part, Eve looked rather disappointed, and barely able to keep her eyes open.

With that, Emil brought his knife back into position over Eve's wrist and pushed the blade in swiftly to open her vein. Eve cried out in pain, as her ruby red blood flowed into the goblet. I held still, holding my breath, morbidly fascinated as I watched Eve's lifeblood spill out of her. The goblet grew heavy in my hands as the crimson liquid rose.

Could this work? Could we really take on some of her power for ourselves?

Perhaps I wouldn't need her at all after this...If such things really did work. I was usually quite pessimistic about spiritual phenomena, but spending time with Eve and observing her abilities had turned me into a believer that magic, in the right hands, was a true thing.

Once the goblet was full, Emil signaled to me to hand it to him. He lifted the goblet up high in the air as he began to chant in a sing-song Creole patois. Father, Teddy and I stayed put, watching the macabre ritual unfold. Blood continued to flow from Eve's wound, spilling onto the Turkish rug below. She quietly muttered to herself under her breath, as her skin grew paler by the moment.

All of the sudden, harsh high-pitched *screeches* made me clap my hands over my eardrums to protect them, and block out the horrific cacophony. I turned around just in time for -

BAM!!

The study's enormous glass window panes shattered inward, spraying us with fragments of glass, as three enormous ravens broke through using their beaks and talons. I felt the sting as a few shards of glass struck my left cheek but before I could even react, I was beset upon by the largest, most vicious raven I had ever seen in my life. Its wingspan was at least three feet across, and its onyx black feathers fanned out in a most ferocious manner.

Another screech issued from the devil bird, and caused my eardrums to ache. I raised my arms to protect my head as the beast raced towards me. Its claws were open, revealing razor sharp talons.

I glanced over and saw that Teddy and Father were similarly being attacked by the black-feathered beasts. Like me, they had their arms up to block and parry the birds away.

Losing my focus on protecting myself cost me dearly. In the next moment, the hell bird managed to get past my arms and clawed its way down the left side of my face and down my neck. The pain burned intensely, as though I had been punctured by burning hot knitting needles. I could feel hot blood course down my face. I screamed in pain and horror. Oh no - not my face!

Meanwhile, Emil, disregarded by the ravens, finished his sing-song chant of what sounded like gibberish. He raised the blood-filled goblet to his lips. The man was determined to complete this ritual when -

CRACK!

A gunshot rang out. Emil looked down and simply said, "Oh."

With a warrior cry, Eve broke through her bonds and leapt off the table. Chaos reined as the ravens attacked all three members of my family. How did everything suddenly turn so awful?

Chapter 35

The Curse

Eve

With that burst of magic still sizzling on the tip of my tongue, I used a broken leather straps to tie a rough tourniquet above my forearm. I was already so weak and woozy from a lack of blood, that I needed to preserve my energy as much as possible. I twisted the leather until the blood stopped pouring from my arm. But with only one hand holding it in place, I wasn't going to be able to stem the flow for long.

A hole the size of a human fist had been punched through Emil's gut. Emil looked down and simply said, "Oh." Blood and guts had flown out behind the man, spraying the carpet and wall with a vermillion spray as his white shirt turned red around the ragged edges of the bullet's pathway.

Just beyond the shattered window, past the row of perfectly manicured hedge stood Isaiah, a smoking rifle in his hands.

"Go to hell, you blasphemous bastard!" he yelled at Emil.

Emil looked up, eyes and mouth wide open with shock. His hand dropped the skull cup. As the goblet struck the floor, it bounced, and I watched my blood fly out across the rugs and nearby club chair. As for Emil, he seemed to move in slow motion, his legs buckling under him, until he collapsed on the floor, looking like a deflated scarecrow.

Rennard roared, "Isaiah! You goddamn sumnabitch! After all we've done for you!" He ran to the wall to grab another rifle.

But Isaiah did not bat an eyelid. He stood his ground, as he worked to reload the gun.

Out from behind him a second figure peered out towards us, then stepped forward with a limp. It was Peggy! She wore an expression of steely determination, feet planted, beside Isaiah, her tattered bloody dress blowing in the wind, and a butcher knife in her hand. I had never been happier to see anyone.

Meanwhile, Teddy had armed himself with a Caspian curved sword and adopted a fencer's attack stance. He guarded himself as one of the ravens approached, and ducked at the last moment. From below, he slashed upward at its underbelly. But the blade found nothing but black smoke and vapor, swirling through the air like a phantom.

Meanwhile, Peggy, braver than brave, scrambled over the window sill into the fray. "Oy, ye bastard!" she cried as she charged at Teddy with her knife. She came close, but Teddy was a skillful and adept fighter. He spun around and brandished his blade, slapping her knife away effortlessly. Peggy fell back and onto the floor, scuttling away from Teddy.

His look was murderous as he raised his arm to strike Peggy down.

What Teddy didn't realize, was that I would not allow the Rennards to kill another human being.

"You'll not harm her!" I cried. I summoned every inch of my powers, my arms burning and prickling all over as I wove together a hurricane-strength wind which blew Teddy up and away from Peggy.

"You bitch!" He yelled as he flew across the room, arms and legs flailing. He let out a sudden high-pitched cry, as he was impaled upon the head of a particularly majestic stag. Antler points burst through his chest, neck and abdomen - gore and blood dripped down from the buck's face onto the floor below.

Teddy put up a feeble struggle to free himself, but to no avail. His injuries were too severe, and if he wasn't dead, the young man had at the very least lapsed into shock.

Rennard screamed at the sight of his son broken and bloody up above him on the wall. He turned to attack me, his blade gleaming menacingly back at me.

Suddenly, someone was at my side. Peggy had come to stand with me, stoic and steadfast! Her support lent me the strength I needed to continue to fight. I heard the voice of the Morrigan inside my mind, encouraging me. All at once, I was clear in what to say and what to do. I raised my arms in the air, and cried out, "I summon all of the spirits who have died by the hands of this accursed family."

Susurrations and whispers rose as a ball of gray mist soared into the study and took form. The mist spiraled out of the bonds of the ball, and each tendril assumed the appearance of a woman. I saw my mother, then Frances and Nan, Bette and many more women whom I had never met rise up and surround Rennard. It was a posse of dead women's spirits, angry and vengeful.

The spirits were thick and tightly packed around the patriarch. Suddenly as a unit they raised the man up as they flew high into the air. Rennard struggled, but his efforts were futile. He cursed and swore at the spirits, screaming to be released, but they were determined and relentless, as they carried him out the window into the night air.

Peggy and I watched the spirits soar up together raising Theodore higher and higher into the air above the forest.

Suddenly, the spirits let go of the man, and turned back into a soft silvery mist. Rennard tumbled head over heels, helpless and wailing into the forest below. I listened hard to hear...

The breaking of branches...

A distant thud...

And then, silence.

The wind picked up then, but only a gust or two, as if to say *All is right, now.*

The moment of peace was broken, as Saskia ran towards us.

"You filthy peasant!" She shoved Peggy aside, causing the woman to lose her balance and fall. With a sickening thump, Peggy hit the back of her head on a corner of the desk. Peggy folded like a deck of cards.

Saskia did not slow down. She rushed forward and tackled me to the ground. My back smacked against the carpet, but I was not going to submit. I raised up my elbow and jammed it directly into Saskia's nose, eliciting a sickening crack as cartilage and bone gave way. Saskia screamed in pain as her nose spouted blood.

Enraged, she pinned me down with her hands on my shoulders and her knees on my hips. She loomed over me on all fours. I tried to push her off, but she held tight. Her broken nose and clawed cheek dripped wet hot blood onto my face, which made my stomach churn. I breathed through my nose and clamped my jaw shut to avoid getting any blood in my mouth.

"I suppose I should thank you. With my father and brother gone, I am now the *heir apparent*," Saskia said as she went to retrieve her blade from its scabbard on her hip. I realized what she intended, and so before she could reach her knife, I reached and grabbed it, then bent my legs into springs and thrust myself and Saskia up and over, so that she landed face up, now with me holding the blade to her neck. Her cold clear eyes bore into mine. Where I had once seen warmth and beauty, I now beheld only icy hate. I held the knife still at her throat for a moment, blood still flowing from my unbound forearm.

I saw how pathetic and weak Saskia truly was. All of the attention she had lavished on me was a means to an end. There was no kindness or compassion in her, only naked greed and fear. I realized that although I wanted her to suffer, a part of me could not possibly kill her. I had cared for her, and vestiges of those emotions caused me to lower the blade to the ground. I could not kill her in cold blood, but retribution and justice demanded punishment in the form of a curse upon this evil woman. My eyes unfocused and my voice sounded deep and husky to my own ears.

"You will never be satisfied, no matter how much you drink, no matter how much you eat."

Saskia squirmed above me. "No! Stop, don't do this."

I ignored her pleas. *"You will find no friends and take no lovers. You will have no peace."*

"Eve, please!" Saskia begged, tears mingling with the blood on her cheek and around her mouth. "Think of what we had, Eve!"

"You will rue the day we met."

A gust of wind soared through Saskia, leaving her shaken for a brief moment. Saskia locked her eyes on me. She reached for her knife and then raised her blade with both hands, aiming to plunge it into my chest. At the top of the arc, Saskia paused for a moment.

"Take back the curse, witch!" she commanded. Her face a rictus of fury, Saskia swung the blade towards my chest.

I shook my head and closed my eyes, summoning aid.

Devil's Own jumped through the broken window at lightning speed.

Before the blade could touch me, Devil's forelegs kicked her off me. She screamed as she flew back into a wall.

"Go to hell!" I said.

Saskia rose up and raced to her horse. She leapt onto the stallion's back, turned him back towards the broken window, then guided him to leap out.

Outside, she urged her horse into a gallop and aimed straight towards Isaiah, who barely escaped being trampled.

Saskia raced her horse down the main path. Just before the curve in the lane, she looked back for a moment, hesitant, then kicked her horse into gear. Two ravens made a beeline for Saskia as she galloped away.

And then darkness fell.

Chapter 36

Unbound At Last

Eve

I awoke to bright, warm sunshine and the chirpy singsong of birds. I opened my eyes and discovered I was lying on a simple bed in a pine-wood paneled cabin. The wood floor was covered by a hand-woven rug. Plain wood shelves held a few pots, pans and oil lanterns. A rifle was mounted on a pair of pegs by the front door. I scanned my body and saw white cotton bandages wrapped around my forearm, shoulder and thigh.

"Easy does it," a man's voice came to me from the shadows. Stepping into the light was Isaiah. He raised his hand to signal me to wait. He had been sitting in a rocking chair across from me, reading from a worn Bible. He put down his spectacles and came over.

"Here let me help you," he said as he helped prop some pillows behind my back.

"Peggy?" I asked.

"I'm right here," she said, and she limped towards me, holding a steaming mug of hot broth. "Drink this. It will help." Peggy was dressed in one of Bette's long skirts and dress shirts. Her face was bruised, as were her hands, with cuts and scrapes in various states of healing.

I took the mug and inhaled the delicious smell of chicken soup, which triggered my salivary glands and my stomach to growl. I wasn't just hungry, I was ravenous. As I drank the broth, Peggy came and sat on the bed.

The nourishment helped to ease my stomach and mind. I put the mug down, and reached over to take Peggy's hands.

"I'm so sorry," I said. Peggy leaned in and hugged me. Tears filled her eyes but she wiped them away with the back of her hand. "For Nan, for Frances, for all of it, Peg."

"It's not your fault," she said. "Not one bit of it." She let go of me and I turned to Isaiah.

"I'm so sorry for your loss," I said to Isaiah.

He looked out the window into his cottage garden, and was quiet for a few moments. "She was my sunlight..."

I followed his gaze and saw fresh grave mounds, each marked with simple wooden cross.

Isaiah harrumphed, then said, "I'm sorry about your Mother..."

A wave of grief welled up inside me and tears spilled down my cheeks.

Isaiah brought over a chair, and sat next to us. He reached out and took my hand in his.

"Why did you come back?" I asked.

Isaiah shook his head. "We were trapped by that family. By the time we understood what was happening, we couldn't leave. After losing Bette, I had nothing holding me back. I knew that if I wanted to get right in the eyes of the Lord, I would have to start making amends for my past mistakes. I came across Peggy fleeing, as I was making my way to Greythorne from my cottage. When she first saw me, she 'bout ran me down with her horse," he said.

"We had some words, and when it was clear that Isaiah was determined to help, I decided to come with him and take a stand against the family. I felt like God was calling upon me to help. I knew what I had to do, I suppose," Peggy said.

I nodded and said, "I know what I have to do, too."

Peggy looked at me and I reached out my hand. She took it.

I hadn't realized until that moment, that I had been holding my breath. I let it out with a sigh.

Peggy and I stood together on the gravel path beside Isaiah's cottage, and watched the sun drop below the horizon. Isaiah stood on the front porch of his patio. In the background, Greythorne Mansion loomed. I turned away from the building and faced my friends. The fresh scent of grass and flowers blooming perfumed the evening air.

Uncomfortable with any sort of non-Christian ritual, Isaiah had opted to compromise by standing back and offering a few Christian prayers. His beautiful melodious voice vibrated in the night air as he sang a spiritual -

Precious Lord, take my hand,
lead me on, help me stand,
I am tired, I am weak, I am worn;
through the storm, through the night,
lead me on to the light;
take my hand, precious Lord,
lead me home.
When my way grows drear,
precious Lord, linger near;
when my life is almost gone,
hear my cry, hear my call,
hold me fast lest I fall;
take my hand, precious Lord,
lead me home.
When the darkness appears
and the night draws near,
When the day is past and gone,
at the river I stand,
guide my feet, hold my hand;
take my hand, precious Lord,
lead me home.

When Isaiah was done, I took a long stick to draw a large circle, and then a pentacle within. At this, Isaiah excused himself and stepped back. He wouldn't be party to such rituals, but he wouldn't stop us. I could respect that.

As I traced the lines, Peggy lit a torch and raised it high. Flames flickered as the evening shadows lengthened. I lowered the stick and picked up a small yellow ceramic bowl that I'd borrowed from Bette and Isaiah's kitchen. Inside the bowl was a handful of pungent tobacco leaves. I limped over to Peggy and raised the bowl.

"Go ahead and light it," I said.

Peggy lowered the torch and lit the tobacco. Smoke curled into the night air.

"How do you know what to do?" Peggy asked.

That was an excellent question, to which I had only the barest sliver of an answer. "I don't. The Morrigan guides me," I said.

The first stars appeared above us in the night sky, as I slowly began to walk around the circle, waving the burning tobacco leaves, wafting the smoke into the air.

"Mother, Father, Gods and Goddesses, We ask for your presence."

A golden light began to glow and spread around us from the torches.

Isaiah and Peggy bowed their heads.

"We invite all beings to enter the Light of your Divine Energy," I said.

From the ground within the pentacle a thick mist began to build up. As it rose, it separated into distinct shapes. Peggy's sisters Nan and Frances rose up in silvery form before her. They floated gently in the evening air, holding hands with one another. Peggy's eyes filled with tears, and from her came only the soft sound of "oh."

Isaiah was stunned by the sight. He dropped down onto the ground on his knees and crossed himself. A portion of mist separated and formed before him into his beloved Bette. I heard his voice speak softly with tenderness and beauty. His face shone in the moonlight.

I shivered as Ma rose up before me. A second glow became the shape of my father, Sean, whom I had not seen since I was tiny. A sob escaped me, as my parents held hands and smiled upon me.

And then, other spirits emerged - women who had died at the hands of the Rennards. They were innocent women, like ourselves, who'd been caught in a web of evil and had not found peace in the hereafter.

I heard soft sounds of weeping from Peggy, and perhaps from myself as well.

"We open our hearts to those in fear. We shine our light to those in darkness. We invite all spirits to move into the Light. We will not forget you. Your memories will be a blessing now and always. We release you from your suffering. May the Morrigan lift you up and guide you to eternal shelter and peace," I prayed.

A deep resonant vibration began in the air around us. I could feel my rapid pulse subside, the tightness in my muscles relax, and my breaths deepen. The trees that surrounded the cabin rustled and swayed in a rhythmic dance, although there was no breeze or wind. The silvery moon glowed and illuminated the darkening night sky as it rose above. The ghosts softened their forms, and became a grey mist, rising up to be absorbed by the moonlight.

"Take care my love," Isaiah said.

I waved my hands in the air to end the ritual. The all too familiar prickles now felt more like a tickle and tingle than a painful sensation. The torches flamed out. It was done, and I was alive. Thank the Morrigan, may she ever flourish.

Part Five

Chapter 37

Epilogue

Dublin, Ireland - Spring 1908 - Eve

I breathed deep, the crisp Irish air filling my lungs, as I walked with purpose through the city streets. The rain had moved on, but had left Dublin's streets a labyrinth of muddy cobbles and pools of rainwater. But now, the sun was starting to shine through dappled clouds, fighting off the storm's chill.

As I made my way, I did my best to avoid stepping in the largest puddles. My leather boots, though well made, would be a misery to walk in if they got soaked. Fluffy clouds scudded by overhead. A stiff breeze blew down from the North, causing people to huddle together for warmth, or more preferably to stay indoors. I pulled my olive green aran wool shawl close around me to ward off the chill. The rough fibers felt comforting to my fingertips. The sweet and smokey smell of burning turf belched out of cottage chimneys into the air. I was home.

I cut through Henrietta Street (a shortcut, albeit a very unpleasant one), lined with cramped dark tenement homes, filled to the brim with large families in the darkest and dankest of conditions. The smell of unbathed bodies, food cooking and uncollected rubbish hung thick in the air. I passed by a stoop where half a dozen wee lads and lassies sat together, playing jacks with knucklebones, ignoring the bustle of the city around them. Their faces were pale and little bodies thin - food was scarce, and jobs were scarcer for those who had no education.

Dublin in some ways reminded me of my time in New York City, but on a smaller scale. There were posh wealthy neighborhoods like Rathmines that lay mostly to the south, while the north of Dublin (including this very street) was filled with some of the most horrid tenements and poverty I'd ever seen. They were at least as awful as the first miserable tenement Ma and I had shared with another Irish family, the O'Reillys (there were seven in the family, plus us two in a tiny two room flat), on Orchard Street on the Lower East Side. After Da had died, we'd come to the city, Ma desperate to find work.

The so-called "Sisters of Charity" (though "Sisters of Cruelty" would be more appropriate) ran a Magdelene Laundry at number 10 Henrietta, where "fallen women" were kept in the most dire conditions, working for barely any food or shelter, as though they were slaves. Mind you, "fallen" included any women without family support, not just streetwalkers. The nuns' halfway house was anything but kind, comforting or protective.

It was no wonder Ma and Pa, and so many others had left the fair isle to seek their fortunes in New York and beyond. But my calling and my life lay here in this difficult place....

I finally reached my destination on Eccles Street - A four-story red brick inn stood facing a tiny green park area, filled with large oak trees. Just down the street was the Mater Hospital, but that's a story for another time.

I paused for a moment to gaze up with pride at the hanging wooden door sign: KELLY INFIRMARY & HOSTEL. Carved and burned in charcoal, below the words into the wood were three ravens circling a Celtic shield knot. Every time I came home from running errands and looked up, the sign made me smile. I walked up the wide stone steps, and opened the butter yellow-painted front door and headed in.

The entry led into a warm and cozy sitting room with a wooden counter and back office behind it. The chairs and sofas were of mismatched chintz, with wool rugs below to provide warmth. A fire glowed in the fireplace, and my heart felt full at the sight of it all.

Behind the counter, stood Peggy, bright eyed and confident, dressed in plain but beautiful Irish woollies. She'd been scratching notes in the account books, tracking bills and payments, no doubt. She had become my most dear and cherished friend, and her loyalty was beyond measure. She cocked her head towards the infirmary.

"There's a new patient for you," she said. "She's had a very rough go."

I nodded and dropped my shawl and bag behind the counter, then went to the infirmary door. I knocked gently and a woman's voice quavered from behind the door.

"Come in," she said.

I opened the door to my infirmary. Cluttered surfaces overflowed with all sorts of tinctures, and books. My favorite piece of furniture was the oak bureau with multiple shelves and cubbyholes for holding my medical tools. A pair of wooden chairs and a wood examining table took up the center of the room. Stretched out in regal fashion on top of the table was my cat, Quinn, who deigned to open one golden eye in my direction.

"Off with you," I said as I waved at her to get down. She ignored me.

In the far corner of the room, stood a young woman in her early twenties, shifting from one foot to another. Her left eye was black and swollen shut. Her face bore bloody cuts and bruises, and she held her right arm close.

"*Fáilte romhat,*" I said.

"*Go Raibh maith agat.* I'm here to see the Healer."

"Aye, you've come to the right place. What's your name?" I asked, using a gentle tone.

"Sally. Sally Keats," she said.

"Welcome Sally, I'm Eve Kelly, the healer here," I said. I waved my arm to invite Sally to take a seat. She flinched, then moved to follow my suggestion.

"It's me arm... Me husband..." Sally shuddered.

"It's okay Sally, I understand. May I?" I asked, reaching out.

She nodded.

I gently examined the woman's injured arm. The forearm was bent just above the wrist at an awkward and unnatural angle. It was clear as day that both the radius and ulnar bones were broken. The skin around the break was bruised and swollen. I checked the wrist and hand and was relieved that no significant nerve damage had been done. Healing the long bones would be an easier and faster recovery.

"Sally - I want you to close your eyes and breathe slow and steady. Can you do that for me?"

"Aye," Sally said. She closed her eyes. As she did so, I began to focus and lay my hands gently on the break. The familiar prickles of energy filled my hands and a silvery shimmer of light and heat flowed from my hands into the broken forearm. The forearm glowed internally and the bones became visible to me at the surface.

Sally groaned.

"Just keep breathing," I said. "You're doing so well, Sally."

I guided the bone ends to move under the skin towards one another with ripples of energy. They straightened and realigned. With my heart, I reached out to the Morrigan and beseeched her for aid. Though I could not see it, I could feel the bones start to knit together. I lifted my hands away, and the glow faded from her forearm.

"You can open your eyes now," I said.

Sally opened her eyes, flabbergasted at the restored alignment of her arm. She rotated her wrist, winced in pain. "What did you do?" Sally asked.

I pulled a simple cotton sling out of a drawer, and gently placed it over Sally's neck and under her arm.

"Just some old-time healing. It should feel better, but you will need to wear this until it fully heals. It will take about six weeks. I'll give you some willow bark tea, which will help with the pain and swelling."

"Thank you," Sally said. She grasped my hand in hers and looked me in the eye. "I mean it, *An Bhean Feasa*. You're a miracle."

"Do you have somewhere safe to stay here in Dublin?" I asked.

Sally shook her head, no. Fear and worry crossed her face. "My family are all out in County Meath..."

"No matter, just come with me." I offered her my hand, and she rose up as I opened the infirmary door and guided her out to the sitting room.

"Peggy, Sally will be staying with us for a bit. What's available?"

"Oh, no I couldn't impo--" Mrs. Keats was about to refuse, but good old Peg wouldn't let her.

"There's an opening in Room Seven," Peggy answered. "It's a little small, Sally, but it is warm and safe and you can stay as long as you need."

"Really? I...I don't know what to say," the woman mumbled. "Thank you. Thank you both so much."

"Perfect. Peggy here will get you settled."

"Aye," said Peggy.

I reached into my pocket and pulled out a pendant on a leather cord. "This is for you," I said. I put the pendant in Sally's hand.

"What's this?" She asked.

"This is our sacred symbol. It signifies that the wearer is under our protection," I replied.

Peggy brought Sally a cup of the willow bark tea. As she leaned forward, Peggy showed our guest that she also wore the identical pendant around her neck. Peg winked and Sally's eyes filled with tears.

!CAW! CAW!

I gazed out the window, startled by the agitated sounds. Perched in a large oak, my three ravens fluttered their wings and cried up in an upset manner, as they looked below. They were there as a constant eye on the Inn below.

A shadow passed behind the tree. I caught a brief glimpse of a familiar silhouette - a once beautiful face now marred by white thick claw marks, and the lines and early graying of her hair. My heart sped up, and a spike of cold fear shot up my spine. I rubbed my eyes and looked again. Saskia was gone.

Dear Reader

Thank you for supporting independent authors. Every book you pick up, every story you share, makes it possible for voices like mine to be heard. Your support means more than I can say.

If you enjoyed *Pearl Bound*, I'd be deeply grateful if you left a short review on **Amazon** or **Goodreads,** or whatever platform you prefer. Even a sentence or two helps new readers discover the story — and it makes an enormous difference for indie authors.

Acknowledgements

While writing is a solitary act, bringing it into the world is anything but. I am profoundly grateful to all who have stood beside me on this journey.

My heartfelt thanks to Mike Braff, whose editorial insight, care, and belief in this story helped me bring *Pearl Bound* fully to life. His guidance has been a steady light through the shadows.

I'm also grateful to my writing group — a circle of generous, perceptive minds who challenge me to dig deeper and write truer, in every medium. Your insight and camaraderie have strengthened my storytelling across both page and screen.

To my family and friends — thank you for your encouragement, your patience, and your faith in me when the writing felt impossible.

To my readers, thank you for opening your hearts to Eve's story. Independent authors thrive because of readers like you.

This book carries with it the voices of countless women who came before, and the strength of those who continue to carve out their own destinies. I am honored to add my voice to that chorus.

What Comes Next?

To be the first to hear about my next sapphic release — and get sneak peeks, extras, and behind-the-scenes notes — join my mailing list at:

www.roseandpearlproductions.com

Until then, thank you for stepping into the world of *Pearl Bound*. May its shadows and light stay with you.

About The Author

Natalie G. Bergman's debut novel, *Pearl Bound*, is a queer, female-led story of love, power, and the fight to claim one's own destiny. Born in Sydney, Australia, to Holocaust Survivors who survived World War II, her fascination with the immigrant experience and the desire to belong continues to shape her work. An award-winning screen-writer, Bergman has been recognized for her TV pilots *Angels of War* and *Exposed*. She also holds a Doctor of Chiropractic degree, bringing an eye for both the body and the spirit into her storytelling. A mother of two adult daughters, Natalie pivots between Los Angeles and New York City with her wife of forty years and two endlessly fluffy Persian cats.